A Season for Spies

GOLDEN ANGEL

GOLDEN ANGEL LLC

Contents

A List of Characters & Titles   v

Prologue   1
1. Present Day: Anthony & Evie   9
2. Late Night at Camden House   16
3. It's A Trap!   24
4. An Unexpected Breakfast Guest   31
5. Investigating the Staff   39
6. Dinner and the Warrens   46
7. Spilled Wine   53
8. The Tramp's Den   60
9. A Fitting Punishment   68
10. Henry & Yvette   75
11. Elijah & Josie's Return   82
12. New Arrivals   90
13. The Society of Sin   98
14. Quickly   106
15. Unfaithful   115
16. An Awkward Breakfast   123
17. Nothing but Tea and Gossip   131
18. An Unexpected Arrival   138
19. A Lady Needs Her Friends   146
20. The Gentlemen Convene   152
21. The Tramp's Message   158
22. Mitchell   165
23. A Private Discussion   171
24. The Best Laid Plans   179
25. Paying the Penance   187
26. The Belt and the Hand   195
27. An Untimely Arrival   202
28. Explanations   209
29. An Unexpected Apology   215

30. The Chase   223
31. Say Yes   230
    Epilogue   237

Acknowledgments   243
About the Author   245
Other Titles by Golden Angel   247

A List of Characters & Titles

A List of Characters & Titles
Captain Anthony Browne – third son of Viscount Browne
Miss Eveline Stuart - niece of the Marquess of Camden
Oliver Stuart – the Marquess of Camden
Elijah Stuart – Earl of Durham and first son of the Marquess of Camden
Josephine Stuart – Countess of Durham, married to Elijah in A Season for Scandal
Joseph Stuart – second son of the Marquess of Camden
Adam Stuart – third son of the Marquess of Camden
Captain Nathan Jones – the Earl of Talbot
Lily Jones – Countess of Talbot, married to Nathan in A Season for Smugglers
Sebastian Jones – the late Earl of Talbot, Nathan's elder brother
Rex – Michael Hartford, the Marquess of Hartford and founder of the Society of Sin
Mary Hartford – the Marchioness of Hartford, married to Rex in A Season for Treason
Lucas Beckett – the Earl of Devon, childhood friend of Rex
Julian Mitchell – former secretary to Lord Warwick and former spy under the direction of the Marquess of Camden

Prologue

Two Years Earlier

Evie

"Someone tried to assassinate the Duke of York?" Evie burst into her uncle's office, no longer content to listen at the keyhole as her eldest cousin reported in. Though her uncle was the Crown's spymaster and all three of her cousins assisted him in one capacity or another, all four of the men were dedicated to keeping her out of the 'men's business.'

Despite surviving the streets of London on her own when she was a mere child and had proven her usefulness over and over since her uncle had found and taken her in. She wanted to be part of the family business, and since she did not consider herself a 'lady' of the *ton*, she did not particularly care if such things were not fit for ladies. High Society did not fit her.

Uncle Oliver groaned, rubbing his forehead with his hand.

"I thought you were in your room resting."

Evie narrowed her eyes. She was very aware he would have been happier leaving her out. She did not need him to say it out loud.

"I was. Then I saw Elijah return home in a hurry from my window, and I wanted to know what the problem was." Evie kicked the door shut behind her and crossed her arms over her chest, lifting her chin defiantly. "If there has been an assassination attempt on such an important personage, you are going to need all the help you can get."

"It is too dangerous," Elijah said immediately, raking his hand through his dark hair. Like father like son, Uncle Oliver and her cousin were cut from the same cloth, though the grey in her uncle's hair made their age difference clear. "The Duke was nearly killed."

"As if I have never been in dangerous situations," Evie retorted, rolling her eyes. "Need I remind you how helpful I was in France?" She had spent two years there during the war and had done just as much work as any of her uncle's operatives. Even saved one of them from capture when he had been set up in a trap—she pushed that memory away.

She did not need her thoughts distracted by *him.*

"You were very helpful, even if you were supposed to be in Denmark at the time," Uncle Oliver said through gritted teeth. He was honest to a fault, even when he did not want to admit the truth. Telling her she had not been helpful when she had provided him with information that none of his other operatives had been able to suss out was beyond him, no matter how much he likely wished he could.

Evie smiled thinly.

"Then let me help now. I can be even more helpful here than I was in France." England was her home, so she should be able to do more in familiar territory than in unfamiliar.

The two men exchanged a glance, and Evie's jaw locked into place. Stubborn fools. They were going to deny her again! When would they learn? As determined as they were to keep her safely tucked away in the manner they thought best, she was even more determined to live her life on her terms. To make her own choices.

Though she would never bring public or societal shame to her family, not after Uncle Oliver had rescued her, and so she ensured no one ever knew of her extracurricular activities. No lord or lady would believe their eyes, even if they saw her in one of her myriad disguises— not that they ever looked—especially among their social set. The *ton* was so convinced of its own importance, they rarely paid attention to anyone who was not on their level, often to their own detriment.

"If we need you, we will certainly call on you," her Uncle Oliver said carefully.

Truthful to a fault. In his opinion, they never needed her, so he was not telling a lie. Evie knew she would not be included in their escapade, regardless of her work in France, which had assuredly been far more dangerous.

Unfortunately, the one witness to her most brilliant rescue had no idea who she was, nor did she want him to. Captain Browne was alive because of her... but only because she had infiltrated a brothel. It was not a rescue she had been able to take the claim for with her uncle unless she wanted to admit that she had masqueraded as a whore. Despite the outcome, she knew it would not help her cause.

Bloody daft men.

"I see." Attuned to her tone of voice, both her uncle and cousin were still watching her warily, ready for her outburst. Evie was tired of the fighting, though. France had been much more productive after she had slipped her 'leash,' the companion her uncle had sent with her, and taken matters into her own hands. She would learn from that lesson and apply it here.

Nose in the air, she turned on her heel and yanked the door open.

"Thank goodness. Browne should be here any moment," Elijah muttered, likely under the impression she either could not hear him or was so upset, he was not paying attention. He must have forgotten she had unusually excellent hearing.

Evie's back stiffened as she slammed the door shut behind her. Hopefully, the two men would think she was in a snit and not give her another thought, especially when they had such important matters to deal with.

She needed to clear out before Captain Browne arrived. The operative had never met her as Lady Eveline Stuart, and she intended to keep it that way. If he recognized her, it would be an utter disaster.

* * *

Anthony

An assassination attempt on the Duke of York.

Things had been so quiet since the war ended, Anthony had wished for a bit of action, but it sounded like this had come a bit too close to actual tragedy for comfort. The war was over, dammit. It was one thing to find action for himself, quite another to nearly lose the second in line to the Crown.

"How can we even begin to investigate this?" he asked irritably. The Duke was a public figure, so any number of people may have wanted to assassinate him. This was a thorny puzzle and not one he was looking forward to.

"To start with, I believe we must have been betrayed by one of our own," the Marquess of Camden said seriously.

Anthony started in his seat. A traitor? That was a very serious accusation.

"The Duke's trip was not widely advertised," Elijah said. "It was also rather sudden. Too sudden for it to be likely that a foreign power organized the attempt."

As the Marquess' son, Elijah would one day hold the title, the lands, and his father's position as spymaster, but for now, he had the ceremonial title of the Earl of Durham. He and Anthony had been friends for years and had given each other permission to use their Christian names years ago.

"Unless it was already organized, and they were waiting for their opportunity," Anthony murmured, his mind already working. Mistrustful and often accused of being a pessimist, Anthony could always see the worst possible scenario. The other two men grimaced.

"I do not know whether or not to hope for that," Camden said, running his fingers through his greying hair, a mannerism mimicked a moment later by his son. Their hair had already been mussed, likely because this was not the first time they'd done so. When stressed, they both reverted to type. "That would indicate something bigger than we know is on the horizon. On the other hand, I would rather have to deal with almost anything than a traitor."

Anthony nodded, fully understanding the dilemma. Britain did not need another war so soon on the heels of the last when they were finally recovering from the previous one. He was regretting wishing for a bit of action. He had only wanted some excitement back in his life, not another damn war.

Knowing someone was willing to betray their country and attempt to assassinate one of the heirs to the Crown, his deeply ingrained sense of honor was infuriated by the very notion. All the years he had spent protecting the Crown, putting his life at stake in service of it, it was a personal slap in the face from one of his own countrymen.

A foreign power or one of their own… there were no good options.

"What do you need me to do?" It was luck he had been nearby, and Elijah had known of it to call him in. The house party he had allowed himself to be talked into at his family's behest had been both dull and dangerous—the danger was he might find himself affianced before the end of it. The matchmaking mamas were very determined, and Anthony was of the right age. Unfortunately for them, he had no interest in marriage. He did not do long-term relationships. They did not appeal to him.

The one and only time he had the thought of setting a woman up as his mistress, she had disappeared in the middle of the night after saving his life. He had never found out who she was, though he had searched for her. All he knew for certain was she was not a whore in a French brothel—though she had pretended to be.

So, he had no mistress and no interest in leg shackling himself to some young, wide-eyed debutante whose sole ambition in life was to become someone's wife.

"I am sending you and Elijah to York to question the Duke and his retinue. You will take the same route, stop at the same places, and investigate every angle you can. In the meantime, I will depart for London." The Marquess leaned forward on his desk. There was mounting fury in his eyes, though Anthony knew from experience, the man would keep it tightly leashed. "I am writing to several agents to meet me there. I believe Mitchell is already in London. I am going to send him into the underground to see if the assassins were hired there."

Mitchell was another operative, although, unlike Anthony, he had no connection to the *ton* other than being employed by one of them. Anthony might not be a lord, but his father was a viscount, and eventually, his eldest brother would be. Although Anthony could disguise himself and change his manner of speaking to fit in with the less reputable denizens of Society, no one was more adept at it than Mitchell. He was a chameleon, equally blending in with both the upper and lower echelons.

"Yes, my lord," Anthony said, nodding his head and glancing at Elijah. The two of them had worked well together in the past. "Whatever there is to be found, we will find it."

* * *

<u>Evie</u>

Chewing her lower lip, Evie listened from her position at the tiny hole she had carefully drilled between her uncle's office and the drawing room beside it. She did not like to use it often for fear of discovery, but in instances like this—before her uncle had finally explained things to Captain Browne—it was far safer than the keyhole, which her cousin now had a habit of checking, thanks to catching her.

As their little meeting broke up, she fingered the bit of wood that slotted into the space to cover the hole on this side, keeping any light from getting through between rooms and giving her away. Unless someone looked extremely closely at the decorative wood paneling, the piece was practically invisible to the eye.

She was about to slide it into place when she heard her uncle speaking to Elijah again.

"I am going to take Evie with me to London."

"What? But..." Elijah's voice trailed off.

"If we leave her here, you know she will be after one or the other of us within a day."

Yes. Yes, she would. Choosing which would have been difficult, but she likely would have gone to London after her uncle. He would be the hub of incoming information, so this suited her.

"Are you going to give her a debut?"

Evie froze.

The very last thing she needed was a husband. She certainly did not *want* one. The relationships she had seen among their social set had convinced her that her parents' love had been an anomaly, and she was unwilling to settle for anything less.

The usual *tonnish* marriage consisted of two people forced together by circumstance or finances, and woe betide the bride who thought her new husband actually meant all those pretty promises. The men were completely in control of everything. There were so many bitter, heartbroken women whose husbands had betrayed them, who then went on to take lovers themselves, but they were still stuck with the man they'd married. They could not take a lover and find even a glimmer of their own happiness until they had born their husband an heir.

The only exception she could think of was Lady Brooke, and the only reason she had not become a complete social pariah was her estranged husband had not allowed it. They were no longer estranged, and it seemed to be a love match, but Lady Brooke's story was highly unusual.

Not that Evie cared about being a social pariah, but she did not wish that for her family. Her uncle and cousins had taken her in the moment they found her, nevermind that she had been wild, dirty, unmannered, nearly feral, and completely jaded by her time on the streets. They had loved her. Cared for her. Given her food, shelter, and the familial support she never thought she would have again.

No, Evie would never do anything to dishonor her family, but she would not give up her life and her control to a husband for them either.

"I do not have a sponsor for her," her uncle replied in a tired tone, and Evie relaxed. "I do not even know if Evie wants to debut. She will come with me and run the household. I will give her full control over it, which should keep her busy enough."

Evie snorted softly. Hardly. Running a household was a difficult and involved task, but their housekeeper and butler had it well in hand. She saw no point in micromanaging them the way some ladies of the house did, though she should not be ungenerous. Those ladies needed something to fill their days, and Society did not provide many options. She shuddered at the thought of becoming one of them.

They had little to no choice. She did.

"Do you really think there is a traitor?" Elijah asked.

Evie went absolutely, completely still, her ears straining for the answer.

"I do. I did not say so in front of Browne, but I have long thought there was a traitor somewhere in the network. I think it must be someone at the home office. We lost several spies in France during the war, and... I do not know if Browne ever told you, but he was nearly caught in a trap there. I think at least some of the others must have been as well. That could only have been done by someone who knew where those agents were and how to contact them."

Heart pounding in her chest, Evie felt herself flush. She had been the one to save Browne from that trap. They had shared a rather intimate time together, then he'd decided he wanted her for his mistress. Obviously, he had not known who she was.

That the trap had been set by a traitor... she had not even considered such a thing.

Yes, she was going to help her uncle find this person... whether he wanted her involved or not.

CHAPTER 1

Present Day: Anthony & Evie

nthony

Entering Camden House through the back door, Anthony paused to listen. After riding through the night, it was well past four in the morning, and the house was quiet, but he did not want to take any chances.

He was chasing a traitor, one who'd nearly killed him twice and a few weeks ago, had put the Marquess of Camden at death's door. Granted, he had used hired hands, but Mitchell had been the traitorous mastermind behind the attempts.

The same mastermind behind the attempted assassination of the Duke of York two years ago.

Anthony still could not believe Julian Mitchell had fooled all of them for so long.

He was the reason Anthony was in London, in Camden House, instead of at Brentwood Manor with his friends and fellow agents. They had gathered there for the funeral of Nathan Jones' brother, who had been killed when he'd uncovered proof his father had been working with Mitchell during the war to smuggle French spies into England. Now Nathan was the Earl of Talbot instead of his older brother, and all because of one man.

Mitchell's treachery stretched back years, and the burning anger that filled Anthony was all the fuel he had needed to stay awake for the ride.

He had not been the only one to chase Mitchell back to London. Miss Eveline Stuart's horse had been in the yard when he had finally given up searching for Mitchell in the streets and headed to Camden House to tell the Marquess everything that had been discovered.

Miss Eveline Stuart. Even thinking her name made him burn as much as saying Mitchell's did, but for an entirely different reason and in a completely different way.

Striding through the house, he paused when he thought he heard something.

Voices.

Yes.

He turned from the stairs he had been heading for. Once he'd seen Miss Stuart's horse, he had assumed she would have gone to wake her uncle, and they would have their discussion in the family quarters, but the voices were coming from the library. As he approached, he could see light flickering from the opening between the door and the frame. Walking as softly as he could, he was relieved when he only heard the two familiar voices of the Marquess and Miss Stuart, and neither sounded in distress.

Mitchell was not here.

Setting his shoulders back, Anthony strode forward, no longer trying to be quiet. As his footsteps sounded, the voices in the room stopped. When he stepped into the doorway, hands raised, he was unsurprised to find two pistols pointed at him.

"Browne." The Marquess sighed with relief, dropping his arm immediately.

Miss Stuart studied him, considering her options. Anthony narrowed his eyes at her, and she smirked, finally dropping her arm and bringing the pistol to rest in her lap.

"Evie said you had gone after Mitchell."

"He disappeared in the Warrens," Anthony replied, coming in to seat himself in the high wingback chair next to Miss Stuart and across from the Marquess. Sitting so close to her was sheer torture, yet better than having to sit across from her.

He was not sure how much of his feelings he would give away if he had her in his sights. Her uncle was far too observant, and Anthony did not know how the Marquess would react if he knew about his and Miss Stuart's past.

The one thing he was sure of was that the Marquess had no idea his niece had once masqueraded as a whore in a French brothel. Anthony would have had no problem informing the man if he had not... well... It had been a very passionate night since he'd had no idea she was actually an English lady.

Suffice to say, if his goal was to remain out of the parson's trap, telling her uncle about his time with Miss Stuart at that brothel would have the opposite effect. As it was, Anthony could barely look the Marquess or Elijah in the eye since he met Miss Stuart *as* Miss Stuart and not as Yvette, the French whore who had saved his life, or a nameless maid he'd uncovered in a noblewoman's household—both disguises had completely fooled him.

He would never have guessed she was part of the upper crust of British Society, yet after engaging with her over the past week, he knew she played this part as well as she had the others.

Anthony described his chase after Mitchell through the Warrens, doing his best to ignore the beauty at his side. He assumed she had already caught her uncle up on the pertinent details of Mitchell's unmasking as the traitor at Brentwood Manor. The Marquess listened intently, but Anthony could see the exhaustion in his eyes.

Perhaps it was the firelight or his recovery from the gunshot that had nearly ended his life, but the Marquess appeared older than usual. Like he had aged years in the space of a month. Considering recent events, Anthony could not blame him.

The Marquess had trusted Mitchell. They all had. His betrayal did more than infuriate... it hurt.

When Anthony finished, the Marquess leaned back in his chair, closing his eyes for a long moment of thought.

"Damn," he finally uttered under his breath.

Anthony risked a look at Miss Stuart. She appeared to be lost in thought, one hand under her chin, staring into the fire to her left. Away from him. The urge to reach out and poke her, to make her look at him, was disturbingly strong.

Clenching his jaw, he looked back at the Marquess.

"I imagine Elijah and the others will rejoin us shortly. My overnight disappearance will hardly be remarked upon, but the others will need to follow protocol to avoid stirring unwanted interest." The gossip surrounding the late Earl of Talbot's death would already be thick on the ground after the drama at his viewing. Mitchell had stabbed his own employer, the Earl of Warwick, as he had fled.

Anthony did not know if Warwick was alive, but he certainly hoped so. There would be many questions for him, considering how long Mitchell had been in his employ.

"We will have to take new precautions." The Marquess took a deep breath, shaking his head. "I need to warn... everyone. Change all the general code words." At least that part was done fairly regularly for safety's sake. "Figure out what Mitchell knows and what he doesn't..." He let out a long breath. "Too much. He knows too much."

* * *

Evie

On that, Evie was in perfect accord with her uncle. Mitchell knew far too much about everything. She had always disliked the man and never understood why her uncle trusted him so much, but saying 'I told you so' was hardly helpful, even though keeping her tongue in check was painfully difficult. If her uncle did not look so overwrought, she might not have had the restraint.

"At least we now know who he is," she said briskly, brushing her skirts, far too aware of Captain Browne's presence next to her. Though they had both spent the past few days at Brentwood Manor, he had been easier to avoid there. Now, he was right next to her, and between her exhaustion and distraction, she could barely think straight. "I will help write the letters and change the codes."

She put a challenge in her words, looking directly at her uncle as she said them. Something in his gaze flickered, but he nodded, and she nearly sagged with relief. He could not do this all on his own. Elijah would have been the obvious choice to help him, but tomorrow was the late Earl of Talbot's funeral, and Elijah would be unlikely to return to London until the day after at the earliest. Joseph was on his honeymoon with his new bride in Scotland, and Adam... well, who knew where her youngest cousin was? He was a very good operative when the time called for it, but he was dismal at organization.

Evie, on the other hand, loved nothing more than planning and organizing.

They needed to warn all of her uncle's operatives that Mitchell was a traitor. If they could summon a manhunt for him as well, that would not be amiss... she would suggest it tomorrow.

Her uncle looked worn out. Old. He needed sleep and time to recover from the blow. She might have never trusted Mitchell, but he had. Now he was struggling to reconcile his own judgment, along with protecting his family, his other agents, and his country.

"Thank you, Evie. I appreciate your willingness to help."

Uncle Oliver did not actually accept the help, she noted. She bit her tongue. There would be plenty of time to bully her way into helping tomorrow. She *really* had to bite her tongue when her uncle continued.

"Captain Browne, would you mind checking the house to ensure it is secure, then joining me upstairs for a moment? There is something in my chambers I wish to give you."

"I can check the windows and locks," Evie said, though her far greater annoyance was with her uncle's attempt at obfuscation. He had something for Captain Browne? She would eat her best hat if that was true.

He wanted to discuss something with Captain Browne without her listening.

He wanted to leave her out.

Again.

No matter how helpful she and her friends, who she had recruited to help her, had been, her uncle's first instinct was to leave her out. Evie swallowed. Hard. The grief, self-recrimination, and pain on her uncle's face were the only reason she did not unleash her temper. Captain Browne's presence kept her in check as well. This was not dirty laundry to air in front of him.

"Captain Browne can check the windows and the house. I need you to help me to my room." Uncle Oliver grimaced as he got to his feet, his hand going to his side where he had been shot. In a flash, Evie was beside him, supporting him.

No matter how angry he sometimes made her, she loved him and knew he loved her. He was misguided in his attempts to control her life, but he had never punished her for going her own way. Not a word had been said about her year-and-a-half-long disappearance when she had turned up again after the attempt on his life. She'd been welcomed back into the family's fold as if she'd never left, the same way she always was.

"Lean on me," she said, sliding under his arm as he picked up his cane.

"I can still walk on my own." His voice was gruff, but she heard the relief.

"But now, you do not have to," she replied matter-of-factly. "If you request my help, you are going to receive it. That or I can assist Captain Browne with securing the house."

A bald-faced lie, and when Evie caught a glimpse of the captain's expression, she knew she was right to avoid being alone with him. However, the words had their intended effect. Not only would her wandering about the house at night with a man be scandalous, but with the possible threat of Mitchell lurking in the darkness, her uncle would not want her in even that slim amount of danger if he could help it.

None of them believed Mitchell was there, but she knew neither she nor her uncle would be able to sleep unless someone checked.

"Very well," her uncle grumbled, leaning on her a little more than she expected. Not that she minded, but it made her worry.

There was very little her uncle hated more than to appear weak. That he was using both his cane and her for support was not a good sign. Evie hoped it was because of the late hour and his lack of sleep, two things she could not have helped.

Behind them, she could hear Captain Browne moving to the windows, checking the latches. There were few people she would have trusted to secure her home, but as relief seeped through her veins, she realized he was one of them. She would not need to come back down and recheck. She would sleep soundly, knowing that he had done a thorough job.

"I do not want you going back and checking Browne's work," Uncle Oliver said as they ascended the staircase. "He will make sure the house is secure. I trust him."

Evie nodded. She was certainly not going to explain to her uncle that she did as well. He would want to know why and how she knew the captain. Evie was not someone who trusted easily, and her family knew it. She also knew her uncle needed reassurance that his instincts could be trusted.

Mitchell's betrayal likely had him questioning them.

"You can say it, you know," Uncle Oliver said in a low voice. "You told me you did not like Mitchell."

"I did not." She would not rub it in, but she was not going to lie. Knowing her uncle remembered it was enough. For now.

CHAPTER 2

Late Night at Camden House

Anthony

Prowling around Camden House, Anthony tested every window, every door, every lock he could. Mitchell had been to the house often enough, it would have been easy for him to sabotage an entrance. Thankfully, it did not seem he had thought that far ahead —or perhaps the Marquess had already had them checked after the recent assassination attempt.

Regardless, the house was as secure as it could be unless Mitchell came in through the servants' quarters, which was a possibility, though the staff seemed devoted to the family. That would have to be looked at separately. Anthony finished his inspections in the family wing. Though he did not know which room was Miss Stuart's, it became fairly obvious as soon as he stepped into the hall. Light flickered from beneath only two of the doors, and he knew which belonged to the Marquess' room.

Doing a quick check of the other rooms along the hall, all currently unoccupied, Anthony came to the Marquess' door and knocked.

"Come in." Though the Marquess' voice was as strong as ever, when Anthony opened the door, the man was sitting in one of the chairs by the window. He was again struck by how much older the Marquess looked. Much more tired. The long hunt for the traitor, only to discover it was Mitchell, had clearly taken its toll on him.

"The house is secure," Anthony said, sitting across from him. That much, at least, he could reassure the other man on. "The only rooms I did not check were those that were occupied."

"Those are secure enough. The servants have all been warned about Mitchell, and the only other person in residence is Miss Rutherford." Camden glanced away from Anthony. "I checked her windows myself before she moved in."

"Miss Rutherford?" Anthony asked, raising his eyebrows. That explained the occupied room in the guest wing. He had started to go in, then realized there was someone inside and immediately backed out. Hearing it was a miss and not a lord or mister... well, that was not what he had expected.

Camden scowled, though he was still not looking at Anthony.

"The nurse Evie hired to look after me while she was at Brentwood. The woman is a termagant." Camden's scowl deepened.

Ah. Well, that changed Anthony's thoughts considerably. He had never known Camden to have a lover, which meant the man must be exceptionally discreet. Moving a woman into the house was hardly his style. But he could only imagine what kind of nurse Miss Stuart would hire to manage her uncle in her absence. If anyone was going to have a chance at managing him while he was injured, they would need to be strong-willed, patient to a fault, and beyond stubborn.

"Now that your niece has returned, surely she will retake those duties," Anthony suggested, though even as he said the words, he felt doubt creeping in.

"Hardly." Camden snorted. "Not while Mitchell is still at large, which is exactly what I wanted to talk to you about." Camden leaned forward. Despite the late hour and his evident exhaustion, his dark eyes glittered with a grim intensity that seemed to energize him. "I need you to keep an eye on Evie. Include her in the investigation before you have to."

Anthony's immediate reaction was to shake his head, and Camden held up his hand to forestall any verbal objection.

"I am not saying place her in danger, but you must understand my niece is not... she is not the usual sort of young lady." Camden shook his head, thankfully missing the expression on Anthony's face.

That was something Anthony knew intimately, but he could hardly admit it.

"Her parents were killed when she was eight, and the woman who was supposed to care for her until I arrived... well, Evie ended up running away. She spent several years on the streets of London before I found her."

Several *years*? Anthony nearly choked on his tongue. At eight years old? An orphan? He could only imagine how horrific that would have been for her, but she'd survived. That, in and of itself, was a minor miracle.

"Because of the circumstances, I was more permissive than perhaps I should have been at times. Evie has all the skills expected of a debutante, but even after I found her and brought her home, she was raised with a group of rowdy boys." Camden lifted his hands, palms up, in a gesture of resignation.

"She taught *them* a few tricks about fighting and sneaking, and they did the same in turn, as well as teaching her how to shoot, track, and live as easily in the country as she did in the city. She also overheard far too much about my operations."

It explained *so* much. Anthony rubbed his forehead where he could feel a headache starting. She truly was a wildcat. He had wanted her to be *his* wildcat the first time they met. He'd wanted to tame and keep her. Wanted to make her his mistress. Now, knowing who she was, obviously, it was not an option.

"I cannot lose her, but she has inserted herself into the family... business more than once. Always with incredible results, no matter how much I would prefer her to remain safe over what information she brings me." Camden made a face. "I had not seen her for almost two years before I was shot. She disappeared in order to investigate the Duke of York's attempted assassination."

Camden sat back in his chair, slumping and appearing exhausted again. Part of Anthony wanted to go wring Miss Stuart's neck for causing her uncle such stress. Considering his responsibilities, he hardly needed *more* concerns.

"I will not have her disappearing again," Camden said softly. His chin tilted up, his gaze squarely meeting Anthony's. "If that means I must accept her involvement in the investigation, that is what we will do. You will keep her safe and out of harm's way as much as possible. If it comes down to a choice between catching Mitchell and protecting Evie, protect Evie."

Damn.

Letting out all the air from his lungs, Anthony met Camden's gaze. Though he knew the priority should be catching Mitchell, hearing her story, he could understand why Camden felt the way he did. If he was completely honest, he had a feeling it was the choice he would make as well.

Would have made, even without knowing her history.

Somehow, the vixen had gotten under his skin.

He nodded.

"I will. You have my word."

* * *

Evie

Blasted men.

Even though she was exhausted and wanted nothing more than to lie down and let sleep take her, her body buzzed and hummed with energy. If she lay down right now, she would not actually sleep. No, she would stare into the darkness, ruminating, mind racing, thinking of all the things she could—should—be doing.

Only once she had done everything she felt she could do would she be able to properly rest.

Thankfully, this was hardly the only time she'd had to operate on little sleep, and not just when she was doing something dangerous. Many of the *ton* had very little care for how hard they worked their staff, and Evie had begun making note of the worst offenders long ago.

In her mind, if someone could afford to treat their staff well and pay them accordingly but chose not to, it was up to her to see that they lost the funds to afford that staff. She did her best to find new placements for those who were let go from their positions or gave them the ability to leave of their own accord as their wages became less reliable.

She'd found the middle classes tended to treat their help much better than the aristocracy, and with many of their fortunes rising, there were always those in need of good help.

Sitting down at her desk, she worked on writing lists. Evie loved lists. Though she never left paper lying around for someone to happen upon, she found the act of writing a list meant it embedded itself in her memory. Once it was written, she no longer had a need for the physical copy, but without having written it out, she would sometimes forget a thing or two, which was unacceptable.

Writing lists also helped her organize her thoughts, which was certainly necessary.

Elijah and Josie would return soon; she was sure of it. Between his father being injured and Mitchell returning to London, he would not be able to stay away. It was likely Rex and Mary would stay at Brentwood Manor to assist Captain Jones and Lily in their investigation into Mitchell's activities there.

Hopefully, when Elijah and Josie returned, they would have more information. Evie wrote out a list of possible questions to send to Lily and Mary in case Elijah rushed back before getting all the information she wanted. Mitchell had spent a good deal of time on the coast while working for Lord Warwick, and it was likely his treachery stretched back years.

It still burned Evie that neither her uncle nor her cousins had listened when she told them she did not like Warwick. No, she had not had proof against him, but her instincts about who was not a good person had been honed on the streets of London, where it could literally mean life or death. While her cousins and uncle had also cultivated such instincts, they had done so from a place of privilege.

They'd always been able to count on their position, physical prowess, money, and connections. They had always had something to fall back on if they were wrong. Evie had no such guarantees. Not only that, but they also did not have the same internal sense most women unfortunately developed about men.

Even women in the *ton* were not protected from men. If anything, they were more at their mercy since defending themselves could still find them married off to the man who tried—or succeeded—in ravishing them. Evie found the whole thing sickening. It proved her point, though.

When it came to instincts, hers would always be sharper than her uncle's or cousins' from necessity.

Done with her list of questions for those still at Brentwood, Evie wrote down everything she had ever known or heard about Mitchell. That would help her create new lists for items of investigation once she had all the information laid out in front of her.

The knock on her door made her jump. Though it was not very loud, there were no other sounds in her room except her quill scratching across the paper, and she had not been expecting it. Blinking owlishly, she paused before getting to her feet and hurrying over.

If Uncle Oliver needed her...

However, it was Captain Browne waiting for her on the other side of her door, not her uncle.

"You." She scowled, closing her fingers about the wrapper she was wearing over her nightrail. "What do you want?"

"We need to talk." Like the big brute he was, he shouldered her aside as he moved into the room.

Evie rolled her eyes. She could have stopped him if she wanted to. Probably. Certainly, she could have kicked up a fuss, and her uncle would have come running, but she wanted to talk to him. Perhaps she could persuade him to reveal whatever her uncle had wanted to talk to him about privately.

Popping her head into the hall long enough to see it was completely dark, meaning her uncle had put out his own candle and gone to sleep, Evie turned and shut the door behind her.

Captain Browne stood in the middle of her room, arms crossed over his broad chest, his habitual scowl upon his face. Compared to the delicate fripperies she had decorated her room with, he looked exceedingly masculine and rather menacing. As always, in his presence, her body was almost immediately aroused. Those instincts she was so proud of always seemed to go haywire around him.

"Yes, Captain, of course, Captain, please come into my room, Captain." She arched a brow.

Being alone with him in her room at this hour of the night, dressed in nothing but her nightgown and wrapper, was wildly scandalous. If her cousins knew, they would likely throw a fit. Well, Elijah and Joseph would. Whether or not Adam would care was debatable, but he had always been the free spirit. Elijah would definitely be frothing at the mouth, and Joseph would be close behind him.

With good reason, although they had no idea about that.

Captain Browne, as usual, remained unpredictable. He snorted at her jibe, meeting her gaze full on with an interesting glint.

"You can hardly claim impropriety now," he responded, referencing their first meeting.... or perhaps their second... but probably the first when they had fucked in the middle of a French brothel to save him from being outed as an English spy.

Still. For some reason, she thought he would be more of a stickler for the proprieties. Men of his station usually were.

"My complaint was about your manners. Well, get on with it. What do you want to talk about?" She was still buzzing with nervous energy and wanted to get to sleep at some point.

"You will be allowed to help with the investigation into Mitchell... under my auspices."

For a long moment, Evie stared at him. Then she snorted. Her uncle was a Marquess, Spymaster to the Crown, and one of the most authoritative men she had ever met. If her own uncle could not control her, what made Captain Browne think *he* could?

The captain's dark eyes narrowed as though he could read her thoughts—not that she was trying to hide them.

"Do not test me, Miss Stuart. I will not hesitate to put you over my knee and spank you... as you already know."

Her bottom tingled at the memory. It had been both painful and erotic. She would have been happy to experiment further with him if her escape had not been necessary. That was the second time they met, when he recognized her as Yvette, the woman who had saved him in Paris but did not yet know she was actually Miss Eveline Stuart, niece of his commander, the Marquess of Camden. Their past was rather convoluted, but he should know a mere spanking would not stop her from doing her duty.

It had not before.

"Very well, you have issued your threat. Now, begone." She waved her hand, stepping to the side and clearing his path to the door.

"I do not think you understand, Miss Stuart—"

"I understand perfectly," she said, cutting him off with a roll of her eyes. "You will allow me to help with the investigation as long as I obey your orders, and if I do not, then you intend to turn me over your knee." He would have to catch her first. No matter that she had found it somewhat arousing the last time, submission to anything or anyone was not Evie's natural state. "If that is all you have to say, you may go. Or, if you insist on staying, get on the bed so I may get *some* use out of you."

"I... what?" His jaw worked as he stared at her as if she had gone round the bend.

"I am exhausted, Captain. I need to finish writing my lists so I may rest, or I need to tire myself out and release my tension another way. If you are going to hinder me from the former, you might as well assist with the latter."

Clenching his jaw, he dropped his arms from across his chest and advanced on her with fists at his sides and eyes flashing with ire.

"If you think to mock me or manipulate me—"

Oh, forget it. Words were useless with men like him.

As soon as he was within reach, Evie grabbed the lapels of his coat, going up on her toes as she pulled him down for a kiss.

CHAPTER 3

It's A Trap!

<u>A</u>nthony

Danger! Danger! It's a trap!

Even as his brain screamed the obvious at him, his body was reacting to the feel of Miss Stuart pressed against him.

When he reached to push her away, his hands encountered the soft, filmy fabric of her nightgown and robe, so thin, he could feel the warmth of her body through it, and he ended up pulling her closer.

This is wrong. She's a bloody lady, dammit!

A lady who he had already had a taste of—more than a taste—and it had not been enough.

Nails raked over the back of his neck, her lips parting beneath his as Anthony devoured her with his kiss. He had always taken pride in his retention of self, but her sudden attack had stripped away that vaunted self-control. His cock was raging hard against her soft stomach, and his hands seemed to have a mind of their own as he held her against him, squeezing her curves.

They moved toward the bed, clothing dropping to the floor until he was left in nothing but his breeches and boots, and she had been stripped bare. She tried to turn them as if she thought to push him onto the bed the way she had during their first encounter, and Anthony laughed.

Absolutely not.

He spun her around so she was facing the bed and bent her over it.

"Bastard!" She pushed up with her hands, trying to straighten. Anthony freed his cock and grabbed hold of her hips to keep her in place as he lined himself up with her soaking wet cunt.

"Is this not what you wanted?" he taunted as he thrust in hard. *Fuck.* The wet heat of her body enveloped him, the feeling of *rightness* striking him with terrifying intensity as he buried himself inside her.

"Go to hell!"

He knew as well as she did, while she may have wanted his cock, she had certainly not anticipated giving up her power. She had wanted to be on top. Instead, Anthony was going to ride her from behind, his stallion to her mare, in a position that allowed her to do very little while he had free rein over her body.

"Such language." Not that he actually minded, but it gave him an excuse for what he wanted to do... as if he needed an excuse. "I do not believe ladies are supposed to curse like sailors."

Lifting his hand, he slapped her arse as he drew back. The position did not allow him to use as much force as he might have liked, her cheek barely turning pink, but it was enough to make her moan and clench. It was *something.*

The frustration of reencountering her, of discovering who she actually was, had been pent up inside him for days, and now he had the opportunity to work out his grievances on her willing body. His hand came down again as he thrust into her, his own pleasure increasing as she shuddered, her muscles squeezing his driving cock every time his palm cracked against her upturned bottom.

Switching sides, he decorated both cheeks with splotches of pink, his strokes in and out of her body slowing as he took his time. He did not know if he would have this opportunity again and was determined to enjoy it while he did.

She had dropped her head between her arms and her upper body to be braced on her elbows as he fucked her from behind. Abandoning the spanking, now that her cheeks were a nice, rosy pink, he leaned forward, moving his hands along her stomach to her breasts. Hanging beneath her, they swayed with each of his hard thrusts. He filled his hands with them, squeezing and kneading the soft flesh, his grip tightening until she cried out softly.

He pinched and tugged on her nipples to his heart's content, using the tender buds to leverage harder, deeper thrusts. She pushed back against him, muscles clenching around him, as he tormented the sensitive tips. Whether or not she wanted to submit, Miss Stuart had a definite masochistic bent.

* * *

Evie

This should not feel so good.

Evie had always hated this position. She did not like being unable to see the person with her. Did not like being blind to their next move. Did not like the feeling of being at their mercy.

Until now.

With him, it was different... damn him.

She had already been wet, but when he overpowered her, positioned her the way *he* wanted her, then thrust into her... it had made her knees weak in a manner she had never experienced. Having him spanking her as he drove into her from behind both infuriated and excited her.

His rough hands on her breasts, toying with and torturing her nipples, provoked her ire and her arousal. She was burning and aching all over, and with her forearms pressed flat against the bed, there was nothing she could do in retaliation.

She was not even sure she wanted to.

This was not going at all the way she had intended, yet it was having the desired effect. Her mind was focused on only the captain and her growing ecstasy. She could feel the tension inside her coiling and knew when it released, she would finally be able to sleep.

She had not remembered how powerful he was. How seductive his domination was. How easily he turned her world upside down and made her want things she should not want.

The steady thrust of his cock in and out of her body was no longer as wild as he settled into a steady, even pace... but Evie wanted more. Needed it. The heat growing inside her demanded it.

"Oh... harder!" She lifted her hips, her bottom pushing back against him. Her climax was coming, but not quickly enough.

Instead of obeying, he pinched her nipples tightly and twisted, causing her to cry out as the pleasure-pain rushed through her.

"Hush, woman, unless you want your uncle to hear you," the captain snarled.

"Then stop pinching me!"

"You like it."

She could not refute the assertion, but she wished she was facing him so she could slap him for saying it aloud.

As if to show her who was in control, he pinched her nipples again, even more viciously, and Evie bit her lip against the cry that wanted to escape as the pain flowed through her. The burning sting and the throbbing of the little buds added to the ecstasy growing inside her.

The captain released her breasts and straightened, one hand moving to her hair, the other between her legs. He used her hair to pull her off of the bed, so she was still bent forward but in a standing position. Rather than keep his hold there, his broad palm covered her mouth just as his fingers found her clit.

Evie cried out against his hand, grabbing onto his wrists to maintain her balance as he stroked and rubbed the little nub at the apex of her womanhood.

Pure rapture struck her like a lightning bolt, right at the point of his clever fingers. His hand over her mouth made her feel free to cry out as hot bliss erupted, waves of ecstasy washing over her with each short, hard thrust of his cock into her from behind. His body rubbed against the pinked cheeks of her bottom, reigniting the sting from the small spanking and adding to the heady mix of sensations wreaking havoc on her senses.

She writhed against him, shuddering and clenching around him as the waves of her climax washed over her, leaving her breathless and spent.

* * *

Anthony

Feeling Miss Stuart sag against him, Anthony lowered her onto the bed. This time, she did not catch herself with her arms. Her entire torso flattened out on the bed, her head turned to the side, so he could see her lips parted as she panted for breath, lashes lowered.

Withdrawing from her body, he gripped his cock in his hand and pumped hard, the cream from her arousal coating the length of his shaft, making it easy. Groaning as his orgasm came hard and fast, he locked his knees as he sprayed thick ropes of cum over her pink bottom, painting it with streaks of white.

When he dallied with ladies who were members of the Society of Sin, he had been able to enjoy similar tableaux, but he had never committed a greater taboo than knowingly enjoying one with an *unmarried* lady. A debutante, whether she had formally debuted. The niece of his commander.

Yet, he could not bring himself to feel the slightest bit of regret.

Releasing his cock, he used the same hand he had been holding it with to swipe his fingers through the sticky white rivulets decorating her bottom.

"Mmm..." Miss Stuart shivered, turning slightly. Less of a turn and more as though she was leaning on one side, her other side, curling to give her a better view, but she was not trying to squirm away or hide from him. "What are you doing?"

Rather than answering verbally, Anthony moved his lubricated fingers to the crinkled rosebud of her anus and pushed in. Her eyes widened, and her lips popped open. He grabbed her hip to keep her in place, so she could not turn as one of his fingers pushed into that very tight space.

"Now then, Miss Stuart," he said, pushing her hip down firmly as he worked his finger into her bottom. She turned her face away, burying it in the mattress, so he could not see her expression, but he could see her heaving breasts as she breathed in deeply, adjusting to the invasion. He felt the tight grip of her body around his fingers. "I want to be sure you understand who is in charge."

If she thought to be rid of him the moment he reached his completion, she would be disappointed. He found claiming a woman's bottom often invoked a supremely submissive response. Whether it was the taboo, the actual sensation, or the shock, there was no better way to establish who was in control.

He would not be easily manipulated, and he certainly would not forget what they had been discussing just because they had fucked.

What he was not expecting was her sudden turn, her foot coming up despite his hand on her hip to land squarely in the middle of his chest, shoving him back. The quick withdrawal of his finger from her bottom could not have been comfortable, but she showed no sign of it as she pushed to her feet.

Green eyes narrowed, hair falling in tendrils around her shoulders and breasts, completely naked—she was magnificent.

"I am in charge of myself, thank you very much," she said tartly, hands fisted at her sides.

He had no doubt if he made a move toward her now, he would be met with fierce opposition.

"However, at the moment, I am willing to follow your lead since you are open to including me and have greater knowledge of Mitchell." An unspoken 'for now' hung in the air.

Anthony was certain she would stop following his lead the moment he headed in a direction different from the one she preferred to go.

"Very well." He would take what he could get. Tucking his softened cock into his pants, he held her gaze as he fastened the front. "Your uncle has placed me in charge, though, and you would do well to remember it. There can only be one general."

"If you are quite finished, you may go." Miss Stuart pressed her lips together. "I am done with you." Turning her back to him, she went to her wash basin and picked up a cloth.

As enjoyable as he might find watching her clean herself, Anthony decided the safer course was to let her have her way in this one thing. All they needed was to get into a fight and accidentally wake the Marquess of Camden.

He could also use some time to recoup. It had been a night of revelations, and he needed rest before facing the ramifications. He also needed some time to better prepare himself for his reaction to Miss Stuart.

Clearly, he was not as in control as he wanted to be.

Gathering his clothing, he pulled on his shirt as he made his way to the door. Gently, he opened it and peeked into the hallway. The other rooms all remained dark, and he could hear no one moving about. A sound behind him had him glancing over his shoulder.

Miss Stuart had flopped down, stark naked, atop her bed. Grinning, Anthony slipped into the hall, closing the door gently behind him.

Out of three intimate encounters, this was the only one he would call a draw.

CHAPTER 4

An Unexpected Breakfast Guest

E<u>*vie*</u>

Normally, Evie was up with the dawn, but with the long ride to London—then being ridden by the captain—she was more exhausted than normal. Instead of waking with the sun, she woke up when the maid who had been assigned to her came into the room and shrieked.

Jerking her head up, Evie groaned as she realized she was sprawled, stark naked, across her bed.

"Oh, miss... I... sorry... I..."

"No, I should be the one apologizing, Lizzie. I was very hot last night, and I seem to have stripped off my gown." It was a terrible lie, but thankfully, Lizzie was happy to accept it.

The truth was far less believable.

"Would you like me to come back later?" Lizzie asked.

Forcing herself into a sitting position, Evie rubbed her eyes. Now that she was no longer startled, Lizzie was unfazed by Evie's nudity, though she was still hovering in the doorway.

"What time is it?" she asked, rather than answering Lizzie. The desire to lie back down and sleep some more was oddly strong. That was what a good release of tension could do for her, and last night's release had been... splendid. Even if the captain had tried to push things too far afterward.

The memory of his finger pushing into her bottom made her shiver. It had been disturbingly intimate. The slight sting had not bothered her nearly as much as him being the first and only man to have touched her there. From her time as a maid to several of the households whose lord or lady was a part of the Society of Sin, she knew a great many of them enjoyed being touched, even fucked, in that hole, but it was something she had never done.

She had never been particularly inclined to want to, not even after her friends Mary and Josie revealed their own experiences and admitted they found it enjoyable.

Like being bent over before a man, it felt too vulnerable.

Yet she let the captain bend her over.

She let the captain touch her there, enjoying it for several long seconds before she finally forced him away.

"Sorry, what?" she asked as she realized she had completely tuned out Lizzie, her thoughts distracting.

"His lordship said you'd ridden through the night." The maid gave her a sympathetic smile. "It is eleven o'clock. His lordship and Miss Rutherford are breaking their fast, and he sent me to wake you and ask if you wished to join them."

At least she was not the only one getting a late start to the day. Evie got to her feet. She was curious about one thing...

"Miss Rutherford?"

Lizzie's smile widened. "Well, Miss Rutherford is breaking her fast for a second time, so his lordship has some company."

Ah, that made more sense. Miss Rutherford, like Evie and her uncle, was often up very early, far earlier than most residing in London. Camden House tended to keep country hours despite being in the city, and Miss Rutherford had quickly adjusted. Evie had very strict ideas about what her uncle should eat while he recovered, and Miss Rutherford never missed a meal with him.

"Good. Thank you. I'll wear my green morning gown today."

If Lizzie was surprised, she did no more than blink.

Of all her dresses, the green was easily the most beautiful on Evie. It brought out her eyes in a glorious manner. It was also one she rarely wore because it was a bit less comfortable than many of her day dresses and a bit more restrictive. She only wore it when company she wanted to impress was expected.

She did not know when Captain Browne would make his next appearance, but that had nothing to do with why she wanted to look her best today.

Truly.

She let Lizzie take a few minutes to style her hair attractively rather than pulling it straight back into a simple bun the way she normally did. Instead, several soft tendrils came down to frame her face.

It was not *that* different from how she normally appeared, only a few minor changes, although her uncle looked twice when she finally walked into the dining room.

"Good morning," she said, smiling serenely. Though she was still tired, now that she was up and moving, she was feeling more energized. "It is good to see you again, Miss Rutherford."

"And you, Miss Stuart." Miss Rutherford smiled at her. She was only about ten years older than Evie, in her early thirties, and quite beautiful, but described herself as being firmly on the shelf.

Though she was from a good family, they had fallen on hard times, and as the eldest, she had sought employment. As her father had been a doctor before a wasting illness took him, she learned quite a bit at his side, and her skills made her the perfect nurse and companion for Evie's uncle.

Despite her youth, she was very determined when she wanted something, and Evie had noted her uncle was not immune to the woman's beauty. She rather thought Miss Rutherford reminded her uncle of herself, which was also helpful when it came to a battle of wills between the two of them.

"I was telling Miss Rutherford about your nighttime ride." Uncle Oliver shot her a warning look. "After you received a threatening letter at Brentwood."

So, that was the story he was using for her sudden appearance. It was close enough to the truth. There had been no threatening letter—it had been the threat itself. Still, Evie was not sure keeping Miss Rutherford from the truth was the best tack to take. She was already aware the Marquess had been purposefully shot but had been kept in the dark about why someone might want to shoot him.

Uncle Oliver had insisted she did not need to know. Evie had not been happy about it then and was becoming less understanding of his insistence by the moment. It had made more sense when Miss Rutherford had been first brought on, and they did not know her very well, but she had proven herself to be both useful and close-tongued. She was certainly no gossip.

"It sounds exhausting," Miss Rutherford said sympathetically, her hazel eyes following Evie's progress to the table. Sitting beside her uncle and across from Miss Rutherford, Evie smiled at the other woman. "If you need more rest today, you may be assured, your uncle will not be exerting himself."

"Good, I will hold you to that, not because I will be resting, but because there are things I need to do that will require me to leave the house."

"I can speak for myself, you know," Uncle Oliver said sourly.

Before Evie could respond, their butler stepped through one of the doors.

"Captain Browne is here to see you, my lord."

"Oh, good, send him in." Uncle Oliver's eyes lit up.

Evie composed her face, her heart beating faster in her chest.

Blast the man. What was he doing here so early?

* * *

Anthony

Following Camden's butler into the dining room, Anthony was unsurprised to see Miss Stuart sitting at the Marquess' side, green eyes flashing and chin in the air. She looked ravishing in a green dress that matched her eyes, with tendrils of hair curling about her cheeks giving her a slightly disheveled look that had him thinking about their activities the night before.

By her expression, she was not happy to see him, which was not at all surprising.

When he'd slept later than he meant to, he worried she had woken before him and gone off on her own. Seeing her seated at the table relieved him of that particular concern. He had made it to the house in time.

What he had not expected was the woman seated across from her. He could only imagine she was Miss Rutherford, which was confirmed when the Marquess provided an introduction. Anthony made his bow while his mind boggled.

Miss Rutherford was nothing as he had pictured. For one, she was far younger than he had imagined. He was fairly certain she was about his age, perhaps a bit older. She was also beautiful, though not in the same striking way as Miss Stuart. She had clear hazel eyes, and her sun-kissed brown hair framed an attractive face with a beautiful smile.

At first glance, she did not look like the kind of woman who could bring the Marquess in line, but he knew better than most how looks could be deceiving.

"I am sorry to interrupt your meal, but I did not want to let a moment go to waste," Anthony said, sitting next to Miss Stuart. He pretended not to notice the way she stiffened.

"Of course... ah, Miss Rutherford, if you will excuse us, I need to speak to Captain Browne privately," the Marquess said. Miss Rutherford frowned but nodded and started to get to her feet when Miss Stuart spoke.

"No. Miss Rutherford, you should stay. You need to know the highly dangerous individual who tried to have my uncle killed is still at large, and it's possible he will make another attempt." Miss Stuart spoke so swiftly, there was no stopping her, though if Anthony had realized what she was going to say, he would have at least made an attempt.

"Evie!"

"Miss Stuart!"

He and the Marquess spoke together as she finished, but it was far too late.

Miss Rutherford slowly sank back into her seat.

"I think I would like to stay for this discussion," she said firmly.

Anthony held back a groan. Of course, she would. Meddling women.

"Do not glare at me," Miss Stuart said tartly, and it took him a moment to realize she was speaking to her uncle, not to him. "How would you feel if Mitchell accosted Miss Rutherford because she was not properly warned? Or if she were injured or worse because he got into the house, and she did not know a threat was at hand? She has proven herself to be both capable and discreet. With Mitchell in London and exposed as a murderer, even if not everyone knows he is a traitor, he is more dangerous than ever."

Miss Rutherford's eyes widened when Miss Stuart named Mitchell a traitor, but she did not speak, which added weight to Miss Stuart's statement that she was discreet. Clearly, she knew more about when to keep her mouth shut than Miss Stuart did.

Though... he looked at the Marquess and their gazes caught. Held.

Miss Stuart had a point.

"I am so glad you discussed it with me before making a decision," Camden said testily, turning his attention back to his niece.

Anthony looked to see her reaction and was stunned to see her smile sunnily at her uncle.

"Of course, uncle, the way you so often include me in your decisions. I learned from the best." There was a slight edge to her voice.

Anthony decided this was a time when he should keep *his* mouth shut. This was between them as family members and had nothing to do with him.

"So," Miss Stuart continued brightly when Camden did not appear to be able to summon a reply. His face was bright red, his jaw tightly clenched, yet he appeared at a complete loss for words. "Last night, I made a list of where to start. Everyone who might be in danger from Mitchell needs to be forewarned. In case he tries to escape, his name and description should be sent to every shipyard, stables, and as many posting inns as we can reach. Warwick's London house also needs to be searched, the staff questioned, and all of them warned against him."

Anthony opened his mouth.

Shut it.

These were all the very things he had come to discuss with the Marquess this morning. He could not argue with her about what needed to be done, but *he* was the one who was supposed to be in charge, dammit.

"Uncle, I think you need to organize a warning to those who might be targeted by Mitchell, as well as writing the letters to the shipyards and the posting inns to be sent by messenger as soon as possible." Miss Stuart smiled another one of her brilliant smiles. "Miss Rutherford can help you with those, and Captain Browne and I can handle Warwick's London house and staff."

"Or you should help your uncle and Miss Rutherford while I handle the house and staff," Anthony said, bristling. She thought she had everything planned out, did she?

"There will be maids and other female staff who are far more likely to talk to me than to you," Miss Stuart responded without hesitation.

Bloody hell.

Now he knew how the Marquess felt. His own face was getting red, and his jaw was clenched, but he could not think of a single thing to gainsay her.

"Now then, is there anything else I need to know about?" Miss Stuart asked, picking up her cup of tea to take a delicate sip.

"You cannot spend too much time at Warwick's house. I need you back here tonight." Camden exchanged a quick glance with him.

Anthony did not know if he was relieved Camden had another task for her. He did not appreciate her high-handedness, but his heart sank upon hearing Camden was putting a limit on their time together for the day.

"I have been invited to a dinner at Lord Spencer's this evening. It is a political dinner, and quite a few of Warwick's friends and their wives will be there. They need to be questioned as well."

That should also be a good deal safer than the other group of people who needed to be questioned—the criminals Warwick had consorted with. Considering Miss Stuart's comprehensive list, Anthony did not believe she had forgotten the more dangerous set. Keeping her busy at a political dinner should give him the chance to go into the Warrens and ask his questions. Hopefully, by the morrow, there would be no need for her to feel as though she should venture there as well.

"Very well," Miss Stuart said, thoughtfully nodding after a moment.

"That is a good opportunity to question our set, especially those who worked with Warwick. They may have some insight into whether Mitchell has been working on his own or if he was aligned with anyone in particular."

Anthony and Camden let out silent sighs of relief. At least Anthony knew she would be safe tonight. Taking her to Warwick's house today was not ideal, but it was much safer than other options, and she really would be helpful.

He would need to find the opportunity to remind her exactly who was in charge, though.

CHAPTER 5

Investigating the Staff

E*vie*

She was going to murder Warwick.

Slowly.

Perhaps after removing certain male appendages, he was attached to.

Men were rats. No, worse than that. They were fleas on rats. Far more concerned about themselves and blind to those around them, even those who they were supposed to protect, which was why she inserted herself into her uncle's affairs. She could not trust him or the other men to have their eyes open.

She knew a large part of her anger at Warwick was her anger at her uncle and cousins for being so blind to who and what Mitchell truly was, but it was harder to be as angry at the people she loved. It was far easier to be angry at someone she barely knew and did not like. She could hardly wish death upon her own kin—though she would shove this in their faces until they could not *breathe*.

Not a single woman under the age of sixty worked for Warwick. Because of Mitchell. Because he had harassed, abused, and raped the ones who had.

"It didna matter their looks or if they were of an age, he saw them as nothing more than toys for him to break." The hard-eyed housekeeper looked to be on the verge of tears. "I did my best to protect them, milady, but the master… well. I stopped hiring them under a certain age. That was all I could do.”

It was more than Warwick had done, and he had to have known.

It was also more than her uncle and cousins had done. Mitchell had been kicked out of the Society of Sin for attempting to rape a maid at one of their events, yet still, her uncle and cousins had defended him. Kept working with him. Protecting him.

Evie seethed, but she pushed it down. She did not want the house-keeper, Mrs. Pringle, to think Evie was upset with her. The woman had done everything she *could* do.

“You did more than most,” she said, leaning forward in her chair to take the housekeeper’s hands. Seated on the couch, Mrs. Pringle hung her head for a moment and took a deep breath. Clearly, talking about it had affected her. “Thank you for protecting those you could when no one else did.”

“I just wish I could have done more,” Mrs. Pringle said.

Evie knew the feeling. She wished she had dug more into Mitchell. Wished she had pushed her uncle harder about him, but she had not known about his removal from the Society of Sin until this past Season, which was the first time she heard of anything material against him. Before that, her dislike had been based on her own feelings and their few interactions.

He’d never threatened her directly, but she had been protected by her status and her relatives. Probably more by the latter than the former.

There was not much she could do now except catching him and making sure he never hurt anyone again. Well, that and ensure her uncle and cousins never hired or supported anyone like him again.

“We will find him, and he will not escape justice. I promise you.” Thankfully, that was a promise she could make. Too often, members of the ton escaped any punishment for their crimes, especially when those they abused were from the lower classes. At worst, they might be shipped to Australia or America, as if that would stop them from preying on others. All it meant was more people getting hurt elsewhere.

It sickened her.

There would be no chance of that with Mitchell. He was a traitor, which meant the Crown would take the crime seriously, and there would be no brushing it under the rug. Otherwise, Evie would have felt the need to take things into her own hands.

It would not have been the first time.

"Miss Stuart?" Captain Browne appeared in the doorway of the drawing room, where she had been questioning the staff. Tightness banded across her chest at the sight of him. Not because of arousal, like before but from fury.

The very sight of him made her want to slap him across the face.

Just like her uncle and cousins, he had worked with Mitchell.

"Thank you, Mrs. Pringle," Evie said, giving the woman's hand a squeeze before letting go. "I will find Mitchell. He will pay."

"Thank you," Mrs. Pringle whispered, hope springing up in her eyes, softening them.

Evie nodded and got to her feet. She swept past the captain, ignoring his frown, and headed for the front door. The butler bowed as he showed them out.

"Miss Stuart—"

"Do not speak to me right now," she snapped. Anger was seething in her breast. She did not know how much the captain knew about Mitchell, but her temper was hanging on by a knife's edge, and the wrong word would be the end of it. "I do not want to talk to *any* man right now."

Wisely, the captain shut up.

It was a very quiet carriage ride back to Camden House.

* * *

Anthony

Although he was dying to know what had set Miss Stuart off after meeting with Warwick's staff, Anthony did not protest. When they reported to the Marquess, he wanted to hear from Anthony first since he had talked to nearly twice as many people as Evie. Warwick did not have many females on his staff.

"The butler said the same as most of the others," Anthony said, glancing down to check his notes. "Mitchell was snobbish and often put on airs. The butler did note he was cruel to some of the staff and said he did his best to keep Mitchell away from those members."

Miss Stuart snorted. Anthony glanced over at her, but she was not looking at him. Seated in one of the high wingback leather chairs, her focus was on the window, looking outside. A fine tension seemed to grip her, making her sit stiff and straight.

"As he did not live on the premises, there was not much else to tell, though the butler gave me an address on Jermyn Street, which I will visit as soon as I can."

"He will likely have already been by there to remove anything incriminating." The Marquess sighed, rubbing at his temples. "But yes, we should look. Damn the man. What about you, Evie, did you learn anything Browne did not?"

"Why, yes, yes I did, Uncle." Miss Stuart's cool tone was utterly lethal.

Anthony felt the hairs standing up on the back of his neck. Every one of his instincts screamed *danger*, and from the way Camden froze in his seat, his did as well.

Miss Stuart turned her head, no longer looking out the window, and pinned her uncle with a look. Even though it was not directed at him, Anthony could practically feel the heat coming from her eyes.

"For instance, and this should not surprise you, did you know that the maid Mitchell attempted to rape during a Society of Sin event was not his only victim?"

"Ah, well..." The Marquess floundered, and Anthony frowned at him.

He had heard about Mitchell's eviction from the Society, but as he heard it secondhand and had not been there to witness the event, he had not wanted to judge the man on that one incident. Though, as Miss Stuart said, perhaps it should not be surprising that what he attempted once, he had probably attempted before and would again. Anthony had not wanted to think about it.

"I thought so." Miss Stuart's jaw clenched before she spoke again, the anger seething beneath her words a palpable thing.

Anthony pressed himself against his chair, holding his breath as if in hopes that a predator might pass him by.

"He was doing a lot of good, Evie." The Marquess' tone was placating, but even Anthony, who did not know Miss Stuart nearly as well, could have told him that was the wrong tack to take.

"A lot of good? A lot of *good*?!"

As Miss Stuart recounted, in bald terms, Mitchell's treatment of female staff under a certain age in Warwick's household, Anthony blanched, his own anger growing. Had Camden truly not known? Or had he, like Anthony, turned a blind eye because he had not wanted to know?

From the dawning horror on Camden's face, perhaps he had not truly known the extent of Mitchell's misdeeds.

Breathless, leaning forward in the chair and fingers gripping the arms of the chair so hard, her knuckles were white, Miss Stuart looked ready to launch herself across her uncle's desk.

"Now, Evie, I have to take into consideration all sorts of—"

"What if it had been me?" she asked, interrupting him. "If you had not found me, if I had been *lucky*, I might have ended up working for someone like Warwick. I could have been a maid on his staff. What if Mitchell had done to me what he did to those other women?"

Camden paled. Anthony clenched his jaw. His stomach flipped over. It had been hard enough imagining it happening to someone faceless, putting Evie's face on it...

"Ah, so now you care. Because it's someone *you* care about. You were willing to sacrifice young women you did not know, who you did not care about, but as soon as it becomes personal, *then* you care." The very softness of Miss Stuart's voice added to the impact of what she was saying.

Anthony felt as if he had been punched in the gut and could not breathe. She was speaking to her uncle, but he felt every word, knowing he was just as culpable.

Miss Stuart got to her feet.

"I used to think you were a good man. I hate that I am no longer sure I can believe that."

She could not have had any more impact than if she had struck her uncle. He was as white as the day he had been shot.

"Now, if you will excuse me, I will use the information the housekeeper gave me to search for the women he hurt and do what I can to make up the harm he, and by extension our family, caused them." Turning, Miss Stuart headed for the door.

"Evie... I am a good man."

Opening the door, Evie looked back at both of them. Her green eyes were hard as jade as her gaze flitted back and forth between them.

"Then start acting like one."

Exiting, she slammed the door shut behind her.

Anthony felt as if he had just walked in on something intensely private and wished he was anywhere else. He had not liked the look in Miss Stuart's eyes, as though she was judging him by the same stick. If he had known what Mitchell was up to...

But you did not investigate, did you? You knew what he was capable of, but instead of looking deeper, you turned a blind eye.

Because he was useful.

The same reason as the Marquess. As much as Anthony wanted to blame the Marquess because he had trusted Camden's leadership and Camden had trusted Mitchell, he knew he could have acted of his own accord. If someone he cared about had been hurt by Mitchell, he would have.

Evie's words would not leave his head easily.

He could have done more. Should have done more. He was supposed to be protecting his country, which meant protecting its people, including threats at home, not just across the seas.

"Bloody hell." Camden bent his head and ran his fingers through his dark hair.

Was it Anthony's imagination, or was there even more grey in it than before?

Sitting quietly, Anthony leaned his head back against the chair.

After a long moment, Camden took a deep breath and raised his head. If his eyes appeared a little glassy, Anthony would not mention it.

"Alright. Tonight, you will check Mitchell's house?"

"Yes, my lord. Then I thought to go to the Warrens and see if I can find any of his contacts there or any clue where he might have disappeared to." Mitchell had once taken Elijah and his wife to the Tramp's Den to meet a contact. Granted, they had not realized Elijah's wife was with them at the time, but she had followed them there. It was a good place to start.

"Good." Camden nodded. Then said more quietly, "If you find anything at his house about any of his other victims... bring it to me, please."

"Yes, my lord."

CHAPTER 6

Dinner and the Warrens

Evie

By the time she was ready for dinner, Evie's temper had calmed. Mostly. A little, at least. Enough that she sat quietly while Lizzie primped and curled her hair. Having someone else helping her dress always felt odd, but she knew it was a coveted position. She made sure her uncle paid his staff very well, gave them regular rest days, and provided as many other benefits as she could muster for them.

Lizzie had once told her that working for the Camden Household felt like a dream.

Having lived through some of the alternatives, Evie understood, but it still felt odd to be on the receiving end. She liked to make Lizzie happy, though, so she let her maid have free rein over her hair. Lizzie loved to style it and was thrilled to try out new styles as often as Evie would let her.

Considering Evie stayed out of the public eye as much as she could, Lizzie rarely received the opportunity and was making the most of it tonight. Evie watched out of the corner of her eye as her mind worked, going over everything she knew about Mitchell that might have caught the attention of the upper classes.

Most of them would not be overly concerned about how he treated the members of Warwick's staff—even if they thought it was awful, the *ton* was far more concerned over their own affairs. At most, they would say that Mitchell should be fired immediately, but if he had useful information, that would hardly keep them from engaging with him politically or through business.

Her uncle was proof of that, and he was not normally one to overlook injustices or abuse.

Remembering that made her angry all over again, and she had to refocus her mind on the tasks at hand. Losing her temper would not help. She had to spend the entire evening with her uncle, and she would not lose the opportunity to talk to those who would have worked with Warwick and Mitchell.

There was always the possibility there was another traitor among them, one who had assisted Mitchell with his endeavors. He had worked with the late Earl of Talbot, after all. Sadly, being born a nobleman did not make one noble. Something the lords of the *ton* demonstrated on a regular basis.

No matter how angry she was with her uncle right now, she did not want any harm to come to him. She would be there as his guard, as well as to keep an eye on him and ensure he did not overexert himself. This would be his first major outing since he had been shot. She did not count Lily and Captain Jones' wedding, as he had only been a witness. Tonight, he would be in his element, with his people, and much more likely to push himself and his health.

"What do you think, miss?"

Evie had been so lost in thought, she had stopped paying attention to what Lizzie was doing. When she looked in the mirror, she blinked in surprise. Objectively, Evie understood she was beautiful, but in her head, she was still the street urchin who survived by mudlarking and theft, dirty with short, ragged hair that helped hide her gender. So, whenever she caught an unexpected glimpse of herself as a *lady*, it always took her a moment to understand it was her reflection.

Which meant she could truly appreciate how stunning she looked.

Lizzie had worked wonders with her hair. A mass of curls was threaded through with emeralds that sparkled and made her eyes appear even greener and brighter. Little curls framed her heart-shaped face, and her dark hair made her skin appear as smooth and bright as carved ivory.

If she walked into a ballroom beside her cousin-in-law, the effervescent and blonde Josie, they would be midnight and sunlight, causing a stir that would leave all other ladies in the room in the shade. Not the kind of thing Evie was particularly interested in doing, but she knew how one's beauty could be used to advantage. Even without Josie as a foil tonight, she would draw attention.

The lords would underestimate her, seeing only her beauty and thinking she had not a thought in her head, and the ladies would either resent her or recognize her as a power and be drawn to her, so they could be part of her circle. There would be no blending in tonight.

If only the captain was going to be in attendance.

Evie shook her head, trying to dash the thought from her mind the moment it appeared. She did *not* care if Captain Browne saw her. The other night with him should have cleared the need from her body, not exacerbated it. Seducing him was not on the evening's agenda.

"Do you not like it?" Lizzie asked, appearing worried.

"I love it," Evie said, wiping the sour expression from her face and smiling at her maid. "I will be the envy of every woman there."

"Well, dinna let that worry you," Lizzie said with a soft laugh. "The ladies might be eaten up with jealousy, but they will not dare sharpen their claws on you. Not with your uncle being who he is."

Even though the *ton* did not know that the Marquess of Camden was the spymaster to the Crown, he was highly influential. Lizzie was correct. Evie revised her thoughts on how many of the women would try to work their way into her sphere tonight, whether or not they resented her beauty.

"The green silk?" Lizzie asked, moving to Evie's wardrobe and reaching in. Evie had to smile. That had not truly been a question. She was dressing Evie like a doll, and Evie was going to let her. Though Evie was well educated on what a lady of the *ton*'s interests were supposed to be, Lizzie was the one who stayed up to date with the latest fashions.

"Whatever you think is best," Evie said, though privately she agreed. If she was going to make a statement with her appearance, she might as well go all out. It would help divert suspicion from any questions she asked.

As long as men were going to underestimate her because she was a woman, she was going to take that advantage and use it against them.

* * *

<u>*Anthony*</u>

Across from Camden House, Anthony's breath caught in his throat as he watched Miss Stuart descend the front stairs with her hand on her uncle's arm.

She was radiant. Ravishing.

Seeing her dressed as a *lady* did odd things to his insides. When he first met her in her disguise as a whore, he had been attracted to her and wanted to capture her beauty and spirit and keep it for himself. When they'd met again when she was playing the part of a maid, he had been surprised at her ability to hide her capabilities and spirit—at least, until she realized she had been caught out, and both had made an immediate reappearance.

When he finally met her as Miss Stuart, she'd been a beautiful young lady of the *ton*, but not like this. This was seeing her as a lady with a capital 'L.' The kind of beauty one appreciated from afar—look but do not touch... yet he had already touched her.

All over.

Spanked her.

Debauched her.

It confused the hell out of his brain.

His body wanted her. His honor said she was off-limits. Logic told him he had already had her, so what his honor wanted was moot.

But he'd never had her when she looked like *that*.

She was a Diamond of the First Water. If she debuted, she would be a princess of the *ton*. With her uncle's standing and place in Society, a man like himself would not have the hope of getting close to her for so much as a dance, much less anything else.

He did not like the way that revelation made him feel.

"Time to go," he muttered under his breath. Coming here had not been necessary. He told himself it was because he wanted to ensure Miss Stuart did actually accompany her uncle, so he would not have to worry about her pursuing her own investigations this evening, but deep down, he knew the truth.

He wanted to see her. Now he almost wished he had not.

Looking at his hands, which he had dirtied with coal while dressing, a small smile tugged at the corner of his lips. No, the likes of him did not belong with the lady who had been on the Marquess' arm. Though Anthony was not as adept at dealing with the underworld as Mitchell, he knew how to disguise both his looks and his accent to blend well enough—especially if he played the gruff, silent type.

Granted, it was hard to question people while not being able to talk much, but he would make do. He always did.

Slipping into the shadows, he made his way through London to the Warrens, stopping by Mitchell's home on the way and checking in with the landlord to ensure no one had come by. The place was empty, and there had been no correspondence left for Mitchell, which was not entirely surprising since he was supposed to be at Warwick's estates with his employer.

Anthony hoped to hear what had happened with Warwick by tomorrow. The funeral for the Earl of Talbot would have been today, which hopefully meant Elijah would come home soon.

Elijah and his wife. Do not think she will allow him to leave her behind.

Likely Elijah would feel she was safer by his side. Miss Stuart's influence on her friends had them going headlong into dangerous situations, just as she did, and they were even less prepared than she was.

Keep telling yourself that. How many times has she bested you?

It certainly would not do to underestimate her again.

Pressing his lips together, Anthony pushed Miss Stuart out of his mind as he went deeper into the more dangerous parts of London, getting closer and closer to the Warrens. Though some lords made their way to the gambling hells and brothels located in these parts, enjoying the danger as part of the experience, they usually moved in packs. Anthony was on his own, with no backup, so he needed to be twice as vigilant.

Though he knew Mitchell had used the Tramp's Den to meet with Elijah and a contact, the Den was deeper in the Warrens, so he stopped at a tavern first. Not just any tavern but one he knew the shipyard workers frequented.

To his surprise and delight, they were all talking about the notice that had gone out about Mitchell, meant to keep him from boarding a ship. Ordering a tankard of ale, Anthony settled in the corner, listening without having to question anyone.

"Did they say what 'e did?" One of them asked, rubbing his beard and frowning.

"Not on the notice, but…" Another man glanced around, lowering his voice and leaning forward. He whispered something, and Anthony was fairly certain he heard the word 'treason.'

Whatever the man said, it aroused quite a bit of anger from those within hearing, so Anthony thought it was likely the truth. After a few minutes of all of them recounting what they would do if Mitchell were to show up at their yard, Anthony was coming to the end of his tankard and decided to move on. Then a newcomer appeared.

"Hey there, Joe, where were you today?" One of the men greeted the man as he came in to sit down, moving gingerly. "You missed a good bit o' excitement."

"What happened?" Joe asked, holding his hand to his side as he settled into a seat among his friends. For some reason, Anthony's neck tingled. Maybe it was luck, maybe it was instinct, but now and then, he found himself in the exact spot where he needed to be at the right time, and he was getting the feeling this was one of those times.

Joe's companions quickly brought him up to date on the notice and the description of Mitchell. The man's eyes widened, and he shook his head.

"I'll be damned. That sounds like the rum cove I run across this morning… he was stealing laundry from the line. We got into it, and that's why I didna make it to the yard."

"What?! Where'd he go? We can hunt him down." The man pounded his fist on the table. "Show him what happens to traitors."

Yup, clearly, they knew treason was why Mitchell was on the run. It was likely a good thing. Men like this would not lift a finger to help a lord under normal circumstances, but they were loyal to their country. Some of them may have even fought in the war. If not, they certainly knew someone who had, and far too many of those had not made it back home.

From the explanations Joe gave, Anthony was able to glean the general neighborhood where Joe lived and where Mitchell had run after he and Joe had engaged in fisticuffs. Joe was lucky Mitchell had been unarmed at the time. It was also good to know he was attempting to change his appearance.

When he was at Brentwood Manor for the viewing, he'd been dressed in more expensive threads than any denizens of the Warrens could afford. If he wanted to pass himself off as something other than a visitor to the area and draw less attention, he would need new clothing. Mitchell and Joe were close enough to a size, which explained why Joe's clothesline had been chosen.

Taking another tankard, Anthony waited long enough to be sure he'd gotten all the information he could from Joe and his friends. They were gearing up to go on their own hunt even as he made his way out of the tavern.

Anthony would have to find him first. If the others found Mitchell before Anthony did, it was unlikely they'd ever get the answers to the questions they had for him. While the men had their hearts in the right place, it was unlikely Mitchell would survive their attentions.

Thankfully, they were also well on their way to being inebriated, which gave Anthony a distinct advantage.

Once again, he was grateful Miss Stuart was otherwise occupied this evening, though the moment she appeared in his head again, he grimaced. Likely she had several lords of the *ton* fawning over her while he was stuck wandering the dirty streets. She was far safer there, even if such thoughts stirred a hornet's nest of unwanted jealousy on his part.

CHAPTER 7

Spilled Wine

E *vie*

If Lord Belmont attempted to look down her dress one more time, Evie was going to stab his eyes out with her dinner knife.

Except she could not because that would dishonor her family. Which was backward to her ways of thinking. If he was going to make her uncomfortable with his leering, *he* should be the one who was dishonored, but he was allowed to leer all he wanted, and she was supposed to pretend not to notice.

It was enough to make her teeth ache from all the grinding as she kept a composed smile on her face. This was why she hated *tonnish* events and gatherings, but she knew it was necessary.

Next time she would remember *not* to wear the green silk. Especially since the man whom she truly wanted to see her in it was not even in attendance.

Lord Belmont turned away to engage with his dinner companion on the other side, the Countess of Spencer. Evie heaved an inward sigh of relief for the short reprieve. On her other side, the Duke of Manchester was engaged in a spirited conversation with Lady Dunbury about his wife and new baby.

Listening to a man who was obviously in love with his wife and enamored of his child did Evie's soul good after having to tolerate Lord Belmont. She was not at all put out that the Duke had seemingly forgotten she was on his other side. She did not particularly feel like talking to him. A few probing questions at the beginning of dinner had revealed neither of her dinner partners had many dealings with Warwick and none at all with Mitchell.

Which meant she was perfectly happy to let Manchester rattle on to Lady Dunbury while she tried to decide which ladies she should focus on after dinner. She was so focused on trying to overhear the conversations going on about the table, she was not paying sufficient attention to what Belmont was doing and was only reminded of his presence when his hand came down atop her thigh.

Absolutely not.

Evie turned blazing eyes on him, and he had the audacity to smirk at her.

Before she could open her mouth and eviscerate him verbally, he suddenly jumped in his seat, shock on his expression, and his hands were no longer on her person but were covering his crotch, where the spreading red stain on the pale breeches he was wearing made it look as though he was pissing blood.

"Oh dear," said Lady Spencer, looking down into his lap and the rapidly spreading stain. "I seem to have spilled my entire glass of wine on your lap, Lord Belmont."

"Yes, you did. Please, excuse me," Lord Belmont gritted out between his teeth, getting to his feet. He was seething, yet good manners dictated he could do absolutely nothing.

The exact same position he had put her in with all his leering.

Evie appreciated the beautiful symmetry.

A few murmurs went up around the table as Lord Belmont departed, and Evie happened to see Lord Spencer glaring at his wife from his place further down the table... but not as if he was angry. There was a very odd look on his face—a bit of reproach but more anticipation than anything else.

For her part, Lady Spencer seemed completely unperturbed. She beamed at Evie over the empty seat, which a footman quickly removed. While Evie could not condone the extra work for the staff of cleaning the red wine from the seat cushion, she was nonetheless grateful for the rescue.

Lady Spencer leaned toward Evie in a conspiratorial manner, and Evie found herself leaning in as well. There was something very charming about the woman. Compelling. She had heard Lady Spencer was an eccentric and a force within the *ton*, but she had never seen the lady for herself or interacted with her. At first glance, she seemed like a proper lady, with her dark pink gown and elegant coiffure, but clearly, there was more to her than met the eye.

"I have found a properly applied glass of wine can work wonders for a person's attitude," Lady Spencer said, keeping her voice low, but there was a twinkle in her hazel eyes. "You should keep it in mind for the future if you will be attending *tonnish* events regularly."

What an unlikely knight in shining armor. With some amusement, Evie realized Lady Spencer thought Evie was a typical debutante and was imparting wisdom to help her navigate the shoals of the *ton*. It was rather sweet. Many women would *not*... especially if they were threatened by Evie's beauty. While Lady Spencer was buxom and beautiful, she was not as striking as Evie, and they both knew it.

Yet Lady Spencer was reaching out with kindness.

Despite her cavalier attitude about creating a little extra work for the staff, Evie decided she liked the other woman. A bit of spilled wine in the rescue of a beautiful young woman was hardly comparable to the demands others among their social set made.

"Do you find that you spill your wine glass often?" Evie asked curiously. She had heard anyone who earned Lady Spencer's ire tended to regret it but not the details.

"Not nearly as much as I used to," Lady Spencer confided, with a sigh of regret that nearly had Evie laughing. "Once the ladies learned the risk to their wardrobes if they flirted with my husband, I have not had the opportunity to employ it much. These days, I find myself spilling on men more often."

"Because they flirt with you?" Evie asked.

"Oh no, dear." Lady Spencer chortled delightedly. "My husband would not abide that." Lady Spencer turned her head slightly, catching her lord's eye. Though he was conversing with the lady beside him, his gaze was still on his wife, and she cheerfully waved her pinky at him from where she was still holding her glass. The glare he leveled upon her smoldered.

That was when Evie realized the couple was very much in love. She'd heard the rumors, of course, that one of the *ton*'s foremost rakes had been tamed, but it was a revelation to see it for herself. Lady Spencer returned her attention to Evie.

"I spill on those gentlemen who are improper with other ladies, who have not yet learned the benefits of being clumsy with their drinks."

She truly was a knight in shining armor. Evie stared at her with something like awe. It was good to know there was a powerful lady among the *ton* defending the more vulnerable members. With all the myriad rumors about the Countess of Spencer, she had not realized.

"I appreciate the lesson." Their gazes met, and the Countess' expression sobered for a moment. Despite her gaiety, she clearly understood the seriousness of her actions and how they affected the young ladies whose lives she touched. "I shall remember it in the future. I must admit, I was thinking more along the lines of stabbing him with my fork."

"Ah, well, that is the second step if the wine is not enough." Lady Spencer grinned at her, frivolity bubbling up into her expression. It was not a mask. She truly was this effervescent and unrepentant. "I think we shall be friends. You must call me Cynthia."

"Eveline, but my friends call me Evie." It had been a long time since she had made a friend, but she had a feeling Lady Spencer was right.

It would be good to have another set of eyes and ears among the *ton*, especially with her friends still at Brentwood. Lady Spencer moved in slightly different circles than her own friends, who were newly married, whereas Lady Spencer's social activities were centered on the matrons and some of the most powerful movers and shakers among them.

"I must ask you... have you ever spilled wine on Lord Warwick or his secretary, Mr. Mitchell?"

The look in Cynthia's eyes sharpened with interest. She was no fool.

"Neither," she said thoughtfully. "Warwick keeps himself to women who enjoy his attentions. He has no interest in debutantes or in a woman who does not return his attraction. Mr. Mitchell was always perfectly proper in his interactions, hanging on behind Warwick. He struck me as a bit of a toady. I do not think he liked Warwick very much."

Fascinating. And insightful. Evie had no doubt Cynthia's observations were correct. They lined up with what she herself had observed—Mitchell had curried favor with those he considered his betters while treating those he saw as beneath him with disdain.

That Cynthia had cottoned on to Mitchell's dislike of Warwick was even more interesting because that was something Evie had not known. Then again, she had had little opportunity to see the two of them together. She had always seen Mitchell on his own at her uncle's house, reporting in.

"Has something happened with them?" Cynthia asked in a low voice, her eyes sparkling. Every lady of the *ton* had a good nose for gossip, and Cynthia was no exception.

It only took a moment for Evie to decide there was no harm in telling her, and it might actually help. The shipyard and posting stations were being alerted. The *ton* should be as well. Mitchell had enough contacts within the ton that some lord or lady might harbor him without realizing the full extent of his crimes.

"Mitchell is a traitor. He smuggled in spies during the war and continued his activities until he was revealed earlier this week." She did not give the details, nor did she mention the attempted assassination of the Duke of York as that was not common knowledge, but the spies would be enough.

Cynthia gasped with shock. There was a moment of delight as she realized she knew something scandalous others had not heard yet, then the delight was quickly tamped over by mounting fury as the impact of Evie's words hit home.

"That... that..."

"Oh, dear. What did you tell her? I do not think I have ever seen Cynthia at a loss for words." The Duke of Manchester had finally ceased his conversation with Lady Dunbury when Evie had not been paying attention.

It did not escape her notice that he referred to Cynthia so familiarly, and she realized they must be friends.

"I was asking her about Lord Warwick and Mr. Mitchell since Mr. Mitchell's treasonous activities during the war were recently uncovered." Evie kept her voice low. There were plenty of boisterous conversations happening around the table. The only other person who seemed to notice Cynthia's ire was her husband, who was watching Evie and Manchester converse with a curious expression.

Evie was taking a calculated risk, but it was worthwhile. When she had questioned him at the beginning of dinner, Manchester had not responded with any knowledge about Warwick or Mitchell, but hopefully, he would spread the word to his compatriots.

"How do you know this?" He frowned, though he did not reject the declaration out of hand as some men might have.

She appreciated that he did not automatically believe her, considering how damaging and serious the accusation was.

"My cousin Elijah uncovered his perfidy," she said, which was partly true. It would not hurt to give Elijah the credit, especially as it would likely spur anyone with information about Mitchell to seek out either Elijah or her uncle for more information. "Mitchell is believed to be in London, and the Crown has already sent out notices to keep him from escaping."

"What about Warwick? Was he involved?"

"I do not know," she replied truthfully.

Manchester nodded his head, his brow furrowed, and his gaze moved over to where her uncle was sitting, conversing with the ladies on either side of him, as well as their host at the head of the table. Likely he would seek her uncle out after dinner to confirm everything she had said and probe for more.

Her uncle might not thank her, but she would explain her reasoning to him later.

That they had not thought to warn the *ton* earlier was a lapse on their part. To be truthful, Evie rarely thought about their set as being particularly useful in any way. Though this dinner was changing her mind... just a bit. While the *ton* as a whole could be vapid, self-centered, and completely self-serving, there were individuals of honor among them.

At the touch of Cynthia's hand, Evie turned to face the other woman again. She'd had no idea that being seated next to Lord Belmont would turn out to be so lucky for her. The lady's voice was even softer than before, but Evie could still hear her.

"You should know, I heard Mr. Mitchell often gambled at some hell called the Tramp's Den." Cynthia gave Evie a meaningful look, appearing rather worried but determined to pass the word on to someone who would listen. "It is not the sort of place a lady should ever go."

Evie nodded, not bothering to tell Cynthia she was familiar with it. That was the kind of scandalous gossip she needed to avoid, even if she instinctively felt the other woman could be trusted. A lady of their station should never, ever, be familiar with something like the Tramp's Den.

It was also good information. The Den was already on Evie's mind because that was where Mitchell had drawn Elijah to meet the man who had set Josie and Joseph up for a scandal. That had ended up with Josie marrying Elijah instead of Joseph, so he could marry the former Miss Bliss.

At the time, they had thought Mitchell had found the man on his own. When Elijah hustled Josie out of there, they had not realized they would never see the man again. He had failed in his mission, which had been to convince Elijah that the French had been behind that particular plot, thanks to Josie's interference. Then he was killed.

Mitchell had cleaned up his mess before they could pick apart the tangle of his lies any further.

Yes, a trip to the Tramp's Den was definitely on her agenda as soon as possible.

"Thank you," she whispered to Cynthia. "I will pass the word on to someone who can help."

CHAPTER 8

The Tramp's Den

nthony
Making his way through the Warrens, Anthony stopped at several other taverns before finally finding himself at the door of the Tramp's Den. Unlike the first place he stopped, he had not been able to find any word of Mitchell in the others. All of them were filled with news of the hunt for the man, as there were plenty of dock-workers frequenting them, but no one had seen him or seemed to know about him. Or if they did, they were not speaking up, even to help with the hunt. And he did not see anyone who appeared worried or anything other than filled with fury and a desire for justice.

Anthony did not know whether to be frustrated or comforted by that. He did not want Mitchell to have more allies than he already did, but at the same time, it was making it very difficult to find the man. Perhaps Camden would have more luck at his dinner.

Considering how Mitchell operated, it was entirely possible his allies were among the upper classes rather than the lower. Still, he would have had to hire out his dirty work in places like this, including the recent assassination attempts.

Though Miss Davies, now Lady Durham, had said the highwayman who kidnapped her had talked like one of their set. He still had not been found.

Damnation. Was he looking in the wrong place?

After a moment, he realized it did not matter. Either way, he needed to make sure every possibility had been covered. Otherwise, the lapse would bother him. Small lapses could sink a mission. If there was something to discover at the Tramp's Den and he passed it by or missed something because he thought there was nothing to be found, he would never forgive himself.

He knocked on the door.

Opening, a huge man stood in the doorway, filling it up, a bruiser, with a healing cut over his left eye and a frown on his face.

"Butch," Anthony grunted. They'd met before when Anthony was in a similar guise.

"Tony." Butch stepped back, allowing Anthony to step through the doorway, eying him warily. "The Tramp willna like it if there's trouble."

"No trouble." Anthony held his hands up as he passed by the other man. "I'm looking for information."

"Ain't ya always," Butch muttered. There was some truth to that. Anthony shrugged. Butch knew Anthony was not exactly what he appeared to be, and one of the best things about places like the Den was people were not questioned too closely.

Unfortunately, it was also probably one of the reasons why Mitchell had connections to this place.

"I need to talk to the Tramp." It was best to start at the top. If he explained why he was there, the Tramp might be more open to letting him make his own way through the hell. While the Tramp was one of the Kings of the Underworld, he was also loyal to his country.

Anthony did not believe for a moment he would countenance treason being plotted in his Den—if he knew—but he still wanted to look the man in the face when he asked him. Just in case. No stone uncovered and all that. He needed to know he could trust his initial instincts about the man.

Butch blinked. Nodded his head.

"You can go to his office to wait."

"Where is he now?" It was already into the wee hours of the morning. By now, Camden and Miss Stuart would be home and abed, even if the soiree had run longer than usual. Anthony would not allow the late hour to make him sloppy, but neither did he wish to extend it beyond what was necessary.

A smile flashed across Butch's face.

"Putting on a show."

Anthony stifled a groan. The Tramp would not have been out of place in the Society of Sin with his proclivities. He thoroughly enjoyed fucking his lady on the balcony overlooking the main floor of the Den, where everyone below could see and hear her. When he was not putting on a show, he kept his lady plugged with a tail and soft cloth ears that made her look like a puppy.

No one would guess she had once been a debutante. When he first realized, he had been worried about how she ended up here but ascertained she was perfectly happy where she was. After some snooping, he discovered the Tramp had legally married her, with the permission of her guardian. Although Anthony would have mounted a rescue, anyway, if it had been necessary.

Now, instead of being Lady Delilah Darling, she was the Tramp's lady, fucked in front of an audience of all classes on a regular basis. Including quite a few members of the *ton* who could have recognized her if they had paid attention—the way Anthony eventually had.

"You can watch while you wait."

"No." Anthony shook his head. "I'll go to his office if you can let him know I'm there once he's done."

He was no prude, but he did not have any desire to watch the Tramp's antics. He had seen them often enough on previous visits to the Den. As titillating as they could be, they held no interest for him now.

It had nothing to do with a particular black-haired, green-eyed beauty who had taken up all his thoughts.

"As you will." Butch closed the main door and opened the next, which led to the Den's main floor. The small hallway between the two doors was helpful for raids and keeping out unwanted groups of people. Only so many could fit there, creating a bottleneck. While Butch or the Tramp's other main man, Frank, were fighters of the first degree, anyone could be overwhelmed by superior numbers. The door setup helped mitigate that concern. "You know where it is."

Anthony had only been in the Tramp's office once, but yes, he knew where it was.

With the second door open, the wash of sound flowed over him—carousing, shouting, laughter, the sounds of people having a good time. Above them all, the Tramp was on his balcony, his lady in front of him, while he thrust into her from behind. Her dark hair hung in front of her face, so her expression could not be seen, but he could hear her moans as the sounds of everyone else ebbed and flowed.

Some were watching, some were not. Those who came to the Den regularly knew they could expect to see such a show on most nights. By the end of it, when she came, they would cheer, the way they always did.

He moved through the crowd, keeping an eye peeled for Mitchell, but he was nowhere to be seen. Anthony was so busy looking for the man in the crowd, he almost did not notice the woman.

Yvette.

Miss Stuart.

The two names overlapped in his thoughts when he caught sight of her. Yvette, the whore he had met in a French brothel—Miss Stuart, her true identity—was laughing at something one of the gentlemen she was talking to said as she leaned forward. Their eyes were on her breasts, which were in serious danger of spilling out of the top of her dress. Both of them were members of the *ton*, and either could recognize her at a future date.

What the devil is she doing here?

Fury surged through him, gripping the inside of his chest. Not only at the danger she was putting herself in but the way she was flirting with the men.

Mine.

That was the driving thought in his head, not for his country, not for her safety—for him. In his head, he had marked her as his years ago when they'd first met. Circumstances and the knowledge of her actual identity had not changed that primitive reaction, no matter how much he might wish it so.

She was supposed to be in bed, safe and asleep, not dressed as a doxy in one of the most notorious gambling hells in London. That she was not at all bothered by the show happening above their heads should not surprise him, yet it piqued his temper. How many times had she been here? He did not for one moment believe that this was the first.

No one, on their first visit to the Den, could entirely hide their reactions to the Tramp and his lady.

Her complete nonchalance, the way she ignored the copulation happening nearly above her head, spoke of someone who had been here before... not once but many times. The urge to toss her over his shoulder and take her back to Camden House was overwhelming... yet he could not.

He could get her off the main floor.

Stalking through the crowd, he knew the moment she became aware of him.

Her head lifted, green eyes meeting his and widening before they narrowed in challenge. Grimly, Anthony stared her down... until one of the gentlemen she was speaking to placed his hand over hers where it rested on his shoulder, saying something that drew her attention back to him.

Anthony saw red.

The moment he reached her, he scooped her up, tossing her over his shoulder exactly the way he had pictured in his mind.

"Hey!" The young lord she had been speaking with was all affront, but Anthony gave him a glare that had the peacock sitting back in his chair, raising his hands in front of him.

If Anthony had given the man a moment to recover, his pricked pride might have compelled him to confront Anthony, but he was already turning and going through the crowd. Several who noticed Miss Stuart over his shoulder gave a cheer or raucous suggestion as he passed them.

To his surprise, she was not fighting him.

Good. Maybe she had accepted the inevitable.

As he came closer to the hallway leading to the Tramp's office, a burly figure stepped in front of him, glaring. Frank, the Tramp's other main henchman, was as big as Butch and just as mean.

"Put Yvette down."

Miss Stuart's false name—the name she used in a whorehouse—on

Frank's lips in the Den had Anthony wanting to rage again. How often had she been down here, anyway? Had she plied her false trade here as well, looking for information? His grip tightened on her thigh.

For the first time, he felt Miss Stuart move, placing her hands on his back and pushing up to look over her shoulder.

"It's fine, Frank. We know each other. He's a broody one." Her accent was pure East End, with not a trace of uppercrust *ton*, and far rougher than the voice she used at home or in France when she had spoken with a French accent. It appeared her disguises went far beyond appearance.

Anthony was reluctantly impressed.

Then she slapped his ass.

Slapped. His. Ass.

And laughed.

While he understood the scenario she was setting—possessive lover and flirtatious doxy—she was absolutely going to pay for that.

"Always getting into trouble, Yvette," Frank said, shaking his head as he stepped to the side. The look he gave Anthony was pure commiseration. "You must have your hands full with her. My sympathies."

Anthony grunted and nodded, not trusting his voice or put-upon accent. There were enough people around listening, he did not want to risk speaking unless he had to. Since Frank moved aside, Anthony moved forward again, taking long strides into the hall just as he heard the Tramp's lady moan louder.

Whether it was because the Tramp knew someone was waiting for him or because he was coming to the end on his own was unclear, but Anthony knew he would not have much time alone with Miss Stuart.

He intended to make the most of it.

Knowing Frank was guarding the hall, he had no compunction about going straight into the Tramp's office. He kicked the door shut behind him and took several steps before bending to set Miss Stuart on her feet in front of the Tramp's desk. She was not entirely trapped. The two chairs on either side of Anthony were close to the desk, but there was still room to maneuver, but it hemmed her in a bit.

"What the devil are you doing here?" he asked the moment he

straightened, glaring at her. Despite his anger, his body was already responding to the sight and feel of her.

Far from being the untouchable lady who had left Camden House earlier that evening, she now appeared eminently touchable. The elaborate hairdo was gone, though many of the curls remained, half of them pinned up while the other half tumbled around her bare shoulders, inviting a man to bury his fingers in them. One curl trailed down her front, resting atop the creamy swell of her breast on the side where her shirt had fallen off her shoulder.

Where she had gotten the clothes she was wearing, he did not know, but they suited her role perfectly.

Miss Stuart rolled her eyes, putting her hands on her hips.

"I'm here because Mitchell met Elijah and Josie here, and tonight, I heard he came here to gamble often." Her voice was still the rough East End accent she used out on the main floor, and it messed with his head. That was not how a lady sounded. That was how a doxy sounded, and he was already fighting his attraction to her. Keeping hands off would have been far easier if she had still been outfitted the way she had for the dinner.

Which... how on earth had she heard about Mitchell's gambling at dinner? He thought Camden was taking her to the dinner to keep her busy. Gentlemen would hardly speak to her about such things. Pinching the bridge of his nose, he closed his eyes for a moment.

Did it really matter? She was here now, and she needed to go.

Opening his eyes, he took in her stubborn expression and knew it would not be nearly that easy.

"You should have told me you were going to be here."

Miss Stuart opened her mouth, ready to argue, then closed it, appearing flummoxed when what he said sank in. Clearly, it was not what she had expected him to say and not what she mustered her arguments for. She rallied quickly.

"I do not report to you."

"Yes, you do, remember? We already had this discussion." Anthony had a sudden realization. They *had* had this discussion, and breaking the rules came with penalties. "Now you are going to pay the consequences."

Grasping her arm, he sat and pulled her toward him, using gravity to help tug her over his lap. He suspected only surprise, and the quickness of his movements kept her from resisting. Whatever the reason, she tumbled over his lap with a cry of surprise. Anthony felt a sense of supreme rightness as he pulled her skirts up, savoring the feel of her against him.

CHAPTER 9

A Fitting Punishment

E *vie*

Bloody hell. Bloody Captain Browne. Bloody betraying body.

She should resist him, should fight him, but the bloody man tipped her over his lap, and her body lit up like the fireworks at Vauxhall. She should not like this as much as she did.

On the other hand, as long as she did like it, why deny herself the pleasure?

You are treading into dangerous waters.

The warning bells trilling in her head were not nearly as strong as the demands of her body. From the moment he picked her up over his shoulder and carried her off, Evie had been struggling with her desire. She could have forced him to let her go, but she used the excuse of not wanting to draw too much attention to them as a reason not to fight. Now, she was over his lap—what was her excuse?

A rough hand ran over the sensitive skin of her bottom, and Evie had to bite back a moan.

My excuse is I want him to do this.

Any other man, she would have been fighting like a hellcat, but with Captain Browne, all the things that should infuriate her made her want to purr for him.

"I said you would be allowed to *help* with the investigation." Captain Browne lifted his hand and brought it down hard on her upturned arse, making Evie gasp at the hot sting of flesh meeting flesh. The pain was brief, stoking the arousal already churning in her core. "Only one person can be in charge, and that is me."

His hand came down again, making Evie squirm. Was it her imagination, or was he spanking her harder than he had before? Evie closed her eyes, trying to ignore his voice and focus on the sensations. The way her skin tingled where he had spanked her. The growing heat in her belly. The slick wetness between her thighs and the pleasure that rushed through her when she pushed her hips forward, rubbing her front against his hard thigh. She could feel his cock pressing into her side, so she knew he was not unaffected by this either.

Two more swats on her bare bottom, one on each cheek, and Evie gasped as his hand landed on spots that were already smarting.

"If you wanted to come to the Tramp's Den, you should have told me so."

Two more swats.

"Would you shut up?" She turned to look at him over her shoulder. "You are *ruining* it."

Captain Browne stared at her with bemusement, his hand frozen in the air where it had been about to descend again.

"Ruin what?"

"My spanking! Stop *talking!*"

The utter disbelief that filled his eyes was almost comical, and if she was not so aroused and frustrated by his incessant chatter, she would have laughed.

"There is no point in punishing you if we do not go over why you are being punished. You put yourself over my knee easily enough. You know you have earned this, but—"

Evie shook her head, cutting him off. That was enough of that,

"I am not letting you spank me because I think I deserve it." The big oaf would think that. "I am letting you spank me because I *like* it."

Something dark and dangerous flashed in his eyes. Something she should probably be wary of, maybe even scared of, but excitement fizzed through Evie. She knew the captain would never actually harm her, and seeing how far she could push him was as arousing as being over his lap.

"Oh, do you?" he growled.

Evie gasped as he tipped her forward a little more, putting her bottom a little higher. Her hands flung out to keep her from going much farther. Though he had a good grip on her, instinct demanded she catch herself. With her hands pressed flat against the floor, she felt vulnerable, but that added to her excitement as well.

"Then I will have to spank you harder."

Evie cried out as he did exactly that, this time without the commentary. Fire bloomed in her cheeks as he brought his hand down over and over. The swats were much less targeted, coming at different speeds, angles, and spots all over her arse. She writhed as the smarting pain began to overcome the pleasure, shocking tears into her eyes.

Not that she asked him to stop.

He wanted to prove a point, but Evie would not submit—no matter how hard he spanked her—especially because the pain did not seem to affect her arousal.

With each hard swat, her discomfort and her desire grew, and she became wetter and wetter. As she squirmed, her slick lips rubbed together, stimulating the little bud between them, despite—or maybe because of—the burning in her nates.

"We need to work together," Captain Browne growled over the sound of his hand striking her chastened cheeks. "You cannot hie off on your own and not tell me! Especially in a place like this. You might need backup. I might have needed backup."

"You came here on your own," she retorted between gasps, shaking her head against the tears threatening to spill down her cheeks. They were a physical reaction to the pain, nothing more, but she still did not enjoy them.

"Because you were occupied at dinner."

Liar. The word was on her lips, but she did not speak it aloud. She did not believe he would have accepted her intention to visit the Tramp's Den this evening... but also recognized she had not given him the chance. She had assumed he would forbid her, the same way her uncle or cousins would have.

Fine. In the future, she would give him the opportunity to work *with* her, then when he said no, she would do as she pleased, with the sure knowledge he had not been reasonable.

She felt a touch guilty for not giving him the opportunity to show that he would have behaved differently, even though she did not believe he would have. Oddly, that small touch of guilt affected how she felt about the spanking, adding to the storm of emotions and sensations assaulting her in an unexpected way. It did not make the painful part of the spanking more enjoyable, but the pain helped wash some of the guilt away.

The feeling was so intense, it was almost physical, and Evie was fascinated by the phenomenon.

While her friends had said similar things after being married, and she had certainly seen plenty of it both here at the Tramp's Den and when she had infiltrated the Society of Sin, she had never experienced such a thing. Feeling guilty for so much of her life, having even a small part of it lifted was freeing.

Tears might slide down her cheeks, her bottom was thoroughly blistered and burning a hot, roasted red, and between her legs was on fire with need, but she felt good. Light. Almost as though she would float up to the ceiling if Captain Browne was not holding her in place.

The patter of smacks stopped, and she gulped in a breath of air, panting.

"Am I understood?"

It took Evie a moment to remember what the captain had said and what he might be asking about.

Ah, yes.

He wanted her to inform him the next time she planned to do something pertinent to the investigation.

"Yes." She did not even have to lie. "Next time, I will tell you if I plan to embark on an excursion." Then they would see what happened, but she would give him a chance.

"Very good." To her surprise, he moved her off his lap, and Evie found herself on her knees in front of him, his eyes glowing as he stared down at her, his hands moving to the front of his breeches.

"Now, let me show you how you can make amends."

* * *

Anthony

Putting his cock in the vixen's mouth was probably not the wisest idea he'd ever had, but Anthony had always liked to live dangerously. He wanted to feel her mouth on him. He was asking her to put her trust in him. She had already demonstrated she must have some trust in him, considering she *let* him spank her. Anthony was well aware she had not fought back in the slightest.

Now, he would show trust in her and receive pleasure in return.

The push and pull between them, the struggle for who was truly in command, was exciting in a way he would have never anticipated.

Getting to his feet, he freed his cock from his pants, relieved she showed no sign of moving away. Before he could tell her to open her mouth, Miss Stuart reached up and wrapped her slim fingers around his cock, then slid her hand down to the base, gripping him hard. Groaning at the unexpected and entirely pleasurable contact, his hips thrust forward.

The movement put the tip of his cock right at her lips, and her tongue flicked out to taste him, swiping the little bead of fluid at the opening. Again, before he could say a word, she parted her lips and took him between them, causing Anthony's jaw to clench rigidly. His fingers plunged into her hair, though whether he was directing her or holding on to her for dear life was up for debate.

He was unsure of who was in charge at this juncture.

Though he had turned her bottom a bright cherry red that made his cock throb at the sight of it, Miss Stuart's assertion that she allowed him to spank her because she liked it... well, despite this being a much heftier spanking than before, she had certainly shown no sign of not liking it. Despite the tear tracks on her cheeks, she had been wet and ready between her legs before he moved her off his lap.

"Fuck."

The wet heat of her mouth engulfed him, sliding over the length of his cock from the leaking head all the way down to where her fingers were wrapped around the base. It was fucking heaven.

If she had *let* him spank her because she liked it, did that mean she liked this as well? That was what her statement seemed to indicate.

She was enthusiastic as she moved her head back and forth, sucking hard when she slid out, then laving her tongue over the underside of his cock as she took him back in. The head of his cock bumped against the back of her throat, and the muscles there massaged the sensitive tip before she moved up again.

The hot, wet sound of her suckling him filled the room. Anthony wanted to close his eyes, but he could not look away from the sight of his cock sliding back and forth between her lips, the length of his shaft was shiny from her saliva. Her pouting lips were wrapped tightly around it, and when she let go of his dick and took him into her mouth from tip to base, his cock sliding into her throat, his knees nearly buckled.

Hell and damnation.

He had already known she was no virginal debutante, but this was far more skill than he had expected. From feeling as though they were battling for control, he now felt he was losing the fight. The way she worked his cock, her hands gripping his hips for leverage, was driving him absolutely wild.

When she looked up at him, green eyes meeting his while her swollen lips glided over his shaft, it was all he could do not to fall into the seat behind him. As much as he wanted the moment to last forever, his self-control was rapidly unraveling. His fingers tightened in her hair, hips thrusting forward as his need grew, hot pleasure sizzling through him and reaching its torrid peak.

"Evie…" The name slipped from his lips, even though she had never given him permission to use it. Hearing it in his own voice increased his arousal and possibly hers. She hummed around his cock with approval, and the vibrations sent him over the edge of climax.

Anthony groaned as he buried himself in her throat, feeling the muscles working around the sensitive head of his cock. Her lips were pressed against his groin, her nails digging into his flesh as she took him fully, tongue laving against the pulsing underside as he spurted hot fluid straight to her stomach.

"Fuck!"

He heard the door open behind them but did not care. He was too far gone in the hot bliss of her mouth, her suckling pulling wave after wave of ecstasy through his body. The connection between them was all that mattered until he was finally utterly spent, and their grips on each other relaxed.

"I do hope I am not interrupting." The amused tone of Henry Trampine's voice made it clear he did not actually care. At least he was amused instead of annoyed at the use they'd made of his office.

Miss Stuart's green eyes glittered up at him, frustrated they'd been interrupted.

Anthony smirked down at her. He had planned to leave her hot and bothered, without relief, as part of her punishment, so this worked out well in his favor.

While Miss Stuart got to her feet, Anthony finished covering himself before he turned. The Tramp was leaning against the doorframe, his lady kneeling at his side with her head resting against his thigh, a dreamy smile on her face.

"Captain Browne, Yvette.... how very interesting." The Tramp raised a sardonic eyebrow.

Before Anthony could respond or ask the Tramp how he knew Miss Stuart, she was already moving to his side, smiling.

"Henry, Delilah, lovely to see you as always." Miss Stuart deliberately avoided Anthony's gaze. Her voice was a little huskier than usual but perfectly calm, and she spoke with the kind of familiarity that indicated long acquaintance. Not only that, she knew the Lady's real name.

It was all he could do not to reach out and pull her back over his knee.

Obviously, she was still keeping quite a few secrets from him.

He had not spanked her hard enough.

CHAPTER 10

Henry & Yvette

E *vie*

Captain Browne was seething beside her, despite the orgasm he just had. Fine. Let him seethe. She could taste him on her tongue, but her own hot need was still coiling inside her, and it was unlikely she would find any relief soon.

Henry came into the room, Delilah crawling after him in that oddly seductive manner she had when she was on all fours. Evie had become used to seeing it, but it still confounded her. She was sure she would be awkward in such a position, but Delilah managed it gracefully. Not that Evie was going to find out any time soon.

She accepted Henry and Delilah's relationship, though she did not entirely understand it.

Sitting in the chair, she bit back a curse as the pain from her spanking flared. She had almost forgotten in the distraction from the interruption and the arousal that was insistently blooming inside her. It bloody well hurt when she sat. Worse, she could feel Captain Browne smirking at her as he realized the reason for her sudden wince.

"How many times must I tell you not to call me Henry?" Henry asked with a sigh, giving her the hairy eyeball.

Evie was unimpressed. Though he was far more dangerous than when they'd run on the streets of London together, she still remembered the young man he was in the early days when he discovered her hidden gender and protected her instead of selling her out. Even if he was an overlord of the criminal underground, she trusted he would never hurt her.

Henry sat down, pulling Delilah up onto his lap to snuggle with him. The former debutante happily settled against him, though she smiled at Evie before closing her eyes and tucking her head under his chin. The unlikely pairing had turned out happily enough, and considering the dire fortunes befalling Delilah's former family, it was probably for the best she had found a strong and suitable protector.

She turned her attention back to said protector.

"I am sure you will ask me again the next time I visit since I will do it again. I am not calling you Tramp." She wrinkled her nose, and Delilah giggled. While she understood the impetus behind it—'the Tramp' sounded far more threatening than 'Henry'—she thought he could do far better as far nicknames went. "We need to know anything you can tell us about Julian Mitchell."

"We?" Henry's eyebrows went up, and he glanced at Captain Browne.

The speculation in his eyes was not unwarranted, considering what he and Delilah had walked in on. Unlike the other men in her life, Henry could be trusted to let her make her own decisions. His question came from curiosity, not a desire to order her about.

"Yes." Evie would not explain herself and did not know how much Henry knew about Captain Browne. While she trusted him with her own secrets, that did not mean she would share others' secrets.

"I did not realize you and Tony knew each other," Henry said, leaning back in his chair, stroking Delilah's hair contemplatively.

It was probably meant to unnerve them, and it had the first few times after Evie met Delilah, but she had seen far more since then, both here and at the Society of Sin events Lady Greywood hosted while Evie had been a maid there.

"Certainly, I have never seen our Yvette on such intimate terms with anyone else."

Evie put one hand atop the other on her lap, enjoying the hard stare Captain Browne directed at Henry, who was completely unbothered.

She had a feeling Henry was doing his best to needle the captain, testing and gauging his responses to find out more information. Slowly, Captain Browne sat in the chair beside hers, keeping his gaze locked on Henry.

The posturing of the men was hardly material, but it was rather entertaining and thankfully distracting as her bottom throbbed painfully beneath her and the taste of Captain Browne was still lingering on her tongue. She needed distractions from those two things to help her focus on the matter at hand.

"He knows my name is Evie, and you have not seen me on any kind of intimate terms with anyone," she replied with amusement, causing Captain Browne to slant a glance her way. She was very curious about how Henry knew 'Tony,' but that was a matter for another day. The amusement dropped as she pressed on.

"This is serious, Henry. Mitchell has been connected to several acts of treason, including smuggling spies during the war, and it appears at least some of his activities have continued into recent years. We believe he may have met with some of his associates here."

"What?" Henry sat straight up, eyes blazing with fury, causing Delilah to shriek when she was nearly knocked off his lap. His strong arms kept her from the fall, but it was a near-run thing. Tightening his arms around Delilah, he looked back and forth between Evie and Captain Browne, hoping one of them would tell him they were joking. "Are you sure?" The low growl of his voice was full of threat.

Not toward Evie, she knew, but a little shiver went down her spine. *That* question had been uttered as the Tramp, not Henry, and there was a clear difference to her ear. All traces of the young man she had known had disappeared, and she realized Henry had never fully allowed her to see him as he was now.

"As sure as we can be," Captain Browne said, his own emotion evident. "Trust me, you are not the only one angered at the discovery." Just like that, he managed to convey a sense of fellow feeling and sympathetic outrage, Evie could not quite drum up on her own.

She was outraged, but not in the same manner as the men because she had never seen Mitchell as one of her own. They had, even if only in the most general way.

"Did you know Mitchell well?" she asked, wanting to get a feel for how personally Henry was taking the revelation.

"No. By name, by face... but if he was using *my* Den to conduct his business..." Henry flexed his fingers, the knuckles cracking threateningly. On his lap, Delilah shivered. Though she knew, better than anyone, what kind of man she had married, she loved him and chose to stay with him.

"We have questions for him," Captain Browne said. "If you see him, we want to talk to him. He will answer for his crimes, but we need answers from him first."

"Hmm." The sound Henry made was extremely noncommittal.

Evie narrowed her eyes at him.

"We still do not know everyone he worked with or the extent of his machinations." She did not order Henry about, knowing he would not take it well. "I would consider it a favor if I could talk to him before he met a dire end."

"We'll see," was all Henry said.

She could practically hear the gears shifting in his head. Favors were not something Evie gave out lightly, and given his occupation, she rarely offered him one.

Beside her, Captain Browne shifted, unhappiness emanating from him, but he did not gainsay her either.

* * *

Anthony

Safely ensconced in a nondescript black carriage headed away from the Tramp's Den, Anthony clasped his hands together to keep from pulling Miss Stuart over his lap the way he had wanted to for the past hour. As much as he yearned to add to the punishment he had already administered, the answers to his questions were more important, and he did not think spanking her would give him what he wanted.

"How do you know the Tramp?" That was hardly the most pressing question, yet it was the first one out of his mouth when the carriage finally moved, and he could be sure the driver was not paying attention to them.

Sitting across from him on her own bench, Miss Stuart yawned, placing a delicate hand over her mouth. In the dim light filtering through the window, she appeared very tired. He would be far more sympathetic if she hadn't snuck out to the Tramp's Den on her own, putting herself in danger—no matter that the Tramp seemed to know her and would have protected her.

And that she could have protected herself, nitwit.

Anyone could be surprised or overpowered, and Mitchell could have easily recognized her.

There was a long pause as if she was debating whether to answer his question. For a moment, he thought she would not, but then she spoke, her voice softer than usual and far away, as though she was lost in the memory.

"When my parents died, I ran away. The woman who was supposed to be watching me until my uncle could retrieve me... she was foul. I am not sure I would have survived until my uncle arrived if I'd remained in her care. At the time, the streets of London were the better option." Evie fell silent again for a moment.

"Henry was quite a bit older than me and was not... kind, exactly, but he kept an eye out for those of us who were children, as much as he could. He was the first to teach me to fight, and when he discovered I was a girl, he did not sell me out... he helped me maintain my disguise."

Others would not have.

Those were the words she did not say, but Anthony knew them to be true. Miss Stuart was beautiful. The Tramp had helped her maintain her appearance rather than making money by selling her to a brothel or worse... Now he understood the trust she seemed to hold for him.

Miss Stuart leaned her head back against the seat, closing her eyes for a long moment, her expression more vulnerable than he'd ever seen. He realized she must not share that information with many people. She could not. It would ruin both her and her family socially if anyone knew she had been running on the streets of London, no matter that she was a child at the time.

She was trusting him.

Again.

The realization humbled him.

"I looked for you in France."

Miss Stuart's eyes opened, one delicate brow arching in question.

It was awkward to admit, the words making him feel far more vulnerable than he was comfortable with. The confession was nowhere near the same level as hers, but it was what he could offer to her. He had no deep dark secrets, nothing that would ruin him in the eyes of Society were it to come to light, but admitting his feelings for her was difficult for him in its own way.

He was admitting the power she had over him.

Anthony cleared his throat, directing his gaze out the window. It was hard enough to speak about it, but feeling her eyes on him only increased the difficulty.

"Also, after I found you acting as a maid in Lady Greywood's household."

She had disappeared into the night, and he had not known what had happened to her until the day Mitchell's minions had carried out a coordinated attack. Thankfully, Camden had been the only one injured, though the lack of other casualties had been pure luck more than anything else. When he arrived after his own attack, Miss Stuart had been there—still dressed as a maid—holding her unconscious uncle.

He had not blurted out any of their past before discovering who she truly was. He was not sure which would have been more likely—her cousins murdering him the moment the words left his mouth or dragging them to the altar.

Marrying Miss Stuart would be a fate worse than death.

It should have been. That was how he should have felt. Instead, he almost wished it had happened that way.

It would have been far easier than admitting his feelings.

"You could not have found me." The pride in her voice made him smile.

His wildcat vixen.

"I did not find you." As hard as it was to admit, it was true. She had hidden so well, played her parts so thoroughly, he would have never guessed her true identity if they had not come face to face.

There was a long pause between them.

"Did you know about Mitchell?" she asked softly. Her eyes were closed, but he could hear the weight of the question, how important the answer was to her.

"No, not until I heard about his ejection from the Society. By then, we were embroiled in the hunt for him, even if we did not know it at the time. The search took priority over all else." Even though he wondered if he would rouse her anger, he told the truth and could not regret it.

They could not make him pay for his crimes if they could not find him. He had not realized the list of crimes was so long. He wished he had. Perhaps he could have found some way to stop him.

"For me, too." Miss Stuart's reply was heavy with regret and self-recrimination.

Frowning, Anthony leaned forward to pick up her hand. Her eyes flew wide open in surprise.

"You could not have known, and that is not your fault," he said, giving her fingers a squeeze. "We cannot change the past. We do what we can in the present to change the future."

Miss Stuart stared at him, then her lips curved into a smile. It was not her full, brilliant smile, but it was a good deal better than she looked a moment ago.

"That is very insightful, Captain."

"I try. I also hope tonight has changed your heart about including me in your plans in the future." As reluctant as he was to break the moment between them, they were nearing Camden House, and he needed to be sure. Miss Stuart nodded, and Anthony grinned as he settled back against his seat, releasing her fingers.

Miss Stuart's eyes narrowed suspiciously.

"I am agreeing because it is sensible, not because you spanked me."

"I do not care why, only that you agree."

CHAPTER 11

Elijah & Josie's Return

Evie

It was another late morning for Evie. The night before, after Captain Browne returned her home, had been frustrating, to say the least. Her bottom still tingled from the aftermath of her spanking, though all the color had disappeared. Last night, her bottom had more than tingled. She had rubbed herself to completion twice before falling asleep... yet it still had not been enough.

Touching herself was not nearly as satisfying as when Captain Browne touched her. Being on her knees, taking him in her mouth, had been enjoyable but hardly something that would bring her to her own completion.

It had been a frustrating night, filled with erotic dreams of him touching her, kissing her, thrusting inside her... It was a dangerous game they were playing, yet Evie did not want to stop, demonstrating how dangerous he was to her in a different way. She should be totally focused on finding Mitchell and uncovering his perfidy. Both of them should.

They had not talked about Mitchell on the carriage ride home. They had shared secrets. Along with her bottom being sore, she felt oddly sensitive and prickly this morning and knew it was because she had revealed more to the captain last night than she ever had to anyone else. Even Mary, Josie, and Lily did not know about Henry. Her cousins and uncle had heard his name, but they did not know he was also the Tramp.

Only Anthony knew. Last night, it had not occurred to her to secure a promise of secrecy from him. She was slipping, distracted by his mere presence in her life, and it showed.

She could not get away from him entirely. If they were going to catch Mitchell, they needed to work together. As he'd said.

Descending the stairs, Evie heard a hubbub in the front hall. Picking up her steps when familiar voices drifted up, she squealed with delight as she looked over the banister and saw a head of blonde curls and a head of dark hair.

"Evie!" The blonde looked up, delight lighting her face.

"Josie!" Evie rushed downstairs into her friend's open arms. They were not always so demonstrative, but this time, Evie could not help herself. She was so relieved and happy to see Josie, not only because she needed a fellow female for assistance with managing the men, but because Josie was particularly good at flirtation and understanding men in general.

Mary was the best listener when one just wanted to talk, Lily was the best for research and any kind of intellectual questions, and Josie was the best at manipulating men to do what she wanted. Which might sound bad to men, but for women, it was a necessity. When men had all the control, how else could a woman make her way in the world?

Though Evie was accomplished in her own way, she had absolutely no experience when it came to love and was worried that was where her feelings for the captain were leading if they were not already there.

Josie, on the other hand, had spent half her life in love with Evie's cousin, Joseph, but ended up married to Evie's cousin, Elijah, and falling in love with him. If anyone knew about complicated love, it was her.

Whatever was going on between Evie and Captain Browne was very complicated.

"Oh, my," Josie said as Evie squeezed her tight, her only verbal acknowledgment of surprise to Evie's enthusiastic greeting. She hugged Evie back just as tightly. "It is very good to see you. We were so relieved to get the letter that Uncle Oliver was fine, but Elijah insisted on hurrying back as soon as possible, and I had no interest in stopping him."

All of Evie's friends claimed Evie's uncle as an honorary 'uncle,' which had not stopped after he had become Josie's father-in-law.

"It is good to see you, baggage," Elijah said teasingly, pulling her away from Josie for a hug of his own. The tightness with which he hugged her showed his emotion, and if they clung to each other for a few moments longer than normal, neither would mention it.

"Did Warwick live? Did you find out anything from him?" she asked as soon as Elijah let her go. Though she had sent a letter to Brentwood Manor, informing them Mitchell had left Uncle Oliver unaccosted and he was perfectly safe, she had not received a response. Likely because Elijah had figured he would be on the road soon enough to deliver the information in person, which was far safer.

"He did, and we did. Where is Father? And Captain Browne? They should be here for this." Elijah lifted his head, thankfully, missing Evie's blush at Captain Browne's name.

As happy as she was to see her friend and cousin, she realized their presence would make certain things more difficult. It was entirely possible Captain Browne would side with Elijah on keeping Evie out of things, even though her uncle had nominally put the captain in charge. Though, if Elijah did, that would be the immediate end to any intimacies between her and the captain.

The thought made her chest ache in an unpleasant way.

* * *

Anthony

"So, Warwick was being blackmailed into looking the other way from anything Mitchell was involved in. What about the late Earl of Talbot?" Camden asked after listening to Elijah and Josie recount everything Warwick had told them about Mitchell's activities.

"As far as we can tell, Sebastian and Nathan's father was deeply involved with Mitchell and knew exactly what he was doing," Elijah said tightly. "We think it's possible Mitchell killed him to cover his tracks, then murdered Sebastian when he began to uncover what his father and Mitchell had done."

"Which means we may never know exactly what Nathan's father did," Anthony muttered, rubbing his temples. Things were finally coming together, answers finally being revealed, but the large gaps in their knowledge would continue to plague him.

They might not know the full truth until they got their hands on Mitchell, and the man had proved damnably elusive. With the number of things he had kept from them, they had to make wild guesses about where he might be and who he might seek help from. The trip to the Tramp's Den last night had not been nearly as helpful as Anthony had hoped.

At least, not when it came to finding Mitchell.

His eyes strayed to where Miss Stuart was primly perched. Looking at her, no one would guess that last night, she had been over a man's lap or gotten on her knees to take his cock in her mouth. She appeared to be every inch the proper debutante. Arousal stirred as his gaze dropped to her full lips, and he had to jerk his gaze away before his body betrayed him.

"Do we even know if he is still in London?" Lady Durham asked. The blonde beauty was as sharp as she was pretty, though he had a feeling gentlemen regularly underestimated her, the same as they did Miss Stuart. With their respective colorings and combined appeal, they made a potent pair. If there was ever a need to distract an entire ball-room full of men...

Anthony's inner caveman rebelled at the thought of Miss Stuart engaging so many gentlemen in such a manner.

Mine.

No matter how much he told himself she was not, could not be, it did not change his instincts.

"No, but we cannot lower our guard until we know where he has gone," Camden said. "At the very least we have done a good job of making it hard for him to leave. Personally, I believe he is still here. We just need to find him."

"I believe so as well," Elijah said, raking his fingers through his dark hair. "We have thwarted him at every turn, and he was never one to take that lightly. Having talked to Warrick, I believe Mitchell is even more vindictive than I would have guessed. He hates us for the stations we hold. He has already tried to murder everyone in this room except Evie, and that is likely only because he did not know where to find her at the time."

Miss Stuart smirked at her cousin, who shook his head in resignation.

From what Anthony understood, she had gone off on her own because her uncle and cousin had forbidden her involvement in the investigation into the attempted assassination of the Duke of York. They had been frantic with worry about her, angered over her rebellion, yet it had kept her safer than the rest of them. The irony was cutting and not lost on any of them.

"What do we do now? Nathan, Lily, Mary, and Rex are looking into the smugglers and the rest of Warwick's staff on the coast. What can we do here?" Lady Durham asked, clearly as eager to jump into things as Miss Stuart. Despite his exasperated look, Elijah did not put his foot down and inform his wife that she would not be involved, even when his father frowned at him.

Anthony found that fascinating.

"We need a Society of Sin event. That is the only group I can think of that Mitchell had any real contact with whom we have not spoken to —at least, the only group we know of. As he was ousted from their events, they at least have an inkling of what he was like. Someone might know more." Miss Stuart spoke matter-of-factly and was correct in every regard, but it caused the gentlemen in the room to stiffen.

He doubted Elijah or Camden knew every detail of her exploits, that she had been to events in the past and had worked in the household while such things were going on. The only reason he knew was he had caught her out at one event.

"I will look into that," Elijah said immediately. "Anthony can help me."

"You will not be going alone," Lady Durham responded curtly, glaring at her husband.

A muscle in his jaw worked, but he did not immediately deny her statement.

"It is one thing for Josie to go with her husband, another thing altogether for Evie to go." Camden shook his head. "It is impossible."

"Interesting. I believe you put Captain Browne in charge of me for the duration of the investigation, did you not?" Miss Stuart tilted her head at her uncle, her green gaze steady. "Perhaps we should see what he thinks. Captain?"

Everyone turned to look at him. Two pairs of furious dark eyes told him he better put the kibosh on this as quickly as humanly possible. One pair of blue eyes glared at him with the opposite message of Lady Durham supporting her friend. It was the green eyes that held him, though.

Waiting to see what he would do.

Wondering if he would try to stymie her, the way her uncle and cousin did.

Anthony knew there could only be one answer.

* * *

Evie

Heart pounding in her chest, Evie showed no sign of her inner turmoil. Though she wanted to rant and rave at her uncle and cousin for their hardheadedness, what mattered even more was what Captain Browne said. If he denied her this, she thought her heart might actually break.

She would do what she wanted, regardless, but if he denied her now, it would rob her of something she desperately wanted, even if she could not put words to it.

"I think Miss Stuart's knowledge and abilities will be of use. She can wear a mask and a wig, neither of which will be of note at such an event."

As the captain spoke, relief and warmth flooded through Evie, especially as her uncle and cousin's glares increased.

"It will be perfectly safe, and if necessary, she will guard Lady Durham if Elijah and I are distracted or called away."

Oh. Brilliant.

Though Josie could take care of herself in most instances and was underestimated even more often than Evie was, she knew her cousin would not risk Josie's safety for anything. Presenting it as a need to protect Josie was brilliant. It even made her uncle pause.

It also made Evie's insides heat up.

Flowers, poetry, jewelry... none of that would impress her.

But going toe to toe with her uncle and cousin to insist she be included? That she could decide for herself how involved she was going to be?

She wanted to drag Captain Browne up to her room and ravish him.

Pressing her thighs together, she could not help but admire how he stood strong despite the withering glares aimed his way. Then again, Josie was beaming at him, and Evie was hardly unaffected, so he was not without support. Some men would not have counted her and Josie's support as highly for the mere fact they were women.

"I will speak with Lady Greywood. With Rex out of town, she is the best option for an event."

Jealousy rippled through Evie, and she bit her tongue. Lady Greywood had a reputation for enjoying strapping younger men—like Anthony. That did not mean anything untoward would happen just because he requested her assistance.

"Very well," her uncle growled. Clearly, he did not like giving in.

Rather than make her happy, sadness washed through Evie. Yes, he was doing it now that Captain Browne, a man, was insisting she be allowed to help but had never unbent when she had spoken on her own behalf.

She would take what she could get and would warm herself in the knowledge that Captain Browne not only was reasonable but that he found her capable. He trusted her to be able to handle herself as much as he did Elijah.

A knock sounded on the door, then Miss Rutherford opened it and smoothly stepped inside.

"It is almost time for luncheon, my lord. You need to eat something to keep up your strength." Before Evie's uncle could protest, as she knew he wanted to, Miss Rutherford smiled and continued. "Also, your middle son and his wife have just arrived."

Joseph and Priscilla had returned? Evie and Elijah exchanged a glance. The pair were supposed to still be on their honeymoon in Scotland and had not been expected back for another two weeks. Why had they rushed home, and what was this going to mean in terms of the investigation?

"Well, then, by all means, let us greet them," Uncle Oliver said, getting to his feet and reaching for his cane. Miss Rutherford came into the room to stand at his side. Though he offered her his arm, the true reason was so she could help him if he faltered—assistance he would not accept from his son. With Miss Rutherford, he could keep up the illusion he was escorting her rather than acknowledging he occasionally needed extra support.

Evie just hoped Joseph's sudden appearance did not come with more bad news.

CHAPTER 12

New Arrivals

E*vie*

It was a wonder they could not hear the hubbub of Joseph and Priscilla's arrival, what with all the activity. Joseph stood in the center, his wife clinging to his arm with wide eyes as she watched the servants swirling around them, some of them moving the boxes and suitcases of their belongings into the front hall and others taking them up the stairs.

"What are you doing home?" she asked, giving Joseph a hug. The rest of her family was just behind her, though when she glanced over her shoulder, Josie was holding back, standing just behind Uncle Oliver and Miss Rutherford. Evie could not blame her.

Though she was in love with Elijah now, it was still a tad awkward. At least Priscilla did not know about Josie's feelings. She knew Joseph had been set up for a scandal with Josie, but she did not know there had ever been anything more than neighborly feelings on Josie's part. To preserve Josie's pride, they all kept it that way.

"Well, when we got Adam's note about Father's injury, we could hardly stay away," Joseph said, hugging her tightly, though he was anxiously looking over her shoulder at Uncle Oliver.

"I did not want to bother you with something so trivial," Uncle Oliver said, coming forward. Miss Rutherford was still at his side, though she let him go so he could hug Joseph. "Not while you were on your honeymoon. You should have stayed in Scotland."

"You were *shot.* That is hardly trivial." Joseph scowled as he pulled away from his father's embrace, though he seemed calmer now that he had seen and touched his father and knew for himself that Uncle Oliver was hale and hearty.

Well, as hale and hearty as he could be.

"Welcome home," Evie said, turning to address Priscilla, who hung back, like Josie, seemingly unsure of her place. She barely had time to adjust to the family before she and Joseph had left for Scotland. In a family of strong, loud personalities, she tended to fade into the background. Evie thought that might be part of why Joseph liked her so much—she was restful.

Or nervous.

Personally, Evie hoped they would eventually see more of her personality. She would like to be friends with her cousin's wife, even if it was not strictly necessary.

"I am sorry that your honeymoon was interrupted."

"It is fine." Priscilla smiled. Her brown eyes were soft, and her smile was warm. If she was disappointed, it did not show, but neither did she seem thrilled to be there. Priscilla was like tepid water—never hot, never cold, always warm. Pleasant, but hardly engaging. "Worrying over his lordship, we could not have enjoyed ourselves."

Despite Uncle Oliver imploring Priscilla to call him Oliver, Uncle Oliver, Papa, or anything other than 'his lordship,' so far, he had been unsuccessful.

"Of course," Evie said, but she could not help but wonder how this would affect everything. While Priscilla knew Uncle Oliver and Elijah did some unspecified work for the Crown on occasion, she was not yet in on the big family secret. Joseph said he wanted to ease his way into telling her in a manner that would not frighten or worry her.

Evie did not know if Uncle Oliver's shooting had spurred him into speaking, but she could not ask with Priscilla there. She hoped it had. Otherwise, everything had become more complicated.

For now, they took refuge in the usual small talk one employs after the return from a trip. Decamping to the drawing room, so the staff could take care of Joseph and Priscilla's luggage, she made the introductions to Miss Rutherford.

Seating Uncle Oliver on the couch, Evie and Priscilla took up the spots on either side of him while Josie and Miss Rutherford sat in the chairs. It did not escape Evie's notice that Elijah hovered closer to Josie than normal. While he knew she loved him, before Jospeh left on his honeymoon, things had been awkward with both them and him in residence.

One would have hoped that would be over by now, but apparently, some awkwardness lingered. Thankfully, Josie seemed more amused than anything else and smiled up at Elijah, who relaxed.

Joseph and Captain Browne pulled over two of the chairs from the other side of the room to provide them with seats. Interestingly, while Captain Browne moved close to Evie, Joseph settled his between Captain Browne and Miss Rutherford. While he would have had to go around the lot of them to reach Priscilla's side, one would think he would want to be close to his new wife.

Evie wished she could see Priscilla's face when Joseph put his chair down but was sure she would see what she always did—Priscilla's calm, warm smile. She had yet to see anything that knocked that smile from the woman's lips. Either she was the most relaxed woman to ever be born, or she was even more adept at social masks than Evie.

A few minutes later, when Elijah and Joseph excused themselves, taking Anthony with them, Evie narrowed her eyes. Likely they were going to get Joseph caught up on everything while she was stuck in here, listening to Priscilla expound on the beauty of the Scottish Highlands. Though she bristled, she did not take it too much to heart. Uncle Oliver was stuck in here as well, and she doubted there was anything they could learn from Joseph.

She still hated the feeling of being left out.

* * *

Anthony

As luck would have it, there was no need to implore Lady Greywood to hold a Society of Sin event—she already had one scheduled for that evening. As he and Elijah were supposed to be out of town, they had not received invitations, but of course, they would be welcome.

He informed Lady Greywood that Elijah would bring Lady Durham, and he would be accompanied as well.

She raised her eyebrows, but he assured her the lady in question had been thoroughly vetted by Rex, and Anthony would have Rex vouch for her as soon as he returned to London. Invoking Rex's name appeased Lady Greywood. Now, he just had to make sure he could speak to Rex and explain before Lady Greywood did.

Rex *would* vouch for Anthony's mystery lady as soon as he knew the details. Considering he was part of the investigation, he would likely vouch for Anthony when Lady Greywood asked him, anyway, but Anthony preferred not to leave anything to chance.

Dashing a quick note off to Camden House, Anthony spent the rest of his day attending to his business matters. Since he was the second spare, he had much more freedom than his older brothers. He had made some investments, which had returned a tidy sum. He preferred not to be reliant on the family coffers, though he had used his income from them for his initial investments.

By the time he returned to Camden House, he was abuzz with nervous energy about what the evening might bring.

Camden met him in the hall, along with Elijah and Joseph.

"I did not know you planned to join us," he said to the middle Stuart son. Though Lady Greywood would likely have no objection, Anthony would have liked to inform her of their full party. "Does your new wife not have something to say about that?"

"Priss is happy to make me happy," Joseph said, tugging on his shirtsleeves, not quite meeting Anthony's gaze. From the censure in his brother and father's expressions, he had likely already gotten an earful. "Besides, she knows nothing of the Society, much less our investigation."

Well, Anthony was not there to tell him how to keep his marriage happy, though he thought Joseph was making a mistake.

It was one thing when it came to arranged marriages, but supposedly, he and Mrs. Stuart were a love match. Elijah had married Lady Durham specifically because Joseph had been in love with the then Miss

Bliss. A scandal had been constructed around them, likely by Mitchell, to distract and cast aspersions upon the Stuart family.

While Elijah and Josie's marriage had cleared up those disparagements, it would have been far easier and made more sense for Joseph to marry her... except he had wanted to marry Miss Bliss.

Chatter from above made the four men turn to look upward.

Joseph's wife was there, walking in front of the other ladies, her usual demure expression on her face. The constant lack of emotion, the way she always appeared 'pleasant' was unnerving Anthony.

No one was that even-keeled. Underneath that placid exterior, he was worried there were some very deep emotions. As long as it did not affect their investigation, it was not a problem for him per se, but...

I want Miss Stuart to be happy, and she will be happiest if her family is happy.

Anthony had never cared if a woman was happy with her life. While he wanted to ensure her happiness in his bed—or whatever reasonably comfortable flat surface they utilized—what she felt outside of that sphere was her own affair.

He did not want to examine why he felt so differently about Miss Stuart too closely.

There she was, just behind Mrs. Stuart, wearing a low-cut gold dress that shone even brighter against the powdered wig atop her head. She appeared ready to attend a masquerade, and the dress was far more scandalous than a debutante would normally be allowed.

Beside her, Lady Durham was also dressed in a revealing gown, though hers was a sapphire blue that matched her eyes as well as the necklace around her throat. Her blonde hair was curled and coiffed, and when Elijah stepped up to take her hand, she smiled brilliantly at him.

Behind all of them, Miss Rutherford brought up the rear and went straight to the Marquess' side, checking in with him *sotto voce*. Though they could all hear his growling answer that he was fine, so they knew what she had asked.

"A masquerade for Evie and a dinner for Josie. So lovely." Mrs. Stuart clapped her hands together. From anyone else, it could have sounded brittle or resentful, but she sounded perfectly happy for them. "And Joseph, you are off to your club for dinner?"

"Yes, Elijah and Josie are going to drop me off on their way." Joseph adjusted his jacket, seemingly impervious to the glares from his family members. Miss Stuart, in particular, was unimpressed by his lies to his wife. "I will not be out too late."

"Of course." Mrs. Stuart smiled, and a chill went down Anthony's spine, even though her smile was perfectly pleasant.

Just as all her smiles were perfectly pleasant.

Despite her demeanor, his surety that Joseph was making a mistake in how he was handling his life was growing by the moment.

"We will have a nice evening in," Miss Rutherford said, abandoning the Marquess' side to loop her arm through Mrs. Stuart's. "After dinner, perhaps we can play cards."

"I am looking forward to getting to know you better," Camden said, leaning on his cane a little more heavily than usual as he took several steps forward, holding his hand out to Mrs. Stuart. She took it, gracefully moving from Miss Rutherford's arm to his.

"And I you," she replied prettily, then looked at Miss Rutherford. "And you. Cards sounds lovely."

"I will see you later this evening," Joseph said, bowing slightly to his wife. Perhaps he felt odd about being overly demonstrative in front of family, but it struck Anthony as out of place.

"Of course," Mrs. Stuart said, pleasant smile firmly in place. "I will see you later this evening."

The trio walked away, and Joseph turned to the rest of them. He blinked as he scanned their expressions.

"What?" Even though his wife was out of earshot, he kept his voice down. Voices carried easily, thanks to the acoustics in the foyer, so it was a wise decision.

"You need to tell her," Miss Stuart hissed. Beside her, Josie crossed her arms over her chest and nodded firmly, her blue eyes blazing.

"I will... eventually. She does not need to know right now."

"Even Miss Rutherford knows because not knowing could put her in danger." Miss Stuart's glare intensified. "How will you feel if she is hurt or manipulated by Mitchell because she did not know to be cautious?"

Joseph opened his mouth. Closed it. Frowned. Looked at Anthony, then Elijah.

"What do you think?"

Miss Stuart looked murderous that he was looking for another opinion.

"I agree with Evie," Elijah said shortly. "You are doing your wife a disservice by not sharing with her. Not only because ignorance could put her in danger, but because she is supposed to be your partner, your helpmeet."

Anthony nodded. He had nothing new to add to their arguments, but he agreed with Elijah and Miss Stuart.

"Oh, look, you can learn," Lady Durham crooned, smiling widely and sidling over to her husband, wrapping her arm around his elbow. He sighed but smiled down at her, as though he could not help himself. Then she turned her attention to Joseph, her blue eyes nearly as hostile as Miss Stuart's green ones.

"You need to tell her, Joseph. It is not fair that everyone in this household, including the staff, knows of the danger, and she does not."

"Fine," Joseph sighed unhappily and scrubbed his hand over his face. "I will tell her tomorrow or later tonight, but not right now. Will that suffice?"

"Only because we need to be going," Miss Stuart muttered with another baleful glare.

"Come on," Anthony said, offering his arm to her to cut off the sniping he was sure was about to ensue between her and her cousin. Joseph was becoming flushed in the face, a scowl threatening on his brow. They did not need an argument about family dynamics when they had an investigation to run. The rest of it could wait.

Sniffing haughtily, Miss Stuart took his arm.

"I trust you have a mask?" he asked in a low voice.

She held it up, tied about her wrist. The gold matched the gold of her dress and had blended in so well, he had not noticed it until now. While the colors looked well enough on her, he much preferred her usual jewel-tone dresses and her regular black hair. The powdered wig did not suit her nearly as well.

Still, he knew better than to say so.

"You look beautiful," he said as they stepped outside.

Miss Stuart cast an amused glance his way.

"Keep talking like that, and perhaps investigating will not be the only thing we do this evening." Her voice was seductive, husky, and thankfully, far too low for her cousins to hear.

The front of Anthony's breeches immediately felt tighter.

"We need to focus on finding Mitchell," he said sternly.

"We will, but if it turns out there is nothing to be learned from the Society members, I do not see why we should waste the evening."

"You are playing a dangerous game," he murmured as they reached the coach. "Your cousins will be there as well."

"Rather adds to the excitement, does it not?" she asked. Her smile was utterly wicked.

Anthony was not sure if she was serious or teasing him, but either way, he was beginning to worry she would be the cause of his greatest downfall.

CHAPTER 13

The Society of Sin

Evie

Flirting with Captain Browne had helped distract Evie from her anger at her cousin. If he did not tell Priscilla, at least in general terms, about Mitchell and the danger he posed, she would. She did not care if the woman was a ninny; she deserved to know. Joseph was going about this all wrong.

Unfortunately, she did not get the chance to harangue him further as they used the carriage ride to discuss their plans.

"Where is Adam?" Joseph asked.

"Doing his own investigations, I presume," Evie said. She had not thought of her youngest cousin in days.

When his father had been shot, Adam's usually carefree nature had disappeared. Once he had been assured Uncle Oliver would recover, he had stalked out and into London, returning at random times and fairly infrequently. Whether he had found out anything, she did not know, but Adam was smart. He knew the danger and could take care of himself. She trusted he would come for backup for anything he needed.

Unlike Elijah or Joseph, who were more likely to try to handle things on their own for no good reason. Captain Browne suffered from that propensity as well.

And you do not?

Evie pushed away the sardonic voice. She worked alone because she had to, not because she chose to. It was not her fault her uncle and cousins never wanted her involved. She would much rather be able to rely on them, but so far, that had not been the case. They wanted to swaddle her in cloth and keep her safely tucked in the house, useless and bored.

"Hopefully, he'll stop by home soon, and we can find out who he's talked to." Elijah rubbed his chin.

"The last I spoke with him, he was doing the rounds of the young men of the *ton*." That made sense since those were the gentlemen he fit in with best—the bachelors who eschewed the usual social engagements. It was possible Mitchell had made contacts there, though it would have been more difficult since Warwick was of an older generation and engaged mostly with those of his own ilk. Though Mitchell had used Warwick's connections, that did not mean he clung to the man's side. It was entirely possible he had sought out young men on his own.

Perhaps not probable, but Evie's options for engaging with that particular group were low, so she was happy to let Adam handle it.

"How do we want to play things tonight?" Josie asked, shooting a sidelong glance at her husband seated next to her. Evie was squished between Captain Browne and Joseph, while Josie and Elijah had more room on their bench. "Are we going to pretend we are there for the activities, or should we focus exclusively on questioning those who knew Mitchell?" The question hung in the air.

Evie could feel Captain Browne shifting beside her, and heat flared within her, but she knew her priorities.

"We need to focus on Mitchell. As yet, we do not have any leads on where he might be hiding."

She felt, more than heard, Captain Browne's exhalation. Whether he was disappointed, she could not tell, but she knew eventually, she would reward him for the way he pushed for her to be part of the group tonight—she also owed him for leaving her without satisfaction the other night.

Surely, they would be able to come to some kind of mutually enjoyable conclusion.

"Miss Stuart is right. While I do not think we should make it too obvious that we are questioning anyone, engaging fully in the activities might mean we miss something." Captain Browne shifted in his seat, his thigh pressing more firmly against hers. Evie leaned against him, a very tiny amount, far too small to be noticed by anyone else, though she could feel a slight difference.

"We could always approach it with gossip," Josie suggested. "Ask them if they've heard about Mitchell."

"Some of them may be talking about it already," Evie said. "Last night, I told the Duke of Manchester and Lady Spencer about Mitchell. They are not part of the Society, but they run in some of the same circles."

Elijah chuckled.

"Yes, they do, and Lady Spencer would love to be part of the Society, but so far, her husband has refused to request admittance." Catching Evie's frown, Elijah grinned wider. "He says she is hard enough to handle in a regular ballroom. He does not wish to give her further ideas."

"Mmm." Evie made a noncommittal noise, but the back of her mind was already working. If Cynthia wanted to visit a Society of Sin event, Evie did not think she should be excluded on the say-so of her husband.

Evie owed her a small debt. Surely, they could find a way for her to visit for one night. Plus, she liked the woman.

"Word will spread, which is all to the good, though it will be in whispers. What should we say?" Josie asked, which led to a discussion of how much it was reasonable for them to know.

When Captain Browne pointed out that Evie should probably pretend to know nothing so as not to draw too much attention to herself, she nodded—clearly surprising him and her cousins. It made sense. Most who were curious would likely approach Elijah and Joseph for information since they often knew the 'official' line on Crown business.

That left Josie as the empty-headed wife, who might have something worth saying or would at least be an interesting person to tell gossip to. Captain Browne and Evie could pretend to know nothing.

Evie had no problem pretending to be the silent type. Normally, that was what she used Mary for. Mary had a knack for being overlooked and hearing all sorts of things, but she could do it just as well.

Granted, she might have chosen a different dress to wear if she had known this was going to be her part to play, but she would make do. Instead of blending into the background, she would play the mysterious observer and let everyone else do the talking to her. It would work well enough with her mask. Although she would hardly be the only one present hiding her identity this evening—she had seen others at the events in similar outfits—she would ensure she was extra aloof.

When they arrived at the house, they were greeted and allowed to enter by Lady Greywood's formidable butler. Evie took Captain Browne's arm, ignoring the dark looks Joseph and Elijah shot him. They headed into the first room while the others continued down the hall to see what entertainments were being offered.

While the entire Society enjoyed hedonistic shows and most had no problem fornicating in front of each other, that was not all they did at these gatherings. The front room had nothing but conversation, though the topics were hardly fit for 'polite' company. Evie smiled enigmatically as Captain Browne inserted them into the nearest one, keeping her on his arm.

Introductions were not made—this was not the place for them— but several of the gentlemen and one of the ladies recognized him. Evie kept silent beside him, gently fanning herself and pretending the lady's covetous gaze on Captain Browne did not bother her.

She was rather impressed at how he managed to slide the conversation around to Mitchell, taking it from a discussion of whips to Mitchell's treason. The group's voices all hushed. Only one of them had heard about it before Captain Browne broached the subject, but they were all interested. They eagerly each recounted what they knew of Mitchell from before he had been ejected from the Society.

Unfortunately, none of it was new information.

The group broke up when a lady came looking for Lord Arnold, which allowed Evie and Captain Browne to move on without it being obvious that they had only wanted to talk about Mitchell. They moved to another room and another conversation, roaming through each of them. At one point, she caught sight of Josie and Elijah, and in another room, Joseph was speaking with a small group of gentlemen.

She and Captain Browne heard a similar theme—no one had suspected Mitchell of treason. Several of the ladies had not liked him, and all of those said they'd found him pushy and often disrespectful. The men had all been unbothered by him but incensed he had tried to force a woman.

Yet... none of them had given him a second thought after he was evicted.

Evie tried not to let their cavalier attitudes get under her skin. Out of sight, out of mind was hardly an unusual tactic for people to employ. It happened everywhere, in all classes, across a broad spectrum, but was particularly insidious in the upper classes. If something did not affect them personally, they had trouble imagining how it could be a problem.

* * *

Anthony

The evening felt as useless as every other avenue they'd explored. Anthony could only hope the others were having more luck than he and Miss Stuart. The lady on his arm seemed increasingly distracted and lost in thought as the night went on, though she paid close attention whenever they were actually speaking with anyone.

As agreed, she added little to the conversations, but when it seemed appropriate, she spoke—using a fluent French accent, which was miles away from what she had used as Yvette. It seemed she was as adept at aping an upper-crust French accent as she was the lower, the same as she did for English.

Seeing how smoothly she slipped into her role, Anthony could understand why she became so frustrated with her family for keeping her out of things. She made an ideal spy, even if the idea of her in danger made him want to tear someone apart with his bare hands.

"My lady, would you like to experience some of what the Society has to offer?"

Anthony jerked his head around and scowled when he saw Lord Conyngham bowing to Miss Stuart. He had gotten close without

Anthony even realizing. The rake was well known among *tonnish* circles, sometimes skating close to the line of intolerable behavior but never stepping a toe over it. While he was happy to take lovers among the more scandalous ladies of the *ton,* he never, ever touched a debutante or caused a lady's ruin. Discretion was his byword.

If he had known Miss Stuart was a debutante, he never would have approached her, but Anthony could hardly inform him of the fact, despite the jealousy ripping through him. If Miss Stuart attempted to go off with the cad instead of staying by Anthony's side...

Suffice to say... she had better not.

"Thank you, *monsieur*, but Captain Browne is taking care of me admirably," Miss Stuart replied throatily. Behind her mask, Anthony could see her green eyes dancing with amusement.

"I can see that he is an adequate escort, but when it comes to actually experiencing everything the Society has to offer, he seems woefully behind." Conyngham's grin grew when Anthony scowled at him.

"She said she's fine," he snapped, his arm tightening where it was linked with hers and pulling Miss Stuart closer to him. It did not feel like enough, not with Conyngham eyeing her up and down as if he was considering a dive into her exposed cleavage. Anthony pulled his arm loose so he could wrap it possessively around her.

"We could always share," Conyngham suggested devilishly. He looked meaningfully at Miss Stuart. "Have you ever—"

"Mine," Anthony growled, then swung her away from Conyngham, whose quiet laughter followed them down the hall.

"Did you just try to *claim* me?" It was impossible to tell from Miss Stuart's tone of voice how she felt about that.

Yes, he had.

No, he did not want to talk about it.

"It is the only thing men like him understand," Anthony said shortly. That was doing Conyngham a disservice—he understood and respected the meaning of the word 'no,' but he also enjoyed needling his contemporaries. Anthony cleared his throat. "That is to say..." He groped for the correct words to negate his slander of Conyngham's character while protecting himself from exposing his own feelings.

"Oh, I believe I know what you meant to say." Miss Stuart smiled serenely, giving Anthony the very uncomfortable feeling she truly did know what he'd meant. Tugging his arm slightly, she pulled him towards one of the doors coming up. "Let us check in here."

The room was empty when she opened it, as sometimes happened at Society events. Not every room was in use all the time. Anthony sighed, then startled when she pulled him into the room.

"Wha—"

Kicking the door shut behind them, she grabbed his lapels and pulled him in for a kiss.

Duty warred with desire, but the latter won out.

They had already spoken with quite a few members of the Society and heard the same refrain over and over again. Besides, there were three others also investigating. If Miss Stuart wanted an illicit rendezvous with him...

Wrapping his arms around her, Anthony pulled her solidly against him, taking over the kiss with fervor. Miss Stuart moaned against his lips, squirming in his arms as his cock hardened. Pressing her up against the door, he felt around for the lock... and found the door was lacking one.

Anthony tore his mouth away from hers to check. His eyes scanned up and down, searching for what he already knew was not there.

"No lock," he said as Miss Stuart turned her head to see what he was looking at. She cursed low under her breath. "Never mind. We will stay up against the door."

That would keep her cousins from coming in and seeing them. They would just have to be careful about how noisy they were and check the hall before they left the room.

Before she could protest, Anthony claimed her lips again as his hands slid up to cup her breasts. The stiff corset denied him the sensation he wanted, so he dipped into the low neckline to pull the plump mounds up farther, exposing her nipples to his eager fingers.

She kissed him back, twining her arms about his neck, her legs parting as he pushed his knee between them. Letting her body come to rest on his thigh, she shuddered as she rocked against his leg, rubbing herself on his hard muscle through her skirts. Massaging her breasts,

Anthony squeezed the soft mounds, ending the kiss so he could move his lips down her neck while his thumbs stroked her pert nipples.

"More," she demanded greedily, arching her back and thrusting her breasts at him, grinding down harder on his thigh.

Anthony growled against her throat, his hips rocking forward so he could rub himself against her. He released her breasts to pull her skirts upward.

They had little time, and knowing the time limit and the consequences of her cousins catching them together added both urgency and excitement to their movements.

CHAPTER 14

Quickly

vie

E Normally, Evie preferred not to be hurried, but in this instance, she found it added to her arousal. The need for secrecy. The danger of being caught by her cousins. She had no doubt the epic argument that would lead to, yet she did not want to tell Captain Browne no. The risk was part of the delicious forbiddenness.

Captain Browne's mouth moved down her throat, a trail of fiery kisses that left her simmering with need. Her breasts, pulled free from her dress, were propped up almost painfully, her hard nipples rubbing against the stiff fabric of his coat, stimulating the little buds, even though his hands had moved down to pull at her skirts.

"Hush," he murmured against her skin as he shifted, and she felt his cock slip between her wet folds. "We do not want anyone recognizing your voice through the door."

She bit her lip against the moan that wanted to escape, her jaw clenching as he thrust in, his cock easily sliding into her on the slickness of her arousal. The angle was not ideal, but it did not matter. The excitement, her need, did not die down at all.

After the way he left her wanting the night before, feeling him inside her, his thick shaft stretching her open, settled a desire that had been pulsing for hours. Wrapping her arms around his shoulders, Evie found herself hoisted up, and she settled her legs around his waist.

Fingers dug into the soft flesh of her bottom, his hips thrusting so he filled her completely. Her lower back banged slightly against the door, not enough to hurt but enough to rattle the door in its frame.

"Hold on." His voice was a guttural groan.

Evie complied, her arms tightening around his neck as he fucked her, hard and fast, her body bouncing between him and the door. It was primal, forbidden, and utterly wicked. She had experienced nothing like it, and despite the angle and the quickness, her arousal surged higher, her cunt clenching around him as pleasure swelled.

Her head fell back for a moment, the back of her wig rubbing against the door.

"Oh... Anthony..." She was looking at him when his Christian name fell from her lips and saw the hot flash in his eyes in response.

"Fuck."

He pounded into her, his cock sliding in deep over and over, his body rubbing against hers. Evie shuddered, her insides throbbing as he fucked her, uncaring of the small flashes of pain that came from her hips being smacked against the door with every thrust.

She could hear laughter and conversation from the hallway as someone passed by the door, which sent her arousal soaring even higher.

Whoever was passing could hear her and Anthony.

Knew what they were doing, even if they did not know their identities.

If they were still there in the hall when she and Anthony emerged, if they recognized her, it would be a scandal of an epic degree. While she did not want it to happen, knowing it could, excited her even more.

Evie cried out, and one of Anthony's hands released her bottom, his body pressing her hard against the door as his cock shoved in deep, his hand going over her mouth to muffle the sound, which sent her ecstasy raging. Her legs and arms tightened around him, holding him against her, within her, as she pulsed around him.

She could feel him shuddering, a guttural groan working its way out of his throat as he tensed... then relaxed. Hot, wet heat flooded her insides, each spurt causing her to quiver around him, milking his cock.

Fuck!

He'd spilled inside her and the sensation spurred her most intense orgasm yet. Rapture spiraled wildly out of control, leaving her limp and satiated, pinned between him and the door, her limbs heavy with satisfaction.

Panting, Captain Browne released her mouth, his forehead resting against the door, breath hot on her shoulder.

"Fuck," he muttered, echoing her sentiment. "I did not mean to do that." Yet he did not entirely sound as though he regretted it. When he lifted his head, his dark eyes meeting hers, they were ablaze with emotion.

Possessiveness.

Heat.

Desire.

With his cock still lodged inside her, she could hardly deny she felt the same.

She had wanted him, and she had him, without care for the consequences.

"If you are pregnant, we will marry." The statement, his harsh tone, left no opening for argument.

Not that Evie was foolish enough to do so. As futures went, those of unwed mothers were particularly dire, and she would never give up her child and pretend it had never happened as some women were forced to do. While there were other options...

She had been in brothels and had seen women die from those options. She had also seen women die from having the child and being unable to find work to support them. It was a slow, cruel death, and she had intervened when she could, but she had not always known in time. Some women had been murdered for trying to keep the child when the man who impregnated them did not want them to.

Pregnancy was a dangerous business for a woman. Evie knew how lucky she was to have the resources she did, the life she did, and the offer from an honorable man like Captain Browne.

"*If* I am pregnant."

Something in her belly fluttered. A little part of her liked the idea of being married to Captain Browne, but she did not want it to be under forced circumstances. Certainly, it was a better option than going it alone and bringing shame to her family, but she wanted...

She wanted...

Evie did not want to think about what she wanted. It made her feel far too vulnerable while he was still pressed against her, pressed inside her, his gaze peering into hers.

Captain Browne nodded.

She felt his cock slide from her. They took a few moments to adjust their clothing, and he helped her with her wig. There was not much they could do about the wrinkles in her skirt other than shake them out, but they did not show too badly.

Just before she was about to turn and open the door, Captain Browne caught her chin and turned her to face him. His gaze bore into hers, fingers firm but not painfully tight on her jaw. Evie should have batted his hand away, but part of her enjoyed his forcefulness. Reveled in it even.

With her face cupped in his hand, his focus entirely on her, she was even more aware of the filthy sensation of his seed leaking out of her onto her thigh. It was perverse how much she liked the feeling.

"You will tell me if you are with child."

Evie felt her anger flare, but she pushed it down. He was not being entirely unreasonable, but he had better take her at her word now, or they were going to have a different problem entirely.

"I will tell you."

The moment hung between them, suspended in the air, then he nodded.

"Good."

To her surprise, instead of releasing her chin, he dipped his head to claim her lips for another kiss. Despite her stirred temper, she kissed him back just as fiercely, nipping at his lip before he pulled away.

* * *

Anthony

His lip stung where Miss Stuart bit him, but Anthony did not mind. He rather liked it. It was a just punishment for being so out of control that he released inside her.

Listening at the door and hearing no one, he opened it and peeked out.

"Quickly," he murmured when he saw it was empty. Miss Stuart glided out before him. Other than a few creases in her skirt, there was no indication she had just been properly fucked up against the door.

Anthony's hands already itched to touch her again. That little taste had not been enough, yet he knew it was all he could have... for now. More would be far too dangerous.

Two of her cousins were at the Society tonight and the situation at home... It had been foolhardy with just Camden in residence. With everyone else? Impossible.

As if to prove his thoughts, almost the moment he stepped into the hall behind Miss Stuart, two figures appeared at the end of the hall, arms around each other, clearly on their way to a rendezvous. Both men, which was not too uncommon within the Society. Though it was technically against the law, everyone looked the other way at Society events.

Discretion was always key.

"Adam!"

One of the figures jerked his head toward Miss Stuart, a look of horror sliding over his expression—not because he saw her, but because she saw him.

The youngest Stuart son was in the embrace of another man, though he quickly scrambled to change that. It took Anthony a moment to recognize the other man—Lord Lucas Beckett, the Earl of Devon. Handsome, close friends with Rex, and the cause of some melodrama within the Society in the past.

He had been pulled into the investigation for the traitor after being framed by one of Mitchell's associates, Collins. Devon had gone to France on Camden's orders to get some time away from England but also to see if he could discover whether there were any ties between the Duke of York's attempted assassination and the other country.

It appeared he had returned after being unable to discover any such connection.

While Devon was well known within the Society for preferring men, Anthony had not realized the youngest Stuart had such proclivities—and going by Adam and Miss Stuart's reaction, it was news to her as well.

"Evie?" Adam's voice sounded half-strangled, and Devon's eyes widened in recognition.

"Your cousin?" Despite Devon's obvious surprise, he kept his voice hushed. What was more interesting was he recognized Miss Stuart's name, indicating Adam must have talked about his family with his lover.

Both of them glanced back and forth across the hall they'd just come from, then hurried forward. Miss Stuart gave herself a shake, closing her mouth and composing herself as Adam approached. Anthony did not know the man well enough to read his expression perfectly, but he could see the conflict there—the worry, the hope, the fear.

"What are you doing here?" Adam hissed, sudden realization coming over him when he reached Miss Stuart. His gaze darted over her shoulder to look at Anthony, who had hung back since this was clearly a family matter.

"Investigating Mitchell, which you would know if you came round more often," Miss Stuart retorted, though there was no heat to her voice. Her tone had gone rather dry. "I would ask what you are doing here, but it seems fairly obvious."

Adam flushed pink, and Devon looked away, studying the wallpaper as if he suddenly noticed something interesting.

"What I do with my time is my business," the youngest Stuart said. Though he was trying to appear firm, he did not have quite the knack for it his father or eldest brother did.

"Same." Miss Stuart was not taking any prisoners, and Anthony's lips twitched. "Though, you should consider being more circumspect this evening if you want to keep it your business. Elijah, Josie, and Joseph are all here as well."

Adam groaned, rubbing his hand over his face, then shot an apologetic look at Devon, who smiled back at him.

"We can be discreet," Devon said before turning his attention to Miss Stuart. "Lucas Beckett, Earl of Devon, at your service." His bow was graceful.

"I know. It is lovely to meet you officially. I am Adam's cousin Evie, and this is Captain Browne, who is also part of the investigation." Miss Stuart gestured back at him, and Anthony came forward to take her arm.

"We should keep moving. Perhaps we can find the others and see if they've discovered any worthwhile information. If not, we can leave the event to those who wish to be here for its own merits."

"Appreciated. Evie is correct. I should catch up with what is happening." Adam sighed and cocked his head at Devon. "Would you like to join us, or have you had enough of this business?"

"I would love to join you," Devon said, appearing pleased to have been asked.

Well, this should be interesting.

Anthony and Miss Stuart led the way, with Adam and Devon coming behind them. He could hear bits of a whispered conversation between the two men, probably deciding what they would say about Devon's presence or... well, who knows what. Anthony knew neither of them well enough to speculate.

Selfishly, he was happy they both were coming. Even without knowing about their relationship, the appearance of Adam and Devon should help keep Miss Stuart's cousins from questioning her and Anthony too closely about accounting for their time this evening. Anthony would not betray a trust, but he was also happy to hide behind the youngest Stuart to avert attention from himself and Miss Stuart.

Rounding a corner, Anthony was surprised to see Elijah and Lady Stuart there, standing against the wall across from a door. Looking up, Lady Stuart pressed a finger to her lips before Anthony or Miss Stuart could say anything. Her expression was anything but pleasant, so Anthony pressed his lips together.

"What is going on?" Miss Stuart hissed in a loud whisper as they came closer.

Lady Stuart's eyes were blazing. With his arms crossed over his chest,

Elijah glared at the door. Whatever was going on behind that door, they were *not* happy about it, but the entire premise of the Society was that one did not judge. "Not for me, but fine for you" was their byword.

So, what could have invoked this reaction?

Something unsettling flicked through Anthony's chest as another question popped into his head.

Where is Joseph?

"Joseph is in there with Lady Cross." Lady Stuart looked like she wanted to claw someone's eyes out, but she kept her voice low. If Joseph was behind that door, it was unlikely he could hear any of this. "We saw him go in."

"Lady Cross has a penchant for spanking gentlemen," Miss Stuart murmured.

Anthony glanced down to see the cloud descending over her features before her temper flared up.

"Hello, Adam," Lady Stuart said quietly. "Lovely to see you." Though her fury was still threaded through her voice, she managed to sound sincere.

"Joseph is here?" Adam whispered, coming to Miss Stuart's other side. "I thought he was on his honeymoon."

"He was. He got your letter about Uncle Oliver and returned home, and now he's apparently questioning Lady Cross in private." Lady Stuart's tone said that had better be all he was doing. Anthony guessed that was why she and Elijah were waiting outside the door—giving Joseph just enough rope to hang himself with.

He did not like to think of what would be awaiting Joseph if he was foolish enough to engage in extramarital activities with his brother and cousin so close by and on a night when he was still supposed to be on his honeymoon. Lady Stuart looked like she was ready to break down the door.

A moment later, they heard a loud, impassioned, masculine moan—albeit muffled.

Anthony decided retreat was the better part of valor and released Miss Stuart, so he could slowly back away, taking refuge beside Devon. He caught the other man's eye and saw his understanding.

They would not have to worry about anyone caring about *them* tonight.

Joseph, on the other hand, was going to have a rough go of it, and he had brought it all on himself.

CHAPTER 15

Unfaithful

E*vie*

When the door opened to reveal her flushed, satiated cousin, it took all of Evie's willpower not to jump forward and slap him across the face.

What the hell had he been thinking?!

Lady Cross' soft laughter followed him as he looked back over his shoulder at her... then he turned and saw the assembled party waiting for him, and his face paled.

"Uh..." The stammering word was damning.

All of them had been hoping there was some other explanation, but now they knew beyond a shadow of a doubt.

"How *could* you?" Josie's hissed whisper was full of vitriol. If anything, she was the angriest among them, and Evie understood why.

At one point, Josie had been in love with Joseph and had dreamed of marrying him. If she had, she would have been the one in Priscilla's shoes this evening. It was far too easy for her to imagine Joseph doing this to her, to imagine how devastating it would be, even though she was happily married to and in love with Elijah.

"I... this..." Joseph pulled himself up, chin tilting up stubbornly, which only increased Evie's desire to punch him in the nose. "What I do is none of your business. Any of you."

While that was true for Adam, it was patently *untrue* for Joseph, at least when it came to this. Whatever perversions he enjoyed, Evie hardly cared, but tomorrow morning, she was going to have to look his wife in the eyes. She could murder him right now for that alone.

"You married Priscilla." Josie jabbed her finger into the center of his chest. Behind her, Elijah was glaring at him. "You brought *us* into this. You are supposed to be on your honeymoon, but instead, you came home and immediately went searching for another woman, and tomorrow, *we* all have to face *your wife* over the breakfast table."

Evie had not thought it was possible, but Joseph's face paled even more.

"You cannot tell her."

"You should have thought of that before you did *this*." Josie turned on her heel and stormed off. Elijah started to go after her, but Joseph reached out to catch his arm. His older brother glared at him, and Joseph wilted slightly before bolstering himself.

"You cannot let Josie tell Priss. It will hurt her beyond belief, even though, I swear on our mother's grave, I did not betray my marriage vows. It was... it was nothing more than..." Joseph cleared his throat. "I did not betray my marriage vows."

"What he means is, he was unwilling to do more than let me spank him," Lady Cross said from behind him. The lady, several years older than all of them, was watching the goings-on with a certain amount of displeasure. She pressed her lips together. "I heard his wedding was a love match, but many of our members are here without the knowledge of their spouses. However, I did not realize Joseph was supposed to be on his honeymoon right now."

"They came home early, thanks to an injury our father suffered," Elijah said through clenched teeth. The coldness in his eyes as he glared at Joseph had not dissipated.

"I see. Joseph, if you return to me, you will have some serious transgressions to make up for." Lady Cross moved past him, sweeping down the hallway and leaving them all alone.

Joseph flinched at her words, but something like anticipation lit up his eyes.

Stepping forward, Evie slapped him across the face. The look in his eyes was replaced by shock as he stared at her, her palm print bright red on his cheek. Evie *never* slapped. She always hit with a fist, the way her cousins had taught her... the way Joseph had taught her.

A slap was demeaning, especially when he knew she could have punched him. A slap said he was *unworthy* of a fist. It was belittling. It made a completely different kind of impact than punching him in the nose.

"You should have never married her."

"I have needs, Evie. That is what the Society is for. The needs we cannot have fulfilled at home." Joseph's tone was begging, pleading for her to understand.

"Did you even give Priss a chance? Did you ask her if she would be interested? Or did you decide she was better kept in the dark as to your needs instead of allowing her to be fully part of your life?"

The stricken expression on his face was the only answer she needed.

"The rest of us are leaving. Find your own way home."

"You cannot tell her," he whispered.

Pausing before turning away, Evie leaned in, speaking very low and very softly.

"If you do not want me to tell Priscilla *everything,* by lunch tomorrow, you will tell her about Mitchell and the danger our family is in."

That was the only concession Evie was willing to make. She hoped, truly hoped, that given some time, Joseph would come to the correct conclusion regarding his needs and his wife. For now, the danger was the more pressing issue.

She would give him some time and would talk Josie into doing the same. Elijah would not betray his brother, no matter how upset he was with him, and from the look on Captain Browne's face, he was already uncomfortable with the family drama. Mentally, she was already putting a limit on the amount of time she'd given Joseph before he spoke with Priscilla about his needs, especially if she found out he kept coming back to the Society and Lady Cross.

It would be one thing if the marriage with Priscilla had been arranged, but it was a love match.

And Priscilla loved Joseph.

Evie had thought Joseph loved her, too.

Sometimes, people did stupid things and made stupid mistakes. Her own family was not immune, but she would be damned if she would be a part of Joseph's lies. Priscilla deserved to know.

However, Mitchell and the investigation took precedence. For now.

Whirling, Evie stomped away from her cousin, aware of Elijah and Captain Browne following her. The slick feel of Captain Browne's seed between her thighs as she moved no longer felt as arousing. Seeing Joseph, remembering the expectations that many men of their social set had for their wives and mistresses, Evie knew she and Captain Browne needed to have a talk if she turned out to be *enceinte*.

Evie would *not* be married to a man who looked outside of their marriage to fulfill his needs.

* * *

Anthony

Rather than going back to Camden House with the Stuarts, Anthony told them he would see them on the morrow. Miss Stuart was so distracted by her cousin's infidelity, she did not question his statement. She and Lady Stuart were seething, whispering to each other, even as they got into their carriage.

Anthony did not envy Elijah the ride home, but the other man seemed lost in his own thoughts, so perhaps he would be able to ignore the ladies' discussion. While Anthony understood their emotions, he was not involved to the same degree.

Love matches in the *ton* were hardly usual, though Miss Stuart's friends had all found love *within* their matches. He might not approve of Joseph's actions, but he did not take them as personally as they did, probably because he did not know Joseph's wife by more than name and face. It did not affect him.

He was going to take advantage of their distraction to do some more searching on his own.

This time, he went into the Warrens without a disguise, trusting his sword stick and confident swagger to keep him unmolested. He kept to the main path through to the Tramp's Den. While being alone might make him a tempting target, his steady gait and the easy way he swung his cane would make any smart robber think twice about taking him on.

Frank let him through the door with a nod. Entering the main room, Anthony glanced up and saw the entertainment for the evening was over or had yet to start. The Tramp stood on the balcony overlooking the throng, but his lady was not in sight, which meant she was not there or she was kneeling beside him, obscured by the waist-high wall the Tramp leaned against.

The Tramp's gaze met his, and the man gestured for Anthony to join him.

Pressing his lips together, Anthony nodded. He had hoped the Tramp might have more information for him by now. His contacts in this world far exceeded any network Anthony, or even Camden, could hope to build.

Guarding the bottom of the stairwell to the balcony, Butch greeted Anthony as he passed. Walking up the dark staircase, Anthony was unsurprised to find the Tramp waiting for him at the top, away from the balcony where they would be easily seen. He was sitting in a chair, Delilah kneeling on a cushion beside him, her head resting against his thigh so he could stroke her hair.

"Tony, what brings you back to my humble abode? No Yvette with you this evening?" The half-smile on the Tramp's face did nothing to detract from the alert wariness in his eyes.

"Not tonight," Anthony said. Though if she showed up again, he was going to take great pleasure in turning her bottom a bright cherry red before fucking her senseless. Their rendezvous earlier had been a tasting rather than a satisfactory meal. "I will not be staying long. I was wondering if you had any news on Mitchell."

The Tramp silently studied him for a moment, weighing how much he wanted to say, which caused a prickle of alertness to tingle on the back of Anthony's neck. He would be willing to wager his entire fortune, the Tramp knew *something*.

He would have won that wager.

"I know he is hiding out in the Warrens, though we have not found him yet," the Tramp said finally. "There have been a few sightings, but the search started by the dock workers seems to have run him to ground rather than flushing him out."

Anthony grimaced. An unfortunate side effect, though he did not regret the warnings they had sent. If Mitchell made it onto a ship, they would likely never catch up with him.

"Does he have any contemporaries I might be able to speak with?" Even though he was sure the Tramp had already spoken with any he knew about, Anthony figured it could not hurt to question them himself. While the Tramp would be focused on finding Mitchell, Anthony wanted to know if any of them had information about Mitchell's past activities.

The Tramp's lips thinned, his fingers gripping his lady's hair for a moment before relaxing and stroking over her temple in a soothing manner.

Anthony could not help but wonder if Miss Stuart might ever be so docile with him. It was hard to imagine. She was a vixen and a wildcat, not a pet.

"It seems Mr. Mitchell has been cleaning house," the Tramp said. "The two men I knew he occasionally consorted with or hired out were both murdered in the past forty-eight hours."

Anthony cursed under his breath. He should not be surprised. The Tramp tilted his head.

"I have not yet had the opportunity to speak with Mr. Richard Grey, fourth son of Viscount Grey. He normally comes here every night to gamble, but he did not last night."

"Or tonight?" Anthony did not ask if the man had ever interacted with Mitchell. The Tramp would not have mentioned the man otherwise.

"Or tonight. I believe his lodgings are on Jermyn Street." As were many bachelors of the *ton*—those who had the money for it. Anthony raised his eyebrows in question, and the Tramp shook his head, understanding immediately. "He was not a particularly skilled gambler, but whenever he started to wade too deeply into the River Tick, he would hire out for just about anything. Most recently, he was bragging about a job he took as a highwayman."

The pieces clicked together in Anthony's mind. A few weeks ago, the then-Miss Davies had been kidnapped by a highwayman on her way home from London. She was rescued by her now-husband, the Earl of Talbot. She'd claimed the highwayman had been well-educated, and his accent indicated he was from the upper classes.

It made an exquisite amount of sense that Mitchell would enjoy hiring someone to do his dirty work from the very group of people he most despised. Someone like Richard Grey would be exactly the kind of person he wanted—a bored younger son with no morals, too much time on his hands, and a great need for funds his family was unlikely to provide.

The greatest surprise was Richard Gray had survived until now, considering he had botched the kidnapping and questioning. Then again, Mitchell had been out on Warwick's estate at the time, ensuring he was out of the city for the attacks his hired goons had been carrying out. They were probably already dead, too.

"I will go there now," Anthony said, giving the Tramp a nod of acknowledgment.

It would be far easier for him than for the Tramp to venture into that side of town. Not that any of the men there would dare stop him if they recognized him, but it would cause talk. If anyone saw Anthony on Jermyn Street, they would think nothing of it.

He turned and went down the stairs without a second glance. It did not take him long to make his way out of the Warrens and to Jermyn Street. Even though the Season proper was over, the street remained fairly crowded with renters—plenty of younger sons who had no interest in returning to their family's estates and who rarely attended the Season's events, anyway.

A quick question to two passersby as he walked down the street and Anthony had the house number for Richard Grey. The house was dark when he walked up, which did not necessarily mean anything, but Anthony was already grimly certain what he would find.

Walking up to the front door, he rapped on it sharply.

Again.

And again.

No answer. Not a sound from inside the house.

Blowing out a long breath, Anthony looked around. The street was blessedly clear. It took him less than a minute with his picks and he was inside.

He did not have to go far—Richard Grey's body was in a crumpled heap at the bottom of the stairs.

CHAPTER 16

An Awkward Breakfast

Evie

Breakfast was a stilted affair until Captain Browne arrived to break the tension.

Joseph was quiet, focused on his meal and pretending to ignore the glares he was receiving from her, Elijah, and Josie. Adam had shown up for breakfast for the first time in days, appearing rather haggard. His false joviality as he glanced at Evie throughout the meal would have probably caught everyone's attention if they were not so focused on Joseph.

At the head of the table, Uncle Oliver sat with Miss Rutherford and Priscilla on either side of him, the three of them exchanging looks of confusion as they tried to figure out what had happened the night before. Miss Rutherford and Priscilla were probably especially confused. To their knowledge, Joseph had been at his club, Evie had been at a masquerade with Captain Browne, and Elijah and Josie at another gathering, so they were probably wondering how Joseph had made everyone so angry during a short carriage ride.

While Uncle Oliver knew they had all been together, nothing they had reported to him explained why everyone was angry at Joseph. They'd given him that much loyalty, though he did not deserve it.

Poor Priscilla also seemed confused but gratified by the sudden, aggressive friendliness Josie exhibited. Not that Josie had been unfriendly before, but she was clearly dealing with her anger at Joseph by being extra supportive of Priscilla, who was completely in the dark why she might have garnered such support.

That was what Captain Browne walked into.

"Good morning," he said in his deep voice. There were dark circles under his eyes, indicating that he had slept little.

Evie narrowed her eyes at him, studying him closely. He had disappeared when the rest of them had gotten in the carriage to go home last night. Had he gone back to his own place, the way she assumed, or had he gone elsewhere?

She was suddenly gripped by the suspicion of the latter. The bastard. He had not said a word!

Various greetings were muttered from around the table.

"Did you need to speak with me?" Uncle Oliver asked with a slight hint of desperation. Likely, he badly wanted to get away from what was the most awkward family meal they'd ever had.

"Ah, yes, but I can wait until you're fin—"

"I'm finished," Uncle Oliver cut Captain Browne off. Getting to his feet, he waved his hand at Miss Rutherford, who moved to help him. "I am fine."

Evie watched closely, but it appeared he truly was fine and regaining some of his strength, and she was sure it was due to Miss Rutherford's influence. With Evie not able to watch him all the time, she had been worried he would overexert himself, but Miss Rutherford had proven capable of keeping him under control.

"I will come with you, Uncle Oliver," she said, getting to her feet and shooting Joseph a significant look. "Perhaps Joseph will find he has something to say in our absence."

"I will come as well," Elijah said. "Josie?"

"I will stay here." Josie glared at Joseph, then turned her head to give Priscilla a smile. Priscilla smiled uncertainly back. For the first time, she did not seem 'fine.' The undercurrents running through the room had rocked her normally even keel. "To ensure that any relevant details to any possible discussions are not missed."

Joseph winced, not meeting anyone's gaze. Not that it would help him. If Josie had decided the discussion about Mitchell and the investigation was going to happen *now,* it was going to happen now. He should be grateful Evie had successfully convinced Josie that Joseph's extracurricular activities at the Society could wait.

Perhaps this would be good practice for communicating with his wife instead of making decisions for her without her input.

"Very well," Uncle Oliver said, offering Evie his arm while giving her a sidelong glance. She was sure he had plenty of questions for her and Elijah. Adam silently got to his feet, following them.

They left the supremely uncomfortable atmosphere of the dining room and headed to the drawing room. Her uncle was moving very well, Evie noted, though he did not let go of her arm. That surprised her, but she was not unhappy with an overabundance of caution when it came to his wellbeing.

Once she got him seated on the couch, Evie took the place next to him. Captain Browne sat in one of the chairs across from them while Elijah leaned against the fireplace mantle, and Adam tucked himself into one of the window seats. She was going to have to talk to him soon and reassure him she did not care that he was consorting with Lord Devon and that she was happy as long as he was happy.

And that she would keep his business private until, and if, he ever felt comfortable sharing with the rest of the family. Though with so many of them attending the Society events, it was likely to come out eventually if he and Lord Devon continued meeting there.

"What brings you by so early this morning?" Uncle Oliver knew very well if they had discovered anything pertinent, they would have woken him up.

"After our visit to the Society's event last night, I went back into the Warrens," Captain Browne said, looking straight at Uncle Oliver and ignoring Evie's hiss of displeasure.

I knew it!

Bloody men.

She should have been more suspicious when he had taken himself off last night instead of getting in the carriage with them. She had allowed herself to be distracted by the situation with Joseph. Lesson learned. Next time, she would ensure she knew where he was going.

Uncle Oliver sat up straight, and it took Evie a moment to catch up. Obviously, Captain Browne had found something, or he would not have shown up at this early hour to report in.

Blast.

She needed to get her head on straight and stop being distracted by Joseph's misbehavior and her attraction to Captain Browne. That likely meant finding some time to be alone with the captain in the near future. Evie was not so foolish to think fighting her attraction would make it less distracting. Indulging would mean she could satisfy her need, then move forward without her body nagging her.

Last night had not been enough to satisfy her, which was why she was still distracted this morning.

"I visited the Tramp. So far, he has not found Mitchell, but he discovered the bodies of several men known to work with Mitchell." Captain Browne grimaced as Elijah cursed under his breath. "He also sent me to Jermyn Street in search of Richard Grey, fourth son of Viscount Grey, who I believe was likely the highwayman who waylaid Lady Brentwood."

The man who had kidnapped Lily? Evie blinked.

"I assume Mr. Grey is dead?" Uncle Oliver asked in a heavy voice, resigned.

"Yes. It appears he drunkenly fell down the stairs and broke his neck." Captain Browne's voice was grim and frustrated, which was also how Evie felt. Elijah paced, rubbing his face, clearly struck by the same emotions filling Captain Browne.

"Very reminiscent of Nathan's father," Elijah said, making all of them blink in surprise. Uncle Oliver nodded. The traitorous and, fortunately for him, already deceased Earl of Talbot had taken a drunken fall from a balcony.

No one had thought twice about it until his son Nathan, the current Earl of Talbot, uncovered evidence of his father's perfidy. The murder of Nathan's elder brother had also been made to look like an accident.

"The other men the Tramp mentioned, did he say how they were killed?" Evie asked.

"No, but he was sure they were murdered," Captain Browne said slowly. "It is interesting that the deaths among those of the upper classes appear as accidents."

"Perhaps because he knows the law would fall far more heavily on him for those deaths," Evie muttered. Her uncle glanced at her, but he did not argue the assertion. How could he? It was the truth.

It made sense that Mitchell was more careful about making a lord, or the son of a lord, appear to die in an accident rather than an obvious murder. Though having the *ton* in a panic might be entertaining to Mitchell, it was hardly conducive to keeping a low profile.

She was a little surprised he had bothered with Mr. Grey. Perhaps it truly had been an accident. Or perhaps he had been hoping Mr. Grey's body would be found by friends or family and dismissed as an accident. If the Tramp had not sent Captain Browne there, it was likely that was exactly what would have happened.

* * *

Anthony

After such a long night, Anthony wanted nothing more than to go home and flop onto his bed and sleep. Upon finding the body, he contacted the authorities and had to answer their questions before going home and finding that he could not sleep because his mind was whirling. He had stared at the ceiling for an hour before finally getting up and making his way to Camden House, hoping the Marquess would be awake.

He'd been surprised to find the whole family at the table, but perhaps he should not have been. The atmosphere in the room had been tense, likely due to Joseph's indiscretions. He hoped Joseph was finally telling his wife about Mitchell. Though it seemed like Lady Stuart did not plan on giving him a choice, going by her words when she had opted to stay in the dining room.

As if his thoughts had summoned them, there was a knock on the door, then Lady Stuart swept in, a satisfied expression on her face. Behind her came a sheepish Joseph, Mrs. Stuart, and Miss Rutherford. Mrs. Stuart appeared rather pale, but overall, she did not seem upset.

Anthony could only wonder what that smooth social mask hid.

Either the woman really was the most even-tempered person to ever walk the earth, or she was going to explode like a firework when she finally reached the end of her fuse. He was not sure if he hoped to be present for the show.

Elijah strode over to greet his wife, and Anthony got to his feet, relinquishing the chair to the ladies. No sooner had Lady Stuart settled in hers, with her husband leaning on the back of it, than she met Anthony's gaze.

"So, what has happened now?"

Like Lady Stuart, Mrs. Stuart sat down in one of the chairs, and like his brother, Joseph moved into place behind her. Unlike his brother, Joseph hovered, keeping his hands off the chair as if uncertain of his place beside his wife. In the window seat, Adam was staring out the window, lost in thought. Anthony would have to find a moment to speak with him and assure the man that what happened at the Society stayed there.

Anthony cleared his throat.

"Well, Lady Stuart—"

"Oh, please, call me Josie. We are all in this together, are we not?" Lady Stuart—Josie's—instruction set off a round of permissions for them all to use their Christian names. Miss Rutherford was Diana, Mrs. Stuart was Priscilla, and he'd already known Joseph's name. The only one who did not extend the offer was Miss Stuart, which should have bothered Anthony but felt more like a challenge.

One he intended on meeting.

For now, he concentrated on retelling the events of the previous night to his audience. Using the ladies' first names would take some getting used to, but with the number of Stuarts about, it was far more comfortable.

"I do not understand," Priscilla said, her brow furrowing when he finished. Behind her, Joseph's expression blanked, something simmering beneath the surface, which was wiped away by surprise at her next words. "Why would this Mr. Mitchell bother to make it look like an accident?"

Joseph's jaw dropped. Josie and Miss Stuart cast approving looks at her. Uncle Oliver cleared his throat, appearing uncomfortable, and that impression grew stronger when it was Diana who answered her.

"Perhaps he hoped it would go unnoticed?" Diana glanced around at everyone as if looking for confirmation. Miss Stuart nodded at her, making a gesture with her hand for Diana to continue. "If his family found him, they would be quick to call it an accident and keep the details of his death covered due to his inebriated state, whereas they would raise up a hue and cry if they thought he had been murdered."

"That makes sense," Priscilla said. She looked back at Anthony. "Did you find anything when you searched his house?"

Though she was not as demanding as Josie or Miss Stuart, she was clearly interested in his answer. Behind her, Joseph looked as though he was close to falling over at his wife's reactions, staring at the back of her head as though he did not recognize her.

On the couch, Josie exchanged glances with Miss Stuart, somewhat smug. The Marquess and Elijah were looking at Priscilla and Diana with new eyes, though the Marquess' focus was more on his nurse than his daughter-in-law. No big surprise there. He had been spending most of his time with Diana recently, and until now, she had been quiet about the situation.

"Nothing that pointed to Mitchell," Anthony admitted. "But at least we have a new direction to look in. It is always possible Richard Grey told one of his parents or siblings something about Mitchell. We just need to find them."

"His eldest sister left London with her husband at the end of the Season, his three brothers never came for the Season, but his parents and younger sister all planned to stay in London for the full year," Priscilla recited as if reading off a page, then blinked when she realized everyone was staring at her.

"You remember that?" Elijah asked incredulously. "You remember all that about a random family?"

"Well... yes." She seemed surprised they found that unusual. "Only the eldest son is married, and my mother and the viscountess run in some of the same circles. I think she hoped to match me with either the second or third son. That was before I met my Joseph, of course." A tiny smile curved her lips for just a moment, then it disappeared.

She did not look back over her shoulder, but Anthony got the impression she wanted to and that she was not entirely happy with her Joseph right now, but he might have been projecting everyone else's attitude toward Joseph onto her. If she was displeased with her husband, she did not show it by word or expression.

"I am supposed to remember things like that, but I never can," Josie admitted. She looked impressed. "That's wonderful, Priss. Now, all we have to do is find out where we can run into them."

"Josie was invited to a tea at Lady Brooke's this afternoon, and likely, the Grey ladies will have been invited as well," Priscilla said, surprising them when she spoke up again. Joseph looked as though he was constipated over his wife's involvement.

"I was?" Apparently, Josie had not looked through her invitations since returning from Brentwood, though one could hardly blame her.

"Yes, I saw it along with quite a few others when I sorted the mail for you yesterday afternoon. There are several events you are invited to but did not respond to."

"I will do that immediately." Josie got to her feet. "Who would like to come?"

The Marquess' gaze met Anthony's, and he nodded. He knew Camden was reluctant to add the ladies to the fold, and he understood, but they kept demonstrating how very useful they were. Gathering information from an afternoon tea would hardly be a dangerous mission, but he would accompany them just the same.

"I think all the ladies, of course. Joseph and I can escort them."

"I will stay here with the Marquess," Diana said quietly, folding her hands in her lap. Surprisingly, Camden did not argue. Likely he wanted to be at the center of things as people came back to report in.

"Adam and I will see if we can find Viscount Grey," Elijah said, glancing at his brother, who finally looked up and nodded.

Just like that, they were back on the hunt.

CHAPTER 17

Nothing but Tea and Gossip

E<u>vie</u>

Afternoon tea was something Evie had never attended before. She'd never had her debut, and she had been too young when her mother and her aunt passed to accompany either of them to the teas younger ladies attended. She felt unaccountably nervous as she stepped onto the patio, holding tightly to Captain Browne's arm. This was one of the few arenas where she did not feel completely confident.

Neither did the captain, it appeared. He took one look around and blanched.

"Where are all the gentlemen?" he whispered.

On the other side of him, Priscilla gave him a puzzled look from where she walked on Joseph's arm.

"Over there," she said, tilting her head toward a pack of young men, barely old enough to be off leading strings. From one glance, it was immediately clear Captain Browne would stand out like a raven among songbirds—bigger, meaner, and deadlier. Evie stifled a laugh. He and her cousin were the only gentlemen of their age and stature present.

"The *older* gentlemen." Captain Browne stressed the second word, his voice tight with unhappiness as he scanned the crowd. The crowd was looking back at him from beneath flowered bonnets, surprise and interest in their collective gaze.

"Ah, yes, they do not often come to these events, especially after the Season proper is over," Priscilla said guilelessly. "Perhaps you and Joseph can go talk to the young men while I introduce Evie and Josie to Lady Grey. She is just over there."

Anthony turned his head to look where Priscilla was indicating, and Evie almost laughed aloud. Her cousin's wife was devious. Lady Grey was currently surrounded by the matriarchs of *the ton*, those with the keenest eyes, sharpest tongues, and largest interest in gossip.

They were eying Captain Browne and Joseph speculatively, wondering why they had impeded on what was clearly a ladies' event, and most of them seemed focused on her on the captain's arm. It did not surprise Evie that none of them were looking at her in confusion—these were the ladies who had their fingers on the pulse of the *ton*. No matter that she had only been to one dinner event, they already knew who she was.

"Right then," Captain Browne said hastily. "We shall leave you ladies to that and see if Mr. Grey had any acquaintances from among the gentlemen."

Taking leave of her arm, Captain Browne did not seem to understand the greater danger until it was too late. Evie watched out of the corner of her eye with amusement as he and Joseph made their way over to the gentlemen, only making it halfway there before being mobbed by the mamas and debutantes from the Season who had not yet caught a beau.

Joseph had a defense in that he was already married, but Captain Browne was dashing, handsome, and of an age—unlike the young men in the corner—the *ton* universally agreed meant he should be interested in marriage. Perhaps she should have felt a touch of jealousy, but she could not imagine Captain Browne with a typical *ton* debutante any more than she could imagine herself with a typical *tonnish* gentleman.

They were going to drive him and Joseph batty, and she found it incredibly amusing.

Once he fought his way through the wall of skirts, she doubted he would learn much from the young men over there. Those were the good boys who had yet to rebel against their mothers—hence their presence at the tea—and hardly the kind of crowd a man like Richard Grey would have run with. A bachelor on Jermyn Street who gambled regularly at the Tramp's Den would not have much in common with the popinjays present.

Of course, she had her own challenges to face. Was it her imagination, or did the matrons sit up straighter as she approached?

"Good afternoon," Priscilla said, curtsying to the exact right degree for the highest-ranking lady present, the Duchess of Manchester.

"Welcome to my little gathering," Lady Brooke said with a welcoming smile. She was a beautiful woman, only a little older than Evie, and with her dark hair and bright green eyes, Evie realized they could be mistaken for sisters at first glance. Their faces were different, and she was a good bit taller than Lady Brooke and not as voluptuous, but the similarities were undeniable.

Priscilla made the introductions for Evie, far more smoothly than Josie would have managed. Unless she was directly addressed, Josie was barely paying attention to the conversation, constantly peering around as though looking to see who else was present.

Before Evie knew it, the three of them were seated, and Priscilla was chattering away with Lady Grey while Evie sipped tea and listened. It was clear Lady Grey had not yet heard about her son's untimely death or else she would not have come to the tea, but Priscilla did not seem to have an iota of guilt about chatting with the lady while keeping that bit of information back.

Perhaps she did not want to ruin the lady's day until it was absolutely necessary, letting her have this one tea to enjoy before her life was irrevocably changed. Or perhaps there was far more to Priscilla than Evie had suspected.

* * *

Anthony

· · ·

Finally maneuvering himself away from the debutantes, thanks to Joseph, who was far more experienced at navigating such arenas, Anthony breathed a silent sigh of relief when they reached the group of young gentlemen.

The *very* young gentlemen. Most of them were baby-faced and appeared startled to find themselves in the crosshairs of Joseph and Anthony. They relaxed after a moment as he and Joseph greeted them equably and began the usual tonnish chitchat. Hardly Anthony's preference, but he did not want to rouse suspicion about the line of his eventual questioning.

It was best to ease them into things.

It did not take long to discover they knew absolutely nothing—not about Richard Grey, not about Mitchell, nor any gossip as far as he could tell. He was both frustrated and envious.

This was why he had fought in the war—so that young men could have trivial, enjoyable interests rather than having to go off to fight for their lives. It was frustrating to come up empty-handed again. Turning, he looked across the way to where Miss Stuart and the others were engaged in what appeared to be a very merry conversation.

Just as he was about to head toward her, a footman in dark clothing stepped onto the patio. There was nothing discernible to draw one's attention to him, yet conversation slowed as he looked around, then made his way over to the group of ladies Miss Stuart sat with. They went silent as he approached, and one lady's eyes widened with worry as she got to her feet.

By the time the footman reached her and bent his head down to whisper in her ear, everyone was watching, anticipating something terrible, yet not knowing what it could be.

Except for Anthony, Joseph, Josie, Priscilla, and Miss Stuart.

They knew.

The three women's expressions were tight with sympathy as the older woman let out a wail, collapsing before the footman and a young woman next to her caught her. The footman said something to the younger woman, who also cried as she held her mother tightly.

Despite knowing Richard Grey had been a cad, seeing his family's reaction, his heart clenched with sympathy. Regardless of his character, clearly, he had been loved.

"What happened, do you think?" One of the young men behind Anthony whispered as the two women were led inside, Lady Brooke assisting them along with the footman. Across the patio, Miss Stuart looked up and met Anthony's gaze, her expression somber.

The two groups came together as if their thoughts were united. The men converged on the matrons to discover what had happened and what dreadful news had been brought to Lady Grey. Just as quickly, they separated again, whispering and talking among themselves.

Anthony knew he should move with them, but he leaned down to Miss Stuart's ear.

"Anything of note?" he murmured.

"No. Priscilla had asked after the family before the news was delivered. It seems the Viscountess was under the impression her youngest son was 'sowing his wild oats,' as men his age are wont to do." Miss Stuart's response was soft, impassive, but like him, she was not unmoved, even though he could hear her low opinion of Mr. Grey clearly in her tone.

While many young men sowed their wild oats, they did not become highwaymen or kidnappers. Lady Grey had likely been unaware of her son's activities since he had been living on his own.

"Go," Miss Stuart said, waving her hand at him. "See what news of his death has stirred up."

Even though he wanted to remain by her side—an impulse he did not want to examine too closely—he returned to the young men.

* * *

Evie

"Nothing. All that and we learned absolutely nothing." Evie plopped onto the couch in disgust, tugging off her bonnet and tossing it onto the table. The tea had been full of gossip, but none of it worthwhile to their investigation.

According to the other matrons, the youngest Mr. Grey was known to be a bit of a cad, though they all felt he would grow out of it, eventually. None of them seemed to know the extent of his activities, just that he was doing a good bit of gambling and whoring. Not that they used such stark terms, but that was what it boiled down to.

"At least you were able to talk to the Viscountess before she heard the news," Elijah said gruffly.

They had arrived at Grey House to see if the Viscount was at-home and found themselves too late to speak with him. He had gone to identify his son's body, which likely, was why it had taken so long for news to reach Lady Grey. The messenger had arrived after she had left for the tea and had probably hoped it was a case of misidentification.

Again, Evie's heart ached, though she was not sure his parents deserved her sympathy. From everything she had heard at the tea, they had indulged his every whim until this past Season when they'd refused to pay off his gambling debts... which was when he had turned to making his own money by nefarious means. He'd been raised to be an entitled, thoughtless, selfish young man... true of many of their set. She was torn between hurting for them over their loss and wanting to shake them for raising their son in such a manner.

Neither of which was particularly helpful.

"Perhaps we are tugging on the wrong threads," she said finally. "We have been chasing after Mitchell and those who worked with him here, but I had Lily reach out to her contacts on the Continent to find out who he was working with *there*. We have two sets of foreign dignitaries who could have been involved with him. Perhaps we should take the time to look at them."

"That is not a bad idea," Uncle Oliver said slowly, thinking it through.

Evie pressed her lips together to avoid making a face. Of course, it was not a bad idea. It was a very good idea, so why was it so difficult for him to say so?

There was a very big difference between 'not bad' and 'good.'

"Dammit, she is right. Do we even know what is happening with the trade negotiations?" Joseph asked. Whether Joseph actually thought she was right or was trying to get back in her good graces, she appreciated the spoken support, nonetheless.

"I have been keeping up with them, of course." Now it was Uncle

Oliver's turn to look vaguely insulted at the implication that he had not been. Evie was hard-pressed to find sympathy for him. "They should be wrapping up soon, though there has been some contention between the French and the Russians over some exclusivity clauses."

"Lucas found no evidence the French had anything to do with the attempted assassination," Elijah said thoughtfully.

"For once," Captain Browne muttered. He cleared his throat and spoke a little louder. "That actually brings up the point that relations have improved markedly in the past few years. Why risk them? They are no more ready for another war than we are."

"Yet if the assassination had succeeded, they would have been the immediate suspect." Evie leaned back against the couch, looking at the ceiling as the possibilities whirled through her head. It was like a giant chessboard where every move had a meaning behind it, but it was not always clear what the meaning was. "On the other hand, they would be the immediate suspect, for good reason, whereas we have been on good relations with the Russians for a while now, so why risk that?"

"The man who gave me the note supposedly from Joseph that led to my attack said he had been hired by a Russian," Josie said. "I do not think we ever truly followed up on that."

"Not after he was killed... after we left him alone with Mitchell." Elijah grimaced.

"I have had both embassies and delegations watched, of course," Uncle Oliver said. "So far, no one has done anything the least bit suspicious. And with such grave charges, we cannot even mention it unless we have some kind of proof."

Right now, they had nothing at all.

CHAPTER 18

An Unexpected Arrival

E *vie*

The week following the death of Richard Grey was one of the most frustrating Evie had ever experienced. Nightly, the gentlemen would go out and scour the streets for Mitchell. The first night, she snuck out and visited Henry and Delilah again but ultimately decided it was more important for her to look into the foreign delegations.

So, she spent her days with her uncle, going over everything they'd gathered about each member of the delegations and the trade negotiations. Nothing stood out as suspicious. Nothing indicated that either country would want to harm the Duke of York, who was doing splendidly as he balanced the negotiations. From what she could see, all the emissaries were happy with the job he was doing.

In the afternoons, she, Priscilla, and Josie attended the ladies' teas to see what information they could glean from the gossip. There was plenty swirling in the wake of Richard Grey's death and his very private funeral, but no one mentioned anything about treachery or a connection with Mitchell. There were a few who were willing to whisper about him, but the ladies did not know him at all.

At night, she went to the political dinners with her Uncle Oliver, keeping quiet and listening to everything the gentlemen said. She had tried to bring Mitchell up several times and had immediately been told she did not need to worry her pretty little head about such serious matters. The man would be caught if he had not already fled the country, but regardless, she should not be concerned.

It was not always easy to bite her tongue, but she managed because she found the gentlemen spoke to each *other* about Mitchell, as long as she brought him up, then was quiet. More than one of them seemed concerned, especially those who were friends with or had worked with Warwick, but none of them acted suspiciously, as though they might be hiding him away somewhere or were worried they would be accused of treachery alongside him.

Granted, they could also be superb actors, but so far, that was all Evie had to go on, and none of them rang a warning bell in her head.

It was wildly frustrating.

"Perhaps the assassination attempt had something to do with Mitchell personally?" she said, looking up from another report from one of her father's agents who had been keeping an eye on the French embassy. Behind his desk, her Uncle Oliver looked up from the report he was reading, his brow furrowed in confusion, and she quickly clarified. "Perhaps we are looking in the wrong place. Mitchell has been murdering everyone who can identify him as a traitor. How do we know the assassination attempt was part of the treachery and not another cover-up?"

Uncle Oliver's jaw dropped, and Diana's head swiveled to stare at her with wide eyes, both of them shocked at what she was suggesting.

"Are you trying to say perhaps the Duke of York was involved in Mitchell's smuggling during the war?" Uncle Oliver sounded as if he was choking, but Evie did not know why the suggestion was so farfetched.

"Just because he is a duke does not mean he cannot also be a traitor." Evie raised her eyebrows. "It would hardly be the first time in history."

"He is a man of honor." Her uncle's face might as well have been carved from stone. He did not like her suggestion, which meant, at the very least, she would need to investigate it herself, if only to be sure that was *not* the case. "I trust him."

"Like you trusted Mitchell?" The bitter question popped out before she could stop herself.

She and her uncle stared at each other across his desk, the air between them simmering with emotion. Out of the corner of her eye, she could see Diana sitting perfectly still as if afraid to draw attention to herself.

Evie pressed her lips together as she met her uncle's dark gaze. Even though it was true, she felt the urge to apologize. She knew part of her ire came from the feeling her uncle did not trust *her*, and he was already mired in guilt about how he had allowed Mitchell to play him.

"You are right." Uncle Oliver slumped, his expression turning haggard as his anger abruptly left him. "We should look at the Duke of York. Your instincts have proven better than mine in this case."

As much as part of Evie rejoiced to hear him finally admit that, her chest ached at seeing him doubt himself.

"You are hardly the only one he fooled," she responded quietly. "And I did not realize the extent of his faults, either."

Uncle Oliver rubbed his forehead, dropping his gaze.

"Maybe it is time for me to retire and hand this all over to Elijah."

"Elijah trusted Mitchell as well," Evie argued. "And he did not think about checking on the Duke of York."

"So, maybe I should hand it all over to you."

Evie's jaw dropped open. He did not mean that, did he?

He could not possibly mean that, but her heart pounded in her chest in excitement. Not only because her uncle was finally acknowledging her contributions, acknowledging she was good at this, but because part of her really wanted it.

Would love becoming Crown's spymaster to be her life's work.

Before anyone could say anything, there was a knock on the study door. It opened before Evie had turned around to see who it was, and Elijah poked his head in.

"Rex, Mary, Nathan, and Lily are here." He barely got the words out before disappearing again. Cursing, Evie jumped to her feet. What had brought the four of them back to London with such short notice?

* * *

Anthony

The whole group was back together again, gathered in the Marquess of Camden's drawing room, with the new additions of Diana, Joseph, Priscilla, and Adam. Everyone was talking at once, trying to catch up on what had happened, both at Brentwood Manor and in London. Nathan and Lily were still attired in their mourning garb for Nathan's brother, but the edge of Nathan's sadness finally seemed to have ebbed.

He also noted the couple, though not as outwardly affectionate as Mary and Rex, were wont to stand far closer together and exchange little glances far more often than before. Remembering Nathan's shock at the idea that he could be in love with his wife, Anthony had to grin. Seemed like he had now not only accepted it as fact but had fallen into the reality of it with his whole heart.

Truth be told, all of his friends made marriage look... not so bad.

Anthony had the thought as his gaze alighted on Miss Stuart, then he realized where his thoughts were going and scowled. This particular group of women was far more dangerous to rakes and scoundrels than he could have imagined.

Not that Nathan had been a rake, but Rex and Elijah both had been, and Anthony might not have been a rake, but he certainly had never considered himself marriage-minded. There was no pressing *need* for him to marry—not like Rex or Elijah, and now Nathan, who all had to provide an heir for their titles.

Without a title requiring an heir, there was no reason to saddle himself with a wife.

Unless it was for love.

That was assuming the woman in question loved him in return and wanted to saddle herself with a husband with particular proclivities in the bedroom and a taste for danger. Hardly the kind of husband the women of the *ton* were clamoring to marry.

Miss Stuart was not a typical lady of the *ton*.

Her cousins would murder you if her uncle did not do it first. They know exactly what kind of man you are and would not approve.

When had he ever cared about others' approval? He barely thought of his own family's approval, so why should another family's approval mean more to him than his own? Perhaps it was more that he took his family's approval for granted, and rejection by the Marquess or Elijah would... well, hurt.

"There you are." Finally spotting Anthony, Nathan grinned as he stepped forward for an embrace, which Anthony happily reciprocated. "Finally. I thought you must be lazing about somewhere, letting everyone else do the hard work."

Laughing, Anthony shook his head. Nathan's comment was a holdover from their days undercover in France. They would accuse each other of evading their duties and make up outrageous stories of their own gallant deeds. It had been one of the ways they had fought back against the loneliness that was inherent in being undercover in a country your own country was at war with. They had not been able to see each other often, but when they did, their little exchanges lightened their spirits considerably.

"Oh, no, I have been in town, risking my life at the Tramp's Den, while *you* played Lord of the Manor and shirked all real work."

"The Tramp's Den?" Rex asked, turning his head as he caught Anthony's statement. Before Anthony could reply, understanding lit up his features. "Because of the man Elijah and Josie met there?"

"Yes." Anthony looked around as the conversation finally quieted, everyone listening to him and Rex. "Perhaps we should sit together and catch up all at once, instead of one by one?"

Everyone agreed that was a brilliant suggestion and moved to a place to stand or sit around the room. The Marquess gave a succinct report of everything those in London had been doing for the investigation, including where they had stalled. Nodding as he came to his conclusion, he straightened his shoulders and lifted his chin.

"This morning, Evie suggested we should investigate the Duke of York as well, not for his position in the trade negotiations, but because Mitchell seems intent on killing everyone who can identify him as a trai-tor." The way the Marquess said it made it clear he was unhappy to have to state such a thing out loud.

The room went dead silent, and Miss Stuart sat up a little straighter in her chair, lifting her chin, her jade gaze traveling over the room's occupants as if daring anyone to argue with the possibility. As much as

Anthony wanted to, he could not, and he saw the same expression on the other gentlemen's faces.

What would a duke have to gain from smuggling and treachery?

There may have been something. It was a good point that Mitchell was cleaning up as he went, even though he had been unable to escape London altogether. At this point, his activities were *known*, and he was still acting with murderous intent. It was not so far-fetched to think the Duke was supposed to be the first victim.

"That would be awful with how close he is to the throne's succession," Priscilla said fretfully. "If someone that close to the Crown could turn on us..." She shivered, though her expression remained the same as ever. Beside her, Joseph reached over to take her hand in a gesture of comfort.

"It is certainly not a comfortable thought," Elijah said. He looked more tired than ever as he shook his head. "But one we should have had before now. Especially since we know Mitchell had already dragooned more than one person of our set to his causes. Speaking of, were you able to find out anything more about Brentwood and Warwick's involvement?"

Watching Miss Stuart closely, Anthony saw the flicker in her expression as if she was displeased her cousin was changing the subject, but she did not protest. She must understand that none of them liked to think of a duke as a possible traitor. It went against everything their status represented... yet Nathan's father had actively worked with Mitchell at smuggling spies when he had been alive, and Warwick had been blackmailed into looking the other way from his employee's treachery. Not that he had realized it was treachery, apparently, but that was partly because of his willingness to turn a blind eye.

"Mitchell was as thorough in cleaning up his traces on Warwick's estate as he was here," Rex said grimly. "We found very little among Warwick's staff."

"We did find my brother's notes," Nathan said, his voice a little more hollow than it had been a few minutes ago as if he had just remembered his brother was dead. Grief had a tendency to hit in waves. Everyone listened sympathetically as he cleared his throat. Lily reached over to take his hand, similar to the way Joseph had attempted to comfort Priscilla.

"Sebastian was unable to find out everything, but there were accounting questions that came up in the books, which was what initially set him on the path of searching into what my father had done."

"Payouts?" Elijah asked.

"That's what it looks like." Nathan shook his head. "He had gambled everything down to nothing, then suddenly had a huge influx of money from out of nowhere. Far too regularly for it to be a gambling windfall, and he was not very good at gambling, anyway. I can imagine it happening once or twice, but ten times? A dozen? In two years?" Blowing out a frustrated breath, Nathan tipped his head back and looked at the ceiling—or perhaps to the heavens, appealing to God for patience or absolution.

Not that his father's sins should have been visited upon him or his brother, but Anthony imagined the guilt was there, regardless, especially since Nathan's brother had been murdered while Nathan was in London. Would things have gone differently had Nathan remained at home? They would never know.

"That does seem unlikely," Josie murmured. "This leads us back to the French again."

"It's one of the few connections, yet was long enough ago, it may or may not be significant." Elijah made a face. "I wish we could find something concrete to follow through on... or find Mitchell, so we could question him."

"Are we sure he's still in London?" Rex asked, his tone neutral, genuinely asking.

"We are not, but we think he must be unless he got out after murdering Richard Grey." Anthony grimaced. "Honestly, I think he is still here. Being discovered took everything from him. I doubt he will go quietly into the night, which I would be glad of if we could just find him." Anthony wanted justice to be served, but he did not want anyone else to get hurt or die in the meantime.

Silence fell over the group again, likely because there was no good response. They all wanted Mitchell caught, but none of them knew how to make it happen.

"Well... perhaps we can all gather at dinner?" Camden suggested, looking around. "With all of us together, surely we can think of possible next moves."

As soon as everyone agreed, Miss Stuart got to her feet.

"Rex, Nathan, might I borrow your wives for a bit?" Her smile was sincere, but her request sounded more like a demand. "I would love to catch up with them."

"And I," Josie asserted.

"Of course," Rex said smoothly. He glanced at the gentlemen. "Would any of you like to join me for an afternoon at the club?"

Nathan, Anthony, and Elijah all agreed. Adam said he had other matters to attend to. Joseph declined as well, stating he and Priscilla were going for a drive that afternoon. Since that night he had been caught out with Lady Cross, he had been paying extra attention to his wife, which was probably for the best, but Anthony saw the look Miss Stuart and Josie exchanged. He had no doubt part of the discussion between the ladies would involve Joseph and Priscilla's marriage.

Camden also declined the invitation, much to their inward relief. He stated he was tired and planned on sitting and resting with Miss Rutherford that afternoon. Anthony wondered if they should be worried about the Marquess' health, but with the look Camden was giving his nurse, he realized he probably did not need to be worried at all.

CHAPTER 19

A Lady Needs Her Friends

E*vie*

In the garden with her friends, where Evie could be sure no one was listening—even if they attempted to, the sound of the fountain beside where they'd seated themselves on benches should help drown out their voices—she realized she was relieved to have them all together again. Not that she did not love Josie, but she and Josie were similar in many regards, including their willingness to throw themselves into danger and a certain disregard for following the rules.

Mary and Lily had always balanced them out. Mary could be impulsive, but not to the same level as Josie, and while she did not shy away from danger, neither did she rush into it like Evie. Lily was the most level-headed of them all and preferred to take stock of a situation before taking action. Not that Evie did not stop to think before she acted, but she did not always think it through as completely as Lily did. There was a reason Lily was their information gatherer.

"My goodness, so much has happened yet so little at the same time," Mary said, sitting on one of the benches and spreading her skirts. Her hair glinted reddish blonde in the sunlight, and in her pale green dress, she was as pretty as a picture with the bushes flowering behind her. "Diana seems perfectly lovely, though I will admit I am surprised Uncle Oliver agreed to tell her what was going on."

"He seems to be finally learning his lesson that keeping us ladies in the dark on everything is actually not the wisest, or best, course of action," Evie said, sitting on the bench next to Mary's. The two were set perpendicular, creating a handy little corner, so those seated could easily speak to each other. She wondered if she should tell them about his comment of putting her in charge of his duties to the Crown but could not allow herself to actually say the words aloud.

It would make them too real and too painful if they did not come true. If no one knew, there would be no explanations required if nothing came of it.

"Uncle Oliver clearly has a *tendre* for Diana," Josie said with a snicker from beside Mary, startling Evie. She would have protested, but Evie's brain started working, going through all the little looks she had seen pass between the pair, the way her uncle actually listened to Diana, how he had been acting as though he needed more help than he really did.

"You think they're..." Lily's voice went lower and trailed off as her dark eyes widened in surprise.

"No, I do not... but I think he wants to." Josie grinned. "I think it would be good for him if he did, but so far, it seems to be nothing but an attraction."

Evie probed her feelings, wondering exactly how she felt about that. She had been the 'lady of the manor' for a long time, and if Uncle Oliver were to marry, she would be replaced. She would no longer be his chatelaine, his hostess... all of her current responsibilities to the household would go to his wife.

Granted, she knew that would be Josie's position when Uncle Oliver passed and Elijah became the Marquess, but that had seemed very far away.

She would not mind giving way to Diana, though, if it made her uncle happy and if she could find something else to do. The familial duties had never been her favorite, and she had neglected them every time she had disappeared on her family, so she did not feel a particular sense of propriety over them.

"Do you think Diana returns his regard?" Mary asked curiously.

"I do not know her well enough to say." Josie shrugged, looking at

Evie, who shook her head. She had not even noticed Uncle Oliver's interest until Josie pointed it out. How Diana felt about him was far beyond her.

"Well, I'm sure it will sort itself out." Lily looked between Evie and Josie. "Why are we mad at Joseph?"

"Are we mad at Joseph?" Mary's brow furrowed.

"We are definitely mad at Joseph," Josie practically growled, her hands tightening into fists. Mary's and Lily's eyes widened. As Josie explained, Mary's mouth dropped open, and Lily's eyes looked like they were about to pop out of her head.

All Evie could feel was sadness but relief that their friends were there. With being Joseph's cousin and Josie formerly thinking she might marry him one day, they were both too close to the situation to be impartial. Josie saw herself in Priscilla's shoes, and Evie was infuriated she had been put in the position of lying to a woman who was now part of her family. Mary and Lily's shock and outrage made her feel better about her own.

"That... that..." Lily was at a loss for words, and Mary's pale skin turned bright pink, clashing horribly with her hair.

"I am going to speak with Rex about it," Mary said primly.

"Rex cannot do anything unless he wants to throw out half the Society. Quite a few of them are married, and their spouses have no idea what they are doing in their free time," Evie pointed out. "Besides, that would hardly solve the problem. It might even send Joseph into worse places to get what he needs."

There were all sorts of brothels and whipping houses that could be made available to the *ton* and other 'secret' societies that were far less reputable than the Society. It might be a secret, but they had rules. Not all societies did, and many were filled with men who cared for naught but themselves and their own pleasures.

Evie would not like to see her cousin forced to join one of *those* societies. Being surrounded by such company would hardly help his morals.

"Perhaps we can bring Priscilla with us to an event?" Josie suggested. "It worked well enough for Elijah and me."

"Do you think she would be interested?" Mary looked doubtful.

They all looked at each other.

Truth be told, Evie probably knew her the best of the four of them, and she could not be sure. Partly because her focus had been on the investigation, not her new cousin-in-law, and partly because Priscilla had not been particularly easy to get to know.

She was very... bland.

It was part of the reason she had stayed on the marriage market for so long, despite being pretty, presentable, and well-dowered. Most men had passed her by, but Joseph had seen something in her he had fallen in love with. Evie still was not sure what that had been, but there must be something more to her than met the eye.

"What I am most interested in is what has been going on between Evie and Anthony," Mary said, pinning Evie with a look, startling her.

"What?"

Crossing her arms over her chest, Mary's gaze did not falter.

"You and Anthony. Something has happened, I can tell. The two of you are not glaring at each other the way you were."

The noise from the fountain kept it from being completely silent as Evie floundered, groping for an explanation, then realizing she wanted to tell her friends. It was something she had kept from them for a long time, partly because she had not wanted to answer the myriad questions they would have.

Though she had been sure to give them an education on what happened between a man and a woman and how to defend themselves if it ever became necessary, she had not wanted to answer particulars. Even when pressed, after they'd met Captain Browne, she had not admitted to more than the bare minimum.

Now, they were all married and had their own stories to tell. And because of the men they'd married, she thought nothing she said would shock them.

So, she told them everything, from her and Captain Browne's first meeting in France when she'd been pretending to be a whore—and he had believed it—to when he'd found her and spanked her at a Society of Sin gathering to their encounters since following Mitchell to London.

By the time she finished, all three of her friends were staring at her in shock.

"I cannot believe you did not tell me!" Josie shrieked, throwing her hands in the air in frustration.

"It was hardly important next to everything else that has been going on."

"Of course, it is important, Evie. It is your *life.*" Josie was even more frustrated. "What happens to you is important. You cannot make spying the only thing you ever do. You need to *live.* It would be one thing if you were not interested in him or nothing was happening between you, but you should not dismiss it just because it is not pertinent to the investigation."

"She's right. Has he said anything? Indicated any interest beyond these... encounters? More importantly, do you want him to?" Lily's questions went straight to the heart of things, as they often did, and Evie's chest clenched.

Maybe this was the real reason she had not wanted to talk to her friends. She would have to face the truth—yes, she wanted something from Captain Browne beyond these secret encounters. She did not know exactly what, and yes, it was important because somehow, her feelings had become involved. Feelings she did not understand or know how to reconcile with the rest of her wants from life.

Priscilla might have been unmarried for so long because men found her bland, but Evie would have the opposite problem. There were very few men who wanted to marry a woman with her skills, much less one who excelled at them. Being able to outride, outshoot, and outsmart a gentleman was a fast way to find oneself not only firmly on the shelf but possibly ostracized from Society.

Evie refused to pretend she was something she was not in order to find a husband.

She had had no particular aversion to being an old maid... not until her friends had fallen into their own marriages, which all had turned into love matches, despite the unlikely circumstances.

That had only been a spark of thought that niggled under her skin, to be turned over every now and then like a sore tooth. Reencountering Captain Browne and her shocking attraction to him had truly ignited her uncertainties.

"I do not know." Confessing she might want what her friends had

felt too raw, too vulnerable, even to those she loved best in the world…
especially to them. "I cannot think of it right now."

"We could always try to arrange a scandal…" Josie said thoughtfully.

"Absolutely not." Evie did not think any less of her friends for how
their marriages started, but she would never countenance such a thing
for herself.

The scandal would have to be enormous, something that would
besmirch her entire family, not just herself. Granted, there were a
goodly number of situations she found herself in that could do just
that, but so far, she had not been recognized and did not expect that to
change any time soon. Though she had stepped into the *ton's* arena
more often of late. Uneasiness spread through her. She had made herself
more recognizable, by necessity, with all the events she had been
attending with Uncle Oliver.

That just means I must be extra careful with any disguises I put on.

Most of their social set barely glanced at their servants and others
they deemed lower than themselves, but there were always exceptions.
In fact, if Mitchell got word she was at events, it was always possible he
could try to embroil her in some kind of scandal the way he had Josie.

The very thought was mortifying.

She would not be leveraged into marrying because of Mitchell.

Though I might be if I am pregnant.

That was different. And something she had left out of her talk with
her friends because she was not ready to face it. Her bleeding should
begin any day now, and if it did not… well, she would not only have to
tell them, but she would also have to tell everyone else.

For now, it was another secret she wanted to keep.

To avert their attention, she told them about her interview with
Warwick's employees. They were all properly shocked and angered. Josie
offered to write them all letters of recommendation, while Lily volun-
teered to help Evie track them down. Mary wanted to go back to Brentwood and give Warwick a piece of her mind, but once she simmered
down, she offered her help as well.

As Evie had been rather distracted of late, she gratefully accepted. It
would go much faster with their assistance.

CHAPTER 20

The Gentlemen Convene

Anthony

Comfortably ensconced in one of White's smaller rooms, which they had to themselves, it was a relief to sit and relax. Doing so with three of the people he trusted most in the world made it even better. Rex was the newest addition to their little group, but he had proven to be a worthy one.

"What else did we miss being away?" Rex asked once they had all found their seats and received their drinks, leaving them alone in the room. "And what the devil is going on with Adam?"

Since Anthony had been expecting Rex to say 'Joseph,' the question took him off guard. He nearly answered before remembering Elijah was there. Rex would not care about Adam's proclivities. He was the one who had founded the Society of Sin and set up its rules, though he might care that Adam's current partner was his best friend. But Anthony would not break confidence with Elijah there.

That was for Adam to do when he was ready.

"Adam? What was wrong with Adam?" Elijah asked, frowning.

"He seemed... off." Rex's brow furrowed, trying to think of how to describe it. He took a sip of his drink. "Quieter than usual. Though I've never seen him around family before."

"Perhaps he was thinking of what he could contribute," Anthony suggested. "Or perhaps he has his own business to attend to." Likely the latter, and more like a person to attend to than business, but that was the most Anthony was willing to say.

"It was very loud with everyone there," Nathan said with a chuckle. He leaned back in his chair, looking supremely satisfied with himself. Being married suited him. Despite his grief over his brother, Lily had kept his spirits up. Though his anger and need to get justice for his brother's murder likely drove him as well.

It suddenly occurred to Anthony that there were four gentlemen and four ladies in their little group, and only he and Evie were unwed... as if fate was pushing them together.

Perhaps it is.

If she was with child...

The thought came with a flicker of anticipation and hope, he could not ignore. Possessiveness as well, though he already knew he had that in spades. Miss Stuart was his, whether or not she was willing to admit it yet. Regardless of whether she ever married him.

Anthony had no intention of letting her go.

"What about Miss Rutherford? Can we trust her?" Nathan asked, looking between Anthony and Elijah.

"I believe so. She has already shown herself to be a sensible and discreet woman. Evie insisted she be told of the danger since she could be in harm's way, given her close position to my father." Elijah frowned, his long finger tapping against his glass. Clearly, he did not like the idea of putting a woman in danger, but it was unavoidable. "And she has been an excellent nurse. My father has improved markedly under her care, even though the doctor told us he might never fully recover."

"He seems mostly recovered, but there is probably some truth to that," Anthony said. "He does still have his moments of weakness and needs assistance walking on occasion."

"Or he enjoys having pretty women fuss over him," Rex murmured with a hint of amusement.

Elijah frowned and opened his mouth to defend his father, then closed it, his eyes unfocusing as if he was thinking through Rex's words and seeing if they applied. It was a good point. The Marquess seemed to enjoy having Diana fuss over him, and Anthony could not blame him.

It could also be an act to make himself appear more defenseless and vulnerable, luring their enemy into making a mistake.

Maybe a bit of both.

"He could always remarry. Give Elijah a half-sibling or two." Anyone other than Nathan might have said that jokingly or to tease Elijah, but Nathan made the suggestion sincere.

Elijah paled. "They would be the same age as my and Josie's children."

"Is Josie expecting?" Anthony asked, and the other two men sat up alertly.

"No, that is... but of course, hopefully soon..." Elijah stumbled over his words, and they relaxed. If Josie *was* with child, they would need to be even more careful.

Anthony grimaced inwardly as he thought of trying to keep Miss Stuart from her usual antics while pregnant. No, he did not think that would go over well, but he knew himself well enough to know he would insist.

Was he actually hoping she was with child?

It would certainly make some things easier.

"Ah, well, it was a thought." Rex's lips twisted wryly. "Hopefully, we can catch Mitchell before any of our ladies end up *enceinte*. I can only imagine how much worse everything would be with one of them pregnant. Mary is determined to see this through to the end."

"As is Josie." Elijah groaned, raking his fingers through his hair. "I could curse Evie for dragging her friends into this."

"Yet, without them, we might never have caught Mitchell," Anthony pointed out. "In fact, we might have believed everything he set up to deceive us with."

"That does not actually make me feel any better, Browne," Elijah growled. The fact that he had used Anthony's surname instead of his Christian name was a display of his displeasure.

Anthony shrugged. Whether or not it was comfortable to admit, the ladies had been invaluable to their investigation. Did it sting a bit that they had figured out so many things he and the others had been blind to? Of course, but it was still better than having the wool pulled over their eyes.

"How much trouble has my cousin been giving you, by the way?" Elijah asked, turning his head to face Anthony full on.

Anthony's expression froze, feeling like a mask.

"Not much... once I explained that communication and having one person making the decisions was imperative to ensuring we did not run into any difficulties." There, that was neutral enough and gave away nothing of his feelings about Miss Stuart.

"Ah ha. So far, have you had to tell her 'no' to anything?" The corner of Elijah's lip curled up when Anthony shook his head. "Please, let me know her response to having one person make the decisions when she's the one not getting her way."

Some of the smugness Anthony had been feeling faded. Elijah's thoughts echoed his own when he had initially been given the task of bringing Miss Stuart to heel.

Then again, he had means and methods of dealing with Miss Stuart her cousin and uncle certainly did not. Though how much she claimed to enjoy such methods took away from some of its potency. He supposed he could always withhold spankings from her if it came down to it. There were some in the Society who craved the pain and pleasure enough that denying it to them was a greater punishment than the whip.

There were also other things he could do to her.

Things that he very much wanted to do to her.

That he should absolutely not be thinking about right now while her cousin was watching him so closely. Anthony shifted in his seat, bringing one ankle over his opposite knee to disguise the sudden tightness at the front of his breeches.

"I will cross that bridge when I reach it. So far, I have found her to be reasonable." Truthfully, she had been. It was her uncle's and cousins' insistence on keeping her out of everything that had caused her to behave the way she had. Elijah snorted, and Anthony shrugged. "I believe it is because I have treated her reasonably."

"And I have not?" Elijah scowled at him.

Not backing down, Anthony raised his eyebrow at the other man.

"Can you honestly say you have allowed her the same amount of leeway you have your wife? Or did you constantly tell her no and expect her to fall in line?"

Elijah opened his mouth. Closed it. Frustration flickered across his features. Rather than raise his ire by pushing the point even further, Anthony turned his attention to Nathan, giving Elijah the opportunity to stew.

"How goes it with the lovely Lily?" he asked, genuinely curious. "The two of you seem to have settled in nicely."

"We have." Nathan smiled, his eyes brightening. "I have even introduced her to my machines." He sighed happily. "She loves them. I have been designing new ones... in my free time," he added hastily.

"Truthfully, he has had little free time." Rex chuckled, looking between Anthony and Elijah as he vouched for Nathan, not that Anthony had any doubts. Besides, Nathan had a wife and an estate now, so his life could not revolve around spy games and traitors.

Anthony did not blame him. If anything, he felt envious.

Pushing the emotion away, he shook his head.

"You should be enjoying your wife and your inventions. You are lucky you can share that with her," Anthony said.

"Unlike my nitwit of a brother." Elijah downed the last of his drink and scowled, drawing Rex and Nathan's attention. Which, of course, meant they then had to explain about discovering Joseph with Lady Cross at a Society of Sin gathering. Which then meant talking Rex down from going off and having a talk with the man. That took a bit and another round of drinks.

Rex scowled as he brooded in his chair.

"It would be different if he had not married her for love, but..." Rex shook his head. "How can he call it love if he has hidden a part of himself from her? The entire reason I knew Mary was right for me was she did not flinch away from the Society."

"Were you not married because you were discovered kissing in the gardens?" Nathan asked, his brow furrowed.

"Well, yes, but that was long after Mary first visited the Society." Rex shrugged, unperturbed. "I had already chosen her. The scandal just helped matters move along a little faster. Initially, I do not believe she had any intention of accepting my proposal, though I was working on her.”

“So, in effect, you had already chosen her.” Nathan smiled. “It all worked out in the end.”

“Very well, just as it did for you and Elijah.”

“Except neither of us chose our brides before the scandals,” Elijah pointed out darkly.

Rex rolled his eyes. “You cannot tell me you are unhappy with Josie.”

“I did not say that.” Elijah bristled. “But I did not choose the way you did. I would not have married at all if it had not been required.”

Anthony rather thought he was feeling temperamental after Anthony had pointed out the differences between how he treated Josie and how he treated Miss Stuart. Unable to counter the truth, his temper now seemed shorter than usual.

“Nor I,” Nathan chimed in. “I had no thoughts at all about marriage. What about you, Anthony?”

“Me?” Anthony repeated, blinking and grasping for an acceptable answer. Unsure what his answer actually was because he was contemplating marriage to Miss Stuart if she was pregnant. Part of him was contemplating the possibility even if she was not, though if she was not, that would make things a little less clear and likely more difficult.

“You are the last man standing,” Nathan pointed out with amusement. “As Evie is the last woman, perhaps the two of you can pair off.”

Elijah snorted derisively, putting Anthony’s dander up, but fortunately, he spoke before Anthony could respond.

“My cousin, marry? When Hell freezes over. She’s determined to be an old maid rather than giving another man dominion over her.” Elijah shook his head, bemused, then took another sip of his drink. Thankfully, he was not looking at Anthony when he made his pronouncement. No one was.

Anthony’s chest felt unusually tight, hopes he had barely been entertaining plummeting to the ground.

Of course, she did not want to get married but would be willing to sacrifice herself to the marital altar if she was pregnant.

Anthony no longer knew whether he wished her to be.

CHAPTER 21

The Tramp's Message

E*vie*

It was after dinner when the front door of the house burst open, and at the sound of shouting in the foyer, Evie went running for the front door. She was not the only one. The moment she skidded into the opening, she saw Elijah coming in from the other direction, and Josie, Priscilla, and Joseph all appeared at the top of the stairs.

Her uncle and Diana would be slower, coming from the back of the house, and Adam was not currently at home, but the rest of them had rushed in, ready to defend the place if needed.

Captain Browne stood in the doorway, out of breath, bent over at the waist as he gasped for air. He was fit as a fiddle, so seeing him in such dire shape meant he had run all the way here, as fast as he could. His clothes were disheveled, his hair windblown, and there was a wild look in his eyes.

"The Tramp... has... Mitchell..." The words were barely intelligible, but as their meaning sank in, everyone froze. Hand on his chest, Captain Browne straightened. "Summoned me to the Den."

"We need to go. Now."

"I'm coming," Evie said immediately.

"Me, too," Josie said right on top of her.

"No and no." Elijah did not hesitate in his response. "Absolutely not."

"I did not ask you." Evie retorted before looking at Captain Browne, raising her eyebrows. Would he be reasonable?

"You cannot go dressed like that," he replied.

Finally, someone with sense.

"She cannot go at all," Elijah snarled. "You cannot always say yes to her!"

"And you should not always say no."

The two men glared at each other. Evie was already on the move up the stairs, rushing to her room to change. It would only take her a few minutes. Likely, Captain Browne and her cousin would be engaged in their male posturing long enough for her to change and rush back. They might not even notice she was gone.

Regardless, she was not wasting any time.

Thankfully, she was in an easy dress to pull off, and her pants and shirt were in her top drawer. She also had lots of practice in changing quickly. Taking her time meant more time for others to discover what she was doing. Not stopping to do her hair, she grabbed a cap and some pins. Putting the ends between her lips, she pinned her hair up to hide beneath the cap as she rushed back down the hall.

It was awfully quiet, and she felt a tinge of fear and anger. If Elijah had convinced Captain Browne to leave her behind, and they'd gone on without her... Well, she would follow them, but she would be extremely upset about the necessity of it.

"If Evie is going, I am going!" Josie's shout echoed down the hall, and Evie relaxed. They were still there, though she doubted if Josie would join them. She should have hurried to change like Evie.

Coming to the top of the stairs, Evie paused to take in the tableau. Josie and Elijah were facing off—probably why it had been so quiet—and Captain Browne was finally getting his breath back fully as he stood by the open door. He looked as though he was contemplating dashing back out of it.

"You are not, and do not even think about sneaking out. You will regret it." Elijah's tone was dark and threatening. Not in a way that made Evie think Josie would require help, but in the way that promised

Josie a good spanking if she did not comply. If Elijah were not her cousin, it would be quite stirring. As it was, she felt slightly embarrassed at the display.

"I have a solution," Evie said, coming to the bottom of the steps. She tugged the cap on over her hair. "I can go with Captain Browne, and you and Josie can stay here."

"What?" Elijah straightened, whirling around to face her, his dark eyes flashing. The color in his face, already pink with temper, turned ruddy as he took in her changed appearance. "Absolutely not."

"Evie can come. Josie, you need to stay here and let Diana and Camden know what is happening. We also likely need to prepare a place to keep Mitchell... and possibly some supplies to treat his wounds." Captain Browne made it sound like a suggestion, but they all knew it was an order.

It also made sense.

Josie sniffed and nodded, which made Elijah relax. He turned to Captain Browne, and Josie caught Evie's eye, sending her a wink. Evie had to stifle a laugh. Though Josie might have wanted to go with them, her true aim must have been to give Evie time to change. She was such a good friend.

"Evie should stay here." Elijah's insisted.

"We may need her," Captain Browne said before turning and heading back out the front door.

Evie could have crowed with delight at seeing Elijah so frustrated. The number of times he and Uncle Oliver had denied her, without acknowledging her arguments, were too many to count, and to see the shoe on the other foot filled her with vindicated glee. Elijah could not continue to argue. Captain Browne was already moving, and Evie darted out the door after him. All her cousin could do was follow, cursing under his breath.

Evie glanced over her shoulder to see him give Josie a rough kiss before nudging his wife back inside and pulling the door shut. Captain Browne had already made his way to the mews, where a carriage had been readied. He must have run because it was faster than getting a carriage ready at his own residence.

"Thank you," she said softly as she came up beside him where he was waiting to get into the carriage. He glanced at her, brow furrowed in confusion, then it cleared, and he grinned.

"I was not lying, Evie. We really might need you. I do not know how easily the Tramp will give Mitchell over. His men said they had him, and the Tramp was asking a few questions... and that we should hurry if we wanted a piece of Mitchell ourselves."

Ah. She was being included because Captain Browne thought she might be able to convince Henry to relinquish his prize. She would take it. It was certainly an improvement over being left out, and Evie would rather be useful than not.

That it would drive Elijah batty was a bonus.

* * *

<u>Anthony</u>

Elijah was angry at him, and Miss Stuart was gleeful.

She was also safely under their eye.

He only hoped Josie would stay where she was supposed to be. Thankfully, she'd been amenable once he had explained why. But he'd known the tasks would not hold both ladies, and Miss Stuart likely would be helpful in explaining to the Tramp why he could not keep Mitchell.

Anthony had not been invited to retrieve the man, but that was what he meant to do. They needed to wring every last bit of information from him they could. The Tramp did not know all the right questions to ask and probably did not care. A traitor could do no more harm once he was dead. While Anthony could appreciate the Tramp's position, they still needed the information from Mitchell.

He was also hoping, as Miss Stuart had assisted Diana with her uncle, she might have some medical skills they could utilize if Mitchell required it. While Elijah and Anthony both knew how to wrap a wound, he had no idea what shape Mitchell would be in when they arrived.

No one was speaking in the carriage, but the silence was very loud.

Truthfully, he would have happily left Elijah behind since he was likely to be distracted by Miss Stuart's presence, but he might need

Elijah to help him carry Mitchell and provide physical bulk to their request to take Mitchell with them if Miss Stuart's words alone failed to move the Tramp.

The carriage rolled to a stop, and Elijah leaned forward, opening the door and being the first to spring out. Anthony did not begrudge him the move—he needed to work off some of his emotions. Indeed, by the time Miss Stuart and Anthony stepped down from the carriage, Elijah seemed a bit calmer as he studied the outside of the Den.

"Let's go." Elijah strode forward, Miss Stuart right behind him.

"Wait here. We'll be back shortly," Anthony told their driver, who nodded nervously. Anthony did not toss him a coin. Doing so would only invite those in the shadows to come out. He would reward the footman handsomely upon their return to Camden House.

The door to the Den opened, and a man stood there. Not Butch or Frank, but one of the Tramp's other men. Anthony recognized him, though he could not remember his name. The man glanced at the three of them, his gaze flickering dismissively over them.

"Den's closed." He started to shut the door.

"Wait. I was summoned here. I'm Tony." Anthony shouldered his way between Elijah and Miss Stuart. He could hear Elijah's huff of breath.

The man paused. What was his name again, dammit?

"You can come in. The other two need to say outside."

"Let us in, Dodger." Miss Stuart peered around Anthony's arm. She raised her hand to tip back her cap, allowing the dim light from inside to play over her features. "Henry willna mind." The accent was back.

Elijah jerked in shock beside Anthony, who had to press his lips together to keep back his amusement. He wondered if Elijah had *ever* seen his cousin in action.

Dodger grinned toothily, his entire demeanor changing.

"Yvette! I almost didna recognize you. Come on in then." Stepping back, the man opened the door wide.

Behind him, Elijah made the oddest noise. Anthony glanced over his shoulder to see the man's face had gone bright red, and his jaw was clenched so hard, a vein was popping out on his forehead. He looked like he was about to fall over.

If the circumstances were not so dire, Anthony would be truly enjoying himself.

Miss Stuart led the way into the main room, which was empty except for a small group of three in the center, standing around a huddled heap. The Tramp looked up and smiled, which was hardly comforting with the blood flecked across his face.

"Yvette! I did not expect to see you here."

Now it sounded like Elijah was being strangled. Anthony peeked over his shoulder again, and Elijah's face was nearly purple.

Even if they ended up not needing Miss Stuart, it was well worth having her along just to see Elijah's reactions. Clearly, he had not known about his cousin's connection with the Tramp, even though the Tramp knew about him, which was obvious from the smirk on the Tramp's face when he looked directly at Elijah.

"Henry, of course, I came." Miss Stuart put her hands on her hips. "Is he alive? We need him alive."

The Tramp's lady was nowhere in sight, making Anthony wonder where she was—and if the Tramp had spared her the sight of the beating. If that was the case, he apparently did not think Miss Stuart needed the same, which was interesting in and of itself.

"He's still alive." The Tramp kicked the curled-up man, who moaned slightly. "He's told me quite a bit and is very sorry to have used my Den for his activities."

An answering moan drifted up from the floor.

If he had not been a traitor, Anthony might have felt sorry for him. The Tramp had given him a thorough, painful beating. Not always the best way to get answers since people tend to say whatever you want to hear to make the pain stop.

"For a while, he was working for the French," the Tramp said conversationally. "During the war, smuggling everything from lace to spies. Naughty boy." He kicked Mitchell again, and the man shuddered, groaning. There was an odd quality to his voice, a hoarseness, as though he had worn it out screaming, which was probably the case.

"Lately, he's been working with the Russians." The Tramp smiled, but it did not reach his eyes, which were dark and cold. "Did you know the Russians are hoping to marry the princess to one of their princes?

They thought if they assassinated the Duke of York, she would be pushed to marry faster."

A chill went through Anthony. He could see that scenario playing out. If the Duke of York had been assassinated, the search for a husband for the princess would have been of the utmost importance as he would become the royal consort.

"For sale to the highest bidder." Elijah, finally getting control over himself, stepped forward and glared down at the sorry excuse for a man on the floor between them all.

"Very much so." The Tramp shook his head. "Which is understandable until it comes to selling out your entire country. Even here in the Warrens, we have better morals than that."

"Thank you for your help in finding him." Miss Stuart stepped forward, gingerly moving around Mitchell and keeping a wary eye on him. "We will take it from here. My uncle has many questions for him."

The Tramp raised his eyebrows at her. Elijah looked as if he was about to say something, and Anthony grabbed onto his arm. When Elijah turned to look at him, Anthony shook his head. The Tramp and Miss Stuart stared at each other for several long moments, him considering his options while she smiled sweetly at him.

Finally, he nodded, and Anthony's breath came out in a whoosh of air.

"I suppose I'm done with him." Crouching and tapping Mitchell's swollen cheek, a cruel smile curved the Tramp's lips. "But if you need any more help getting answers from him, let me know. I am happy to oblige."

"Thank you, Henry."

Elijah made that noise again, but he kept quiet. He was very useful carrying Mitchell out of the Den, just as Anthony had hoped. Surprisingly, Mitchell did not give them a lick of trouble, even though he was conscious.

He was probably too relieved to be away from the Tramp.

CHAPTER 22

Mitchell

E*vie*

Checking over Mitchell's many injuries in the carriage ride, Evie sat back, satisfied he would live to face justice. Henry had elicited maximum pain without doing much actual damage. With his wrists and ankles bound in rope, Mitchell did not even attempt to escape. He seemed humbled. Broken.

Good.

If it was up to her, she would have kicked him—hard—a few times between his legs and done her best to ensure he could never use his cock again.

She still might before all was said and done, but they needed him able to speak, and she did not think he could take much more damage without passing out.

The ride back to Camden House was as quiet as the ride there had been, but for entirely different reasons. Elijah was staring out the window, brooding. Once or twice he muttered something under his breath, none of it intelligible, so Evie ignored him.

She was no longer feeling so gleeful. Though she felt satisfied, she was strangely let down. With all the work they'd done trying to find Mitchell, having him handed over to them... She would have liked to be the one to find him. That was all. But she should not have been surprised Henry was the one who had ultimately hunted him down.

If she had been able to go through the streets the way she wanted, instead of having to play the part of a lady, it might have been her who found him, but she could not regret it. She'd needed to keep an eye on her uncle. If she had been out searching the streets, he would have worried about her, and she truly was trying not to worry him as much.

When they reached Camden House, the place was lit up. Josie, Diana, and her uncle were waiting for them, as well as Rex, Mary, Nathan, and Lily. Josie must have sent for them, which was wise. Not only might they think of more questions, but of all of them, Nathan had the right to be there to see Mitchell brought in.

The man had killed his father and brother.

Captain Browne and Elijah came through the door behind her, each of them with an arm under one of Mitchell's armpits, dragging him. They'd kept the rope around his wrists and ankles in case he decided he had enough energy to run—or to force them to kill him before they could get their answers. Bound, he was much less of a danger, both to them and to himself.

In the light of the hall, Mitchell looked worse than ever. Blood matted his hair, both of his cheeks were swollen, there was a cut above one of his eyebrows, his lips were puffy and bloody, and bruises were already forming all over his face, but in his eyes, they could see the real story. Anger was forming in them as he took in the crowd waiting for him—anger and smugness.

Despite his current position, he liked knowing they were all there for him.

The bastard.

His jaw worked, and she realized he was about to speak.

"He's working for Russia," she said, taking away any sense of drama he might have been able to muster. There were gasps around the foyer. She looked away as Elijah and Captain Browne lowered Mitchell to a kneeling position between them. Not allowing him to speak, she quickly repeated everything Henry had told them, which made him angry.

Angry men made mistakes, especially when their egos had been pricked.

It was even better for her to speak for him—he was such a misogynist, Elijah or Captain Browne doing so would not have the same effect.

"Well, that certainly explains a few things," Uncle Oliver said when she finished. His mouth was set in a grim line. "Why did you bring him back if he already told the Tramp everything?"

"Not everything," Mitchell said, straightening, then hissing in pain and slouching back down. His shoulders hunched, his hands were unable to touch where it hurt since they were tied behind his back.

Uncle Oliver's eyes gleamed with triumph. That had been what he truly wanted to know—if there was anything left for Mitchell to tell.

"Well, then. Let's get him into the drawing room." Uncle Oliver tilted his head.

Evie pursed her lips but kept quiet as Uncle Oliver directed Captain Browne and Elijah to untie Mitchell's wrists and seat him in a chair. She rather thought the floor was good enough for him, but she also understood her uncle's tactics. Where Henry had used his fists, Uncle Oliver would pander to Mitchell's ego, soothing it and making him feel important again.

It may not loosen his tongue, but it could not hurt to try—and truthfully, it would probably make his ego even easier to prick if he was feeling indulged.

Uncle Oliver sent for food and water but did not wait before he began his questioning.

"What else could you possibly tell us?" Uncle Oliver asked, sitting in the chair across from Mitchell. The man's legs were still tied together, but Evie did not like seeing him so close to her uncle. She shifted a little closer, which caught Mitchell's attention, and he leered at her.

Captain Browne grasped the man's shoulder, giving him a shake.

"Stop looking at Miss Stuart and answer the Marquess' question."

"If she did not want men to look, she should not wear such revealing clothing." Mitchell chuckled, a hoarse, scratchy sound.

"Interesting, I did not realize trousers were considered so revealing." Evie turned to Josie, who was standing beside her, glaring at Mitchell. "Do you have trouble resisting staring at men wearing trousers?"

Now Mitchell was glaring at both of them.

"I suppose it depends on the man." Josie caught on quickly, tilting her head to the side and tapping her finger against her lower lip. One would think they had nothing better to discuss and no cares in the world beyond this ludicrous discussion. "I find Elijah in trousers very distracting, though not nearly so much as his breeches. He has such strong thighs, you know."

"I have actually never paid attention," Evie responded dryly.

"I find Nathan's thighs very appealing." Lily shot a meaningful look at her husband, who relaxed a tiny bit as he focused on her instead of Mitchell.

Evie could only imagine how difficult this was for him, but Lily came through.

"I find the way they hug Rex's arse to be most distracting," Mary said, drawing gasps from around the room, not just from the ladies. Elijah and Uncle Oliver were staring at her as though they'd never seen her before.

It was all Evie could do not to laugh.

"Would all you chattering ninnies shut up!" Mitchell appeared to have reached the end of his rope, his face such a hot red, Evie could almost see the steam coming out of his ears.

"Well, *you* were not saying anything interesting." Lily's cool, dismissive tone seemed to rile Mitchell to further heights.

"There's another attempt planned for York. How's that for interesting?" Mitchell snapped.

The jovial mood they had created plummeted.

* * *

Anthony

Watching the ladies drive Mitchell round the bend had not only been entertaining, it had also been informative. Mitchell had become so angry, he had said something he did not mean to. The moment he realized, his mouth snapped shut, and his jaw clenched. The man had probably been inwardly celebrating holding back that little tidbit the entire time the Tramp had been interrogating him.

Admitting to past misdeeds hardly qualified. Even though he claimed he had been working for the Russians in the attempted assassination of the Duke of York, without proof, there was nothing they could do, especially since they did not want to disrupt trade negotiations. The attempt had been too long ago, and matters had changed too much since then to disrupt the delicate balance of peace between the countries.

But a fresh attempt?

That was something different altogether.

"When?" Camden barked out the question. "How?"

Pressing his lips together, Mitchell shook his head, and they all exchanged frustrated glances. Hell and damnation. He was not sure the ladies' tactic would work again now that Mitchell was prepared for it.

A footman appeared in the door with a tray. Camden held up his hand, and the footman halted.

"If you would like some sustenance, you need to start talking. Now." Camden's voice was low. Threatening.

Mitchell sneered at him.

The desire to grip the man by the back of the head and smash his face into the table a few times was strong.

"Fine, have it your way. You can spend the night in the gaol instead of a proper room and see if that loosens your tongue." Camden waved his hand at the footman, who backed away.

Elijah and Nathan were the ones dispatched to take Mitchell to the gaol—with his hands properly tied again, this time at the wrists and elbows, despite his grunts of pain. The Tramp must have done a number on his torso because Mitchell's face contorted every time anything strained his stomach or sides.

While Anthony would have liked to go along, in case Mitchell said anything else interesting, he did not mind ceding the duty to Nathan. After what Mitchell had done to his family, the man deserved to be a part of this.

Once they were gone, the Marquess shook his head, slumping.

"I am done in for the night. I need to think. We will reconvene tomorrow, all of us, to make a plan." His gaze moved over the assembled, including the ladies. "If any of you see Joseph, Priscilla, or Adam, please let them know to be at the dinner table."

"Here, Uncle Oliver, let me help you to your room." It was not Miss Stuart but Josie who stepped forward, shooting a glance over her shoulder at Miss Stuart, a look that said 'stay put.'

Interesting.

The Marquess and his daughter-in-law made their way up the stairs as Anthony and Miss Stuart watched. Rex, Mary, and Lily murmured to each other until the pair was out of sight. Anthony was about to turn and join them when Rex looked up.

"Mary and I will take Lily home. We will see you on the morrow."

Rex could have offered Anthony a ride, but he did not. And was it his imagination, or did Lily and Mary wink at Miss Stuart as they said their farewells? Anticipation was thrumming in Anthony's veins.

Elijah and Nathan would be a while setting Mitchell up. There would be forms to fill out, explanations to be made, and guards to be set. It would be a while before Elijah returned.

Who knew where Joseph, Priscilla, and Adam were... but they were not here, and everyone else was leaving them alone, whether in ignorance or by design.

His desire for Miss Stuart flared.

He could have left with Rex and the others, but even without his burgeoning arousal, he needed to talk to Miss Stuart. Privately.

So, he hung back as the others left, and she closed the door behind them. Turning, she raised her eyebrows, questioning his presence, yet there was nothing in her expression that made him feel he was unwelcome or that she wanted him to leave.

"Would you like to sit down again? I feel we have some things to discuss," he said, gesturing towards the drawing-room.

Miss Stuart only paused for a moment before nodding.

"Yes, of course." Chin high, she glided forward as elegantly as if she was dressed in a gown rather than the clothes of a street urchin. Anthony had to admit her bottom looked very nice in her trousers.

Though if Mitchell indicated he noticed Miss Stuart's bottom again, Anthony would see to it that the reprobate lost some teeth for his troubles.

CHAPTER 23

A Private Discussion

Evie

Heart beating a little faster in her chest as she heard Captain Browne following her into the drawing room, Evie knew what he wanted to talk about. She did not have an answer for him, and she could have told him so and sent him on his way immediately...

That is what she should have done. She regretted not doing so as soon as he closed the door behind them, trapping them in the room.

She did not know how to deal with her growing feelings for him. She felt out of control and did not like it. Did he have any feelings for her?

Desire, certainly.

That much was obvious.

But beyond that?

He seemed to respect her and value what she could bring to the table when it came to the investigation, but that was not the same as having feelings for her. If Evie ever married, it would be for one reason and one reason only—love.

Not love found *after* the wedding, the way it had happened for her friends. That had been their choice to make, but she knew it was not one she would make for herself.

Unless I am pregnant.

Two reasons, then.

That would be an extenuating circumstance.

The problem was she was fairly certain she was falling in love with Captain Browne, which made him more dangerous than ever, especially if she was pregnant, and they had to marry. If she ever discovered him with another woman, the way they had found Joseph and Lady Cross...

Well... Ladies of their station were expected to turn a blind eye, but that was not something Evie was capable of. Not when her emotions were involved. He would be lucky to walk away with his manhood intact.

Rather than sitting, Evie leaned against one of the chairs. Captain Browne stood, his back to the doors, and crossed his arms over his chest as he faced her. There was a glint in his eye that sent shivers down her spine.

Yes, he certainly still desired her.

She desired him, but she was not sure the risks were worth it... though they could use a French letter this time or ensure he did not actually spurt his seed inside her.

She gave herself a shake.

"What did you want to talk about?" she asked, then plowed into the obvious before he could answer. "I do not know yet if I am pregnant." Hearing the words spoken aloud made them feel more real, and Evie had to suppress another shiver. She bit the inside of her lip, waiting for his reaction.

"That is what I wanted to know." Captain Browne nodded slowly. "Partly." He stepped forward, and Evie braced herself.

Heat fizzed through her with every step he took toward her, his prowling gait like a predator on the hunt, but she was no prey. A lioness in her own right, she would not run. That would make her far too vulnerable.

"What else did you want to know?"

He was rapidly coming closer, and her head tilted back so she could hold his gaze. When he stopped in front of her, their faces mere inches apart, her breath caught in her throat. Her nipples tightened in aroused anticipation as the front of his body brushed against hers, his eyes searching her face for... something.

"This."

Lips lowered to hers as his hands came up to cup her face. Evie met his kiss, stepping into it, her hands pressing against his chest and sliding up.

Bad idea, bad idea, bad idea...

When his lips moved away from hers, hands moving down to trace the curves of her body and pull her more firmly against him as he kissed her neck, Evie groaned.

"This is a terrible idea."

"Then tell me to stop, and I will." His hand cupped her breast, tweaking her nipple through the fabric, and desire clenched her insides.

"I do not want you to stop," she whispered. "But it is still a terrible idea."

"You did not think so before."

Her heart had not been engaged before, but she could hardly admit to that.

Instead, she turned her head and bit his neck, eliciting a low snarl.

That bite seemed to unleash something inside him, something hot and primal, and Evie found herself pressed down to the floor beneath him. He was bigger than her, caging her as his mouth latched onto her skin.

"Do not leave a mark!" she snapped the words at him, knowing their hypocrisy and not caring.

Anyone who saw a mark on him would hardly comment. He was a man and could do as he wished. If anyone saw a mark on *her* skin, which had obviously come from someone's mouth, it would cause an uproar. And a huge distraction to the far more important business of Mitchell's treachery and the Russian plot to assassinate the Duke of York.

Captain Browne growled his displeasure but obeyed.

Hands pulled at her shirt, buttons popping off as he ripped it open, and Evie gasped. She loved it. Loved his loss of control. Loved seeing him so undone. Loved the feel of his hands and mouth on her breasts, squeezing the soft flesh, his teeth biting the tender nubs as if to punish her for not allowing him to mark her elsewhere. She cried out softly at the sensations, writhing beneath him while he tormented her and tore at his shirt.

Skin met skin, fingers gliding beneath fabric to touch and tantalize. Evie's thighs were spread wide, her legs wrapped around him as she rubbed herself against him. Wearing trousers made it far more frustrating, with more layers of clothing between them, but she loved how she could feel his erection pressing into her.

"Bloody trousers."

Captain Browne, apparently, did not have the same appreciation for her clothing.

His weight left her, and she heard more fabric ripping. Damn him. At this rate, she would have to replace the entire outfit.

* * *

Anthony

Fuck, this woman was driving him wild.

He was aware of the danger they were courting—even more so than their short interlude at the Society of Sin—but only dangerous in the sense they were risking being caught. Being caught risked being forced to marry because of the scandal, the same way their friends had been.

That did not sound so bad to him right now.

He was also risking her cousins' violent reactions, but he could handle them. Since he was more than prepared to do the right thing by her, if only she would have him, there would be no duels at dawn over her honor. Anthony was happy to preserve it.

Bloody hell.

He wanted to marry the woman.

He just was not ready to admit it aloud, not when he had no idea how she felt about him.

Not when he knew her cousin did not think she would ever be interested in marriage.

Lovers was good enough. For now.

As long as she was his lover and his alone.

He wanted to devour her. To taste her. Feast on her.

Stripping the clothes from her body, he rolled them again so she was straddling his face, her knees planted on either side of his head, the sweet peach of her pussy right above his lips while he stared at the pretty curve of her ass. A long lick through her center made her moan, and she leaned forward, sliding her hands down his stomach to the front of his trousers.

Anthony licked her again and again, stroking his tongue through her wet folds, feasting on the ambrosia of her arousal as it coated his tongue. Wrapping his arms around her thighs, he dug his fingers into the soft flesh of her arse, so he could pull her cheeks apart and expose more of her sensitive flesh to his mouth.

Feeling her pull his cock free, fingers wrapped around the thick length, he groaned with pleasure against her slick cunt. Bloody hell, that felt good. It felt even better when she bent forwards and took the tip of his cock between her lips, her breasts brushing over his lower stomach.

He could *feel* the vibrations of her low hum of approval as he slid his tongue up and down. *Feel* her gasp when his tongue moved from her pussy to the crinkled star of her anus, laving the little opening.

From the way she squirmed atop him, the way her fingers dug into his thighs, her teeth grazing the surface of his cock like a warning, he remained fairly certain this was new territory for her.

He wanted to be the man to claim that spot. To take the last of her innocence. Just as he wanted to be her last lover.

His tongue laved against the tight opening and he felt her thighs flex, trying to push up and away. Tightening his fingers on her, not letting her retreat an inch, he formed a little point with his tongue and pushed it inward before pulling away, swiping through her wetness again, and returning to tease that spot. From the way she was moaning around his cock, she enjoyed the sensation, even if she did not want to.

He groaned, thrusting his hips upward as her fingers squeezed his balls, distracting him. The exquisite sensation of her taking the entire length of his cock down her throat was almost too much to bear, stealing his concentration and his breath. Moving his fingers down, he pressed a tip to her anus, pushing past the tight ring of muscle guarding it.

Miss Stuart moaned and shuddered, suckling him with renewed

fervor, her grip on his balls becoming painful as she tugged on the sack, pulling it away from his body.

Fuck.

Pushing his finger in deeper, past the clenching muscle, he stretched the tiny hole while he feasted on her pussy below. They moved together, using each other's mouths for their own pleasure while working to please each other.

Anthony could not remember the last time he had experienced the like—the give and take of pleasure, the mutual exchange, the loss and regaining of focus. This was nothing like what he indulged in at the Society, and he loved every moment. He did not know who was in control. One moment it was him, the next it was her, but it did not matter.

If anything, he was more excited each time he wrested control from her.

* * *

Evie

Pleasure. Heat. Need.

Evie was drowning in it. Her virginal bottom was clenching around Captain Browne's finger as it rudely delved deeper, thrusting in and out, mimicking the sex act. If she would ever allow a man into such an intimate area of her body, it would be him.

She knew her friends had all given up that part of their innocence to their husbands. They had all surpassed her experience in that way, though that was not why she would consider allowing Captain Browne to take her there.

She wanted to do something with him she had not done with any other man. Wanted him to be the first to take her there, to show her the pleasure and the pain of the experience.

Knew she could trust him with such an intimate and delicate encounter.

He would make it enjoyable for her, of that she was sure, and that was not something a woman could say about every man.

His tongue worked her over, her hips moving atop him, as his finger thrust and twisted inside her. Evie cried out around his cock, shuddering, her body tensing as ecstasy gripped her. Sensing her culmination, Captain Browne held her tighter, plunging the full length of his finger into her bottom, filling her deliciously, and she screamed with the hot rush of erotic rapture, but his cock muffled the sound.

Then she had to swallow, her throat working, even as she was in the throes of her own pleasure, as his hot seed spilled down her gullet. Evie sucked and sucked, mindlessly shuddering as the waves of bliss rocked through her. Sparkling heat rolled over her, again and again, until she was left spent with the salty taste of him on her tongue.

With their passion quelled, she rested her head on his thigh, quivering as she felt his finger finally slide from her most forbidden aperture. The sensation was as wicked as it was taboo.

Rolling off him, Evie sat up and took stock of their surroundings, suddenly feeling incredibly awkward. She knew how to deal with men in general. She did not know how to deal with *this* man and the way he made her feel. With any other man from her past, she would already be shooing him out the door.

But she almost wanted him to stay.

But what if he did not want to stay?

"You should be going," she said. "Elijah could return any moment. Or Joseph. Or Adam." Or her uncle could come down the stairs. Very good reasons for him to go, no matter what she wanted.

"Yes, of course." He cleared his throat and sat up.

Evie could not meet his eyes as she grabbed the tattered remains of her clothing, which would need mending. Two of the buttons from her shirt had rolled under the couch.

Silently, they put themselves back together. Captain Browne handed her a button that had rolled beneath him.

Evie could not look him in the eye, and he did not seem able to look her in the eye, either.

Was he regretting their moment of passion?

Worried someone might catch them?

Wanting someone to catch them?

Evie pressed her lips together. He had better not be. She still remembered his offer to make her his mistress. Was he willing to extend that to wife?

Even if he was, waiting to see if they were caught and having her family insist upon their marriage was hardly the best way to propose. It certainly did not meet any of *her* requirements for agreeing to marry a gentleman.

The taste of him was still on her tongue when she finally met his gaze, clutching her ruined shirt closed in front of her.

"Thank you for the pleasant evening. I suppose I will see you tomorrow."

Before he could respond, before he could reach for her, Evie fled the room. She heard the front door open and close as she hurried down the hall of the second floor to her bedroom, hoping no one stepped out to see her.

As usual, Captain Browne had made her lose her head, and she did not have a good explanation for why her shirt was without buttons.

CHAPTER 24

The Best Laid Plans

Anthony

"The Manchesters are throwing a ball in three days." Priscilla pulled the invitation from the stack.

"The French delegation was invited to that one," Lucas said, perking up. The Earl of Devon had joined them in their conference of 'what to do,' now that Mitchell had claimed the Russians were going to make an attempt on the Duke of York's life again. As the original scapegoat set up to take the fall for one of Mitchell's counterparts, he was apparently invested in bringing the whole plot down, and he had great insights into the French. He was also excessively charming when he wished to be and had also made some inroads with the Russian embassy, as much as anyone had. He and Adam, that was.

Adam was seated on the opposite side of the room from Lucas and neither of them was looking at each other. Nor were they looking at him or Miss Stuart. Not that anyone else seemed to notice, other than himself and Miss Stuart.

"If the French were invited, the Russians likely were as well." Adam rubbed his fingers over his chin, bringing them to a point in the center. "The biggest question is whether the French are going. The Russians only show up to those events the French attend."

"It's the Duke of Manchester, so I doubt either will say no."

Priscilla sounded authoritative, and Anthony was fascinated by the change that had overcome her once they'd begun talking about social gatherings. It seemed she knew a little about most everyone and was very in tune with what events were the most socially important.

The other ladies hesitated before answering the questions that Priscilla was confident about, and as soon as she answered, they agreed she was correct.

"This one." Priscilla tapped her finger against the invitation and nodded as if confirming her thoughts to herself. "This is the one where most of them will be. Perhaps all of them."

Exactly what they were looking for. So far, Mitchell had remained very close-mouthed. He was already on the block for treason and would be tried and executed, so he had little reason to help them. With his previous traitorous activities, not to mention the many murders he had committed, there were no lesser punishments available. The best they could do was give him a kinder death than being drawn and quartered, but Camden said the Crown did not want to make that concession.

They were still expected to prove the Russians' perfidy and keep the Duke of York safe from their machinations, even if Mitchell never confessed, which meant finding a time when they could infiltrate the embassy. Easier said than done. A time when the entire delegation would be gone was best. There would be guards, of course, but the fewer people in the building, the better. The entire delegation was staying in that one place, along with the ambassador, which made things a bit easier.

"Who will go?"

"Me." Anthony looked up and around. "It has to be me. Some of you can serve as a distraction, but you cannot go inside. I am the only one without a title unconnected to the Camden family. Mitchell could have told them who you are to the Crown, and if he did then getting caught in their embassy would confirm it. None of you can go."

"He could have told them you work for my uncle," Miss Stuart said. She was sitting poker-straight, hands folded neatly on her lap, practically vibrating from the energy she was holding back.

"There is a difference between being told by a source they can no longer reach and actually being a member of your uncle's family,"

Anthony countered. "If I am caught, you can all disavow me. The Crown can disavow me. I can make something up that has nothing to do with spies or the Duke of York. Even if Mitchell told them something, without proof, they could not act."

Just as *they* could not act without proof other than Mitchell's word.

"We will need distractions," Camden said, speaking up before his niece could interject again. "People to keep watch. But I agree, out of all of us here, Anthony is the best suited for the actual incursion, and only sending one person in makes the most sense."

"There should be at least two," Miss Stuart argued, not about to be put off. "To search most efficiently and in case someone requires a distraction. Exactly how are those keeping watch outside to know if there is a problem?"

"I could bring someone else in..." Camden hesitated, and they all knew why. The only people they could be completely sure of trusting, whom they knew Mitchell had never suborned, were in this room.

"It has to be me. I am the only expendable one." Anthony looked around. "The rest of you either have titles or are part of the Stuart family. You cannot take the risk. The best thing is for me to go in alone while everyone else ensures the Russian delegation stays as long as possible at the ball."

"There will need to be some backup outside," Elijah said. His eyes skipped over all of them. "Adam, Lucas, the two of you outside in the street, in case Anthony needs help."

He would not, and if he was caught, there would be very little anyone outside the house could do—so he understood Miss Stuart's point—but having them there would do no harm.

"If the delegation returns early, you can stall them." Best-case scenario, he would not need them at all, especially if the others did their jobs and kept the delegation occupied long enough for him to search the embassy.

"Well, then..." Camden cleared his throat. "We have three days to prepare."

. . .

Anthony spared a glance at Miss Stuart, but she was sitting very still with her chin held high. She was not arguing, even though she was not happy. He wondered if any of her unhappiness stemmed from worry for him or if it was entirely due to being denied what she wanted—which was surely how her uncle and cousins were reading the situation.

Was it too much to hope she worried a bit for him as well?

* * *

Evie

Bloody blockheaded men.

Captain Browne offering himself up as a martyr, and the others letting him.

She was dressed up in a ballgown, keeping an eye on the Russian dignitaries, along with everyone else. While Captain Browne broke into their embassy with no backup other than the two men outside, who were not supposed to go *inside* for any reason.

Bollocks to that.

Evie had been here long enough.

Catching Josie's eye, she nodded.

Josie turned and tugged on Elijah's arm. A few moments later, they were headed for the dance floor. Lily and Nathan were deep in discussion on the other side of the ballroom, so no worries there.

And...

With a mental salute to Lady Spencer, who had given her the idea, Evie tipped her glass of wine onto her dress.

"Oh, dear!" Evie exclaimed loud enough to draw the attention of several parties around them. The ladies murmured in sympathy as Diana, who ostensibly was there as Evie's companion, stepped forward to help her dab ineffectually at it with a napkin. After a moment, Evie shook her head in mock sadness. "It is no use. I will have to return home. I do not think even water will help. Tell my uncle I went home. I do not want to interrupt anyone else's night."

"Of course," Diana said sympathetically. "Do you want me to come with you?"

"No, thank you." Evie gave her a small smile of appreciation. "I will see everyone at home. You should stay and enjoy yourself."

With that done, and plenty of people witnessing her spill and her conversation with Diana, Evie made her way to the entrance. Glancing over her shoulder on the way, she saw Diana making her way across the room to Evie's uncle.

Priscilla and Joseph were on the dance floor. She did not see Rex and Mary, but she did not need to. Rex would follow Mary's lead on this, one of the things she liked most about him.

Slipping out a side door into the alley, Evie hurried to the spot where she had tucked away some clothes—a simple skirt and blouse, along with pins for her hair.

A few minutes later, she crept out of the alley and down the street. Whereas a lady on her own in a gown would have drawn immediate attention, no one glanced twice at the maid running down the sidewalk.

She did not stay on the main thoroughfare for long. There was an unmarked carriage waiting for her not far away. Coming up from behind, she waited until there was no one on her side of the street before opening the door, hopping in, and rapping her knuckles on the ceiling.

As the carriage lurched forward scant seconds later, she could feel her heart beating faster in her chest.

Captain Browne would not be happy... but then, he might never even know she was there. It was a big building.

This is foolishness. You should have told him you were going to do this, and you know it.

Perhaps, but she would not back out now.

Energy fizzed through her. Maybe there was even a part of her that enjoyed knowing he was going to be angry. Wondered what he would do when—if—he discovered her there. She was not planning on hiding from him. Things would go far faster with both of them there. She also very much doubted, even if they were caught, anyone would look at her twice.

* * *

Anthony.

Not here... not here...

The search was tedious, far too long, and so far, utterly useless. Anthony wished he had extra hands to help him along. Doing this on his own was not easy. He had started in the most obvious area, the ambassador's office, before moving on to the other offices along the hall.

So far, nothing. Not even in the secret caches he'd found in multiple desks.

Footsteps in the hall made him freeze. He crouched, silently moving to insert himself beneath the desk, hoping they'd move on.

The door opened.

Bloody hell.

Hopefully, they would not notice the chair was pushed back from the desk.

The footsteps moved briskly. Not a man's, likely a maid's. He could overpower her... That might be his best chance if she discovered him. Taking slow, quiet, deep breaths, he slowed his pounding heart. Time seemed to stretch as she came closer. Her skirts came into view—definitely a maid or a servant by the looks of them.

Readying himself to grab her—or possibly the chair if she tried to push it in—utter shock stilled him when she crouched, and he caught sight of her face.

"Ah, there you are. Come on. I have what we need." Miss Stuart motioned to him.

A red mist obscured Anthony's vision as sheer rage gripped him. His lungs felt as though they seized as he choked back the need to shout at her.

"Yes, I know, I know, I should not be here, and I should have told you. You can punish me later. We need to be going. It's already been too long."

"What are you doing here?" he growled as he moved from underneath the desk, hating that she got to see him crawling on the floor.

"Searching with you, of course. I figured you would start on this side of the embassy, so I started on the other, in the bedrooms. I found correspondence between Mitchell and the ambassador—there is nothing about the Duke of York in them, but it proves the connection.

And there are some letters that are definitely in some kind of cipher or code, which I bet has something incriminating." Miss Stuart hurried to the door and peeked out, then looked over her shoulder. "Come on, we need to get moving. You could not have dressed more inconspicuously?"

The urge to shake her until she rattled like a baby's toy was hard to resist. His palm was itching to lay down the punishment she had mentioned. She would not sit easily for a week.

A month!

"If anyone saw me, I planned to play the drunken son of a lord on a lark."

Understanding lit Miss Stuart's jade eyes, and she considered it for a moment before nodding.

"It could work, possibly."

"Certainly better than someone on the staff not recognizing me and wondering what I was doing here."

"This time of day, most of the staff is finishing up their last tasks before they can retire, if they have not already. The personal servants are getting what rest they can before the delegation returns and needs their assistance. No one is looking at each other. They're all in a rush to get to their beds." Miss Stuart spoke quickly, keeping her voice low as they approached the corner, which she peeked around, then nodded.

She made a good point. Anthony had a feeling she was very well versed in how household staffs behaved. This was not her first time posing as a servant. Once again, he wondered exactly how long she had worked for Lady Greywood and how many other families of the *ton* had employed the niece of England's spymaster for a short period of time. Likely, more than he wanted to know.

That would not be enough to save her once he got his hands on her.

"How were you planning to get out?" she asked.

"The same way I got in. Window, one story down, into the side alley. The guards do a regular patrol there but never change up the timing." Sloppy work that, but he was not complaining.

Miss Stuart nodded.

"I'll go out through the servants' stair."

Clamping his hand around her arm before she could go, Anthony pulled her to his side.

"You will not," he growled. "You are coming with me." Where he could keep an eye on her. Now that he knew she was here, being separated would give him heart palpitations. "If we *are* caught in the alley, we can be a drunken lord having his way with a merry maid. That's even better than doing it on my own."

"In which case, perhaps you should have let me come along," she whispered as they hurried down the side stair. Thankfully, there was still no one in sight.

"Hardly. That ruse will only work once we're in the alley." He would not let her wriggle her way out of punishment, no matter what excuses she came up with.

Though he might let that she had found something sway him toward a more lenient punishment.

Possibly.

But not necessarily.

CHAPTER 25

Paying the Penance

Evie

Captain Browne was fuming. She could feel it emanating from him.

But it had been worth it.

He would have made his way around to the bedrooms, eventually, but the less time it took, the better. She had halved the chances of him getting caught.

Except in the time it took - with two of you there, it doubled the chances of someone accidentally seeing one of you.

That was why she would be willing to let him punish her. For the first time, she felt she deserved it. Just a little.

That and you want his hands on you again. That might have been why you did this instead of staying where you were assigned.

That was uncomfortably close to the truth.

She could not regret it. They had what they needed, neither she nor Captain Browne had been caught, and she knew he was going to punish her as soon as he got her alone, and...

She could not wait.

Sometimes, at the end of a successful mission, she felt a bit of a letdown, especially if it went well. When things felt too easy, it made her nervy. Not this time, though. As she and Captain Browne emerged from the alley into the street, him leaning on her with his arm tightly clasped around her shoulders while she giggled and played the besotted maid, her blood was just beginning to fizz with heat and anticipation.

The real excitement was with him.

Not with the mission.

It was the first time she had ever felt this way.

She wanted to be done with the mission, not for the satisfaction it would give her—at least not only for that—but because she wanted to fully focus on Captain Browne and what was happening between them.

"You and I are going home, and we will have a... chat."

"My home or yours?" she asked impishly.

"Yours. I do not want to imagine what your cousins would do if they found you at my house."

Fair enough.

"You should know that my menses started today," she murmured. His gait faltered. Was that disappointment she detected? Had he wanted her to be pregnant?

She had felt nothing but relief that she was not, but if he felt disappointment instead of relief... well, that was interesting. If he did not want to be married to her, he should have been relieved.

"That will not get you out of punishment."

Evie had not expected it to. Thankfully, she was on a cycle where her bleed was not very heavy. Her cycles tended to go from light, to medium, to heavy, then back to light again. She had no idea why, but the light ones were always accompanied by less cramping than the heavier ones, and if she had a heavy bleed, he *would* have to wait before she would submit for punishment.

As it was, she was intrigued that he was not at all deterred. Many men wanted nothing to do with a woman when she was bleeding— which a lady might prefer, but not always.

Evie was feeling the heady buzz of arousal that always followed a successful mission, not to mention Captain Browne's closeness and promise of punishment.

As they walked down the street, she saw Adam and Lucas jerk upright from where they'd been sitting and talking. It was a good thing no one from the delegation was out here—they would have given away everything with the expressions on their faces when they saw her.

Evie glared at Adam, who immediately sat back in his former position, his expression blanking. Lucas followed suit a moment later, but she could still feel their eyes following her and Captain Browne down the street. Glancing over her shoulder, she met Adam's gaze and pointed her finger.

He grimaced, but he would not rat her out, and hopefully, he could convince Lucas not to do so either. Out of all her cousins, Adam was the most reasonable and understanding. Usually. Hopefully, he would hold true to that tonight.

She was sure her uncle and Elijah would do their fill of shouting at her later. Not that it would make a difference.

She did feel a little trickle of guilt over not informing Captain Browne, which she knew had put both of them in more danger rather than less, but she did not feel beholden to her family members over it. The only person she felt beholden to was Captain Browne.

"Do we need to worry about Adam?" he asked, his voice low.

"No." She was fairly certain Adam would keep his mouth closed—especially since she knew *his* secret with Lucas. Not that she would ever share it with others out of revenge or because he had shared one of hers. Adam knew she would not rat him out and would return the favor.

"Good. Get in the carriage."

Unsurprised that Captain Browne had a carriage waiting for them at the end of the street, Evie allowed herself to be bundled in. It *was* much faster than walking. Would he start her punishment in the carriage?

Her heart pounded in her chest.

Hmm, perhaps that would not be for the best. While her monthly bleed was not very heavy, they would still risk the seats if he attempted to spank her here. A spanking, then... Evie squirmed on the seat, pressing her thighs together. Her arousal spiked now that they were alone in close confines.

Captain Browne settled onto the seat across from her, crossing his arms over his chest and glaring at her as the carriage rocked forward.

Silence hung between them. Neatly folding her hands on her lap, Evie did not feel the least bit discomfited.

Yelling, silence, it made no difference. She acknowledged her guilt and was ready to pay her penance, but he would not make her feel guiltier by yelling, scolding, or anything like that. Evie knew what she had done wrong *and* what she had done right.

If he wanted to sit in silence the entire way back to Camden House, so be it.

After a few long moments of glaring at her, he finally cleared his throat.

"What the hell am I supposed to do with you, Miss Stuart? You risked the entire mission, not to mention revealing your family's involvement." His voice was tight with anger.

"I did, which is why I am willing to accept there needs to be punishment, no matter how foolish I think your original plan was."

"Foolish!" He sounded as if he was choking.

"Foolish." Evie nodded. "Having someone else search doubled the chances of being caught, but so did searching on your own since it would have taken twice as long. However, searching on your own did *not* have the benefit of someone else in the house to help you if you were caught. Which makes your insistence on being the only one searching foolish."

More choking noises, and even in the dim light of the carriage, she could tell he was turning red.

Taking a deep breath, he closed his eyes. His nostrils flared in repressed annoyance. Evie watched with interest as he reined in his temper, his color slowly returning to normal.

Finally, he opened his eyes and pinned her with a glance. A very intense look that had Evie's thighs squeezing together beneath her skirts. If he wanted to deter her from breaking his rules, he should probably try to appear less attractive when she did.

"You still should have spoken with me and let me know what you were going to do so we did not end up tripping over each other."

"Ah, so you would have agreed had I spoken with you?" Evie smiled as he stiffened in his seat. "That is what I thought. As I said... foolish."

* * *

Anthony

The carriage ride with Miss Stuart was pure torture. Anthony longed for nothing more than to turn her over his knee right then and there, especially when she persisted in calling him foolish. However, the carriage ride would be far too short for what he planned to do with her. Even as a precursor, it was not enough.

No, he would keep his hands to himself until he had the time to deal with her as she deserved... they should have some time before her family returned from the evening's event. Certainly enough time for him to put his belt, hand, and cock to good use.

Desire pulsed through him in anticipation.

Since she had not wanted to risk pregnancy again, he had been carrying around a little vial of oil in case he found a good use for it. He'd known she would eventually do something that would require punishment.

Had looked forward to it.

He wished she had not chosen such a dangerous avenue of disobedience, but it had turned out well enough in the end. The papers they'd purloined crinkled against his chest. Anthony knew little of ciphers and code breaking, but the Marquess had people who excelled at it.

That meant, for all intents and purposes, his job was done once he turned these papers over. Normally, this was the point when he felt a bit let down, but with Miss Stuart sitting across from him, waiting for punishment, all he felt was anticipation. Excitement. Desire.

When they reached Camden House, he helped her down from the carriage and whisked her into the house. The house was quiet, other than the footman guarding the door they came through, indicating the rest of her family was still out. Anthony's anticipation soared even higher. Every step caused his trousers to rub against his stiffened cock, teasing him with the stimulation.

"Your room. Now." If he had to wait any longer, he was going to explode. He was also aware they were on a clock that was ticking down quickly.

The smart thing to do would be to leave her here. Retreat and not look back. If he really felt the need to punish her, he could find another time and place to do so.

Perhaps they should have gone to his home...

If her family returned here, and she was *not* at home, and Adam reported she had left while in his care... No. She needed to be home. He was taking risks either way, but this was the lesser. Just barely.

Leave.

Leave and leave her wanting.

That was the smartest option, certainly, but he knew he would not take it.

They reached her room, and he stepped in with her. Closed the door behind him.

There was no going back.

"Strip," he ordered. "Then bend over the bed."

Reaching down, he undid his belt, and Miss Stuart's eyebrows rose as she watched him. Her head tilted to the side.

"All the way?" she asked, her hands moving to the buttons at the top of her blouse.

"Of course, all the way."

"I will need to lay something down, so my sheets do not stain."

Was she trying to use her monthly to see if she could frighten him off? He had not only been a spy, he had also been in the army. Blood would not send him running off in fear. While he knew some men were put off by the natural behaviors of a woman's body, he was not one of them.

He wanted her. Period.

Nothing about her would deter him, especially not something as natural as her cycle.

"Then do so."

Appreciation lit up her eyes, and he wondered if she had been testing him. A little smile curved his lips. Whatever men she had been with in the past, who made her think such a small thing would be the end of their encounter, they had not deserved her. A woman's body was to be celebrated and revered in all its many forms and functions.

With a sultry smile, she disrobed. Anthony watched as each piece of clothing dropped to the floor, revealing more and more of her creamy skin. By the time she sashayed to the bed, his cock was rock hard and aching, and his hand was gripping his belt so tightly, his fingers were turning numb.

Picking up a bundle of linen from her nightstand, she spread it over the bed, just in front of where she was standing.

"Like this?" she asked as she bent at the waist and rested her elbows on the bed, then glanced over her shoulder.

Her heart-shaped bottom was perfectly smooth, the pale skin shining in the dim light. Bent over as she was, she had spread her legs apart to ensure she remained balanced. The arousal at the top of her thighs had a very faint pinkish hue to it. He felt the faint pang of disappointment again, knowing she was not with child.

Eventually, he was going to have to come forward and confess his feelings.

And hope she returned them.

It was not something he was looking forward to, but to have the future he wanted, it would be necessary. Miss Stuart would accept nothing less, and she deserved all that she wanted, even if part of him wished he could have gotten around such a vulnerable confession.

Knowing she could refuse him was enough to make a man sweat.

He would not think of that right now.

He was going to focus on where they were at this moment.

Her pain.

His pleasure.

"Just like that." He flexed his fingers around the belt in his hand, the supple leather soft against his skin. When it landed on her upturned bottom, it would not feel nearly so soft. "You should have come and talked to me before going out on your own."

Miss Stuart sent him an amused glance over her shoulder.

"We would have still ended up here. You would have said no, and I would have gone, anyway. I acknowledge I put us both in a little danger by not informing you, so I am willing to let you punish me." She wriggled her bottom.

Anthony pinched the bridge of his nose, right between his eyes. She was trying more than his patience and clearly had not learned a thing.

Well, they would see how confident she was when she was taking his cock up her arse.

He raised his arm, and seeing the movement, she dropped her head back into place. Striking with the folded-over leather, it caught her across both cheeks with a hot, red welt. She cried out, nearly a scream, before remembering herself and pressing her lips to the bed, muffling the noise.

The sound made his cock throb.

She did not look so confident now with her legs and bottom quivering, the red stripe clearly showing across her pale skin. Anthony smiled with grim satisfaction. Five with the belt should color most of her bottom red, then he would fill in all the areas in-between with his hand.

CHAPTER 26

The Belt and the Hand

E*vie*

Mistakes had been made.

Evie was no stranger to pain. Life on the streets was not kind. As she donned various disguises, she had been hit more than once. Yet somehow, it had been different.

Perhaps because she had not offered herself up for the blows. Or perhaps because there was something particularly humiliating about being completely naked and aroused while being whipped. Or just because she had not truly expected it to hurt all that much.

Her debutante friends, prim and pampered, who had suffered no physical hardships beyond what she put them through when training them to defend themselves, had all been punished by their husbands. They'd enjoyed it, though Mary said she did not actually enjoy the punishment, only the aftermath. Since Evie had enjoyed her spankings, she had not been particularly worried about the addition of a belt or thought it would be all that different.

But the initial impact of leather across flesh seared her, making her scream, then gasp and clench.

Then, before she could truly catch her breath, it came down again.

And again.

And again.

"Last one."

Evie panted as the final stroke was laid across the tender crease between her buttocks and her thighs, the hot red pain slicing across that sensitive area. She screamed into the bedding again, fists clutching the sheets and going up on her toes as the searing blaze sank into her skin.

She could feel the individual lines where the belt had come down horizontally across her chastised cheeks, each one flaming hot with the final one blistering the hottest. It hurt—a lot—but did nothing to bank the fires of her desire. If anything, she felt warmer all over—outside and within—and the ache between her legs had increased with each bite of the belt.

"Good girl." Captain Browne's deep voice punctured the haze she'd fallen into. The accolade sent warmth through her chest, and her pussy quivered. "Now for your spanking."

Spanking?

On top of the belting?

Her brain barely had time to assimilate the information before his hand came down hard and fast on her already roasted bottom. Evie cried out, both in surprise and pain. While his palm did not hurt nearly as bad as the belt, he was spanking tenderized flesh, which hurt a lot more than his previous spankings.

Not enough to feel like she had made the wrong choice tonight, but certainly enough to help assuage the bit of guilt she felt.

With every smack of his hand against her upturned bottom, the flames of her arousal were stoked higher and higher. The belt had hurt, had been impersonal, and painfully arousing, but there was something about being spanked by hand that felt incredibly intimate.

"Ow!" she protested when his hand smacked against her sensitive crease, atop the welt there, then continued down the backs of her thighs, spanking the unmarked skin.

That hurt more than she had expected. Evie leaned forward, her nipples rubbing against the linens beneath her as she rocked with each hard slap. The extra stimulation did not change the pain, but it made it more bearable. She squirmed every time Captain Browne's hand came down, her body aching for the pleasure she knew would soon follow.

"Beautiful," he murmured, his hand coming down on her thigh and staying there, then sweeping up over her hot skin to cup her buttocks.

Evie moaned when he squeezed, but the painful discomfort hardly signified against the need that rushed through her. His fingers slipped between her cheeks, probing, and she sucked in a breath when she realized how slick one of his fingers was. It pressed against the little ring of her anus and pushed in easily. Her body quivered. Clenched.

Captain Browne's free hand came down hard.

"Relax. You will have bigger things in there soon enough."

Pressing her face against the sheets, Evie moaned again as his slick finger moved back and forth inside her, mimicking the sex act. His cock. He meant to replace his finger with his cock.

Another gush of heat flooded her, her arousal soaring even higher.

She felt utterly wicked as a second finger joined the first, stretching her open for him. Readying her tiny hole for his cock. Even knowing she was the last of her friends to experience this did not make it *feel* any more normal. The strain of her body around his fingers, the sting of discomfort that slowly gave way to strange pleasure, felt like pure, delicious depravity.

Sinful.

Agonizingly intimate.

She was giving him the last vestiges of her innocence, the only one that remained.

To the only man she had ever loved.

Not that she could say the words out loud, but she knew in her heart. Otherwise, things would never have progressed this far.

When his fingers left her, she braced herself, moaning when his hands cupped her bottom cheeks and pulled them apart. The slick head of his cock pressed against her where his fingers had been, pushing against the stretched opening. Evie gasped as he thrust forward, feeling herself open even wider than she had for his fingers.

It hurt.

It burned in an entirely different way than her spanking.

A deep, aching, cramping burn increased as the thick length of his cock pushed deeper. When she clenched around him, her body automatically working to push him out, he groaned with pleasure, and his fingers flexed against her flesh.

She was pinned between him and the bed, his oiled cock sliding deeper inside her, and she could not escape. Her bowels cramped, making her gasp and whimper. She clenched over and over, which did nothing to ease the erotic discomfort of being slowly impaled.

Captain Browne's groin came to rest against her burning cheeks, flattening them as he fully embedded himself inside her. Evie whimpered again, shuddering and clenching. He felt much larger in her arse than he had in her pussy or her mouth.

"Breathe, Miss Stuart." His voice was soft. Soothing. His hands had moved up to her hips, and he massaged the small of her back with his thumbs. That he was still calling her 'Miss Stuart' instead of by her Christian name when his cock was filling her bottom made the entire moment feel even filthier. "You will adjust, then I will fuck this pretty little bottom, hard, and you will think about why you have been punished this evening."

If he thought this was supposed to be a deterrent, he was wildly incorrect.

Did it hurt?

Yes.

It burned, still, as his hips rocked slightly. She was on fire inside and out.

She was also so aroused, she thought she might explode if she did not climax soon.

* * *

Anthony

The grip of Miss Stuart's arse around his cock was exquisite. The tight ring of muscle was flexing around him, the walls of her body massaging his entire length. The tiny hole had opened fully for him, all the wrinkles smoothing out as he inserted himself into her fundament.

Looking down at the white, rimmed hole, so pale against the hot red of her cheeks, stretched around his cock was one of the most erotic sights he had ever had the pleasure of seeing. Knowing he'd taken the last of her innocence, claimed a part of her no man ever had, was a hot thrill he knew would be imprinted on his mind.

He could feel her discomfort in the way she panted, how her muscles convulsed around him, and the fine tension in her back, but she did not complain. Did not ask him to stop.

She took it.

Accepted it.

Submitted to it.

All to please him.

Nearly bringing him to his knees.

After several long moments of her arse clenching around him and her body shuddering beneath his hands, he felt her relax. Felt her press back against him, rocking towards him.

She was ready.

Both of them moaned as he pulled back. His oiled cock was shiny as it retreated half out of her tight hole, then thrust back in, causing her to cry out. Pain and pleasure filled the sound, tightening his balls and heightening his lust. He drew out again, then thrust back in hard, and her bottom came up to meet him, even as she muffled her cries in the bedding beneath her head.

Bloody hell.

Groaning, Anthony let go of his control as he truly fucked her arse good and hard. His cock was throbbing as he rode her, the slick oil on his length keeping her clenching muscles from being able to resist his rough thrusts.

"Oh... oh, please... Anthony..."

She shuddered beneath him, his name falling from her lips, and he groaned. Moving harder, faster, he could feel her quivering beneath him, walking the fine line between pain and pleasure.

The hard, steady rhythm of his thrusts made her reddened cheeks jiggle every time he slammed home. Sliding his hands up her sides, he slipped them beneath her body, curving his fingers around her breasts. She cried out again as he squeezed hard. Using the soft flesh to give him even more leverage, he pinched the little buds of her nipples between his fingers.

"Anthony! Oh please... oh... Anthony!" She squealed as he impaled her on his cock, over and over, shifting beneath him, hips lifting to push against his thrusts.

He was moving inside her easily now, her hole nicely stretching to accommodate him, her discomfort melting away under the steady assault of his cock. Need was throbbing through him, but he did not want to stop. He wanted to make this last. Wanted to feel her ecstasy as he buggered her, to have her writhing in climax before he filled her forbidden entrance with his seed.

One hand moved down her body, pushing between her thighs and seeking the wet folds of her pussy and the little nub of pleasure tucked between them.

* * *

Evie

Agony and ecstasy burned through Evie as Anthony's hands and cock coaxed new sensations from her with every touch, every thrust. Fingers from one hand pinched her nipple tightly, even as the other found her clit, rubbing the little bud and sending hot pleasure coursing through her.

Every part of her body felt invaded by him.

Conquered by him.

Claimed.

The way he was taking her was as raw as it was erotic.

The fevered bliss of climax surged, twisting round and round deep inside her to a point right where his fingers were pressing, then burst outward in an explosion of searing passion. The ecstasy surged through her, from her core to the tips of her fingers and toes, sending her head spinning.

"Anthony... oh God... Anthony!" She screamed his name in the linen, her voice muffled, as the sensations rioted through her, wallowing in the sinful rapture of her wicked climax. Felt him respond by moving even harder, faster, taking her roughly, with all of his own pent-up passion, caused another wave of pleasure to overcome her, swamping her with the sensations.

"Evie!" He uttered her name as he thrust hard, rocking her body against the bed, his cock filling her completely. Leaning forward, his weight pressed against her, pinning her to the bed as he throbbed inside her.

She could feel every hot spurt of seed as it pulsed through his length, pushing past the gripping muscles spasming around the base of his cock and filling her with wet heat. The walls of her body clenched, milking him of every last drop while she sobbed in abject ecstasy.

The weight of him slumped over her, crushing her between his body and the bed, she could barely breathe, yet she did not want him to move.

Warm breath against her cheek, his body all around her, inside her, her needs utterly satiated—she did not want this moment of exquisite intimacy to end.

But, of course, it had to.

Sounds out in the hall made them freeze.

Her family was home.

CHAPTER 27

An Untimely Arrival

A*nthony*

Bloody hell.

Neither he nor Miss Stuart needed to exchange words when they heard the sounds of others in the house.

The very last thing they needed was for him to be caught in her room.

While he would be willing to marry her—wanted to marry her—he did not want to do it like this. It had been one thing when they'd thought she could be pregnant. Now that they knew she was not, if they were going to be married, it would be with a proper proposal and a proper acceptance.

One that she made without pressure from her family.

Which meant he had to get out of here.

Now.

No matter how much he longed to stay pressed against her.

He disengaged as gently as he could, sliding out of her body and straightening and quickly wiping the pink-tinged arousal from his fingers on the linens she had laid out on the bed.

"Is there a way down from your window?" he whispered, shocked when she shook her head. The glance she gave him as she bundled up the linen was sardonic.

"My uncle and cousins thought it would be easier for them if they put me in a room without an obvious escape route." From her smugness, it had clearly not worked the way they intended, although he could not blame them for trying. Then she bit her lip. "You may have to hide until everyone is abed for the night."

Damn. His eyes darted around the room as he pulled his clothes on, straightening them. Miss Stuart picked up her blouse and put it on, covering her to the tops of her thighs. It was a wholly appealing look on her.

Blast her family.

They came home even earlier than he had expected... than she had expected.

The door burst open behind him.

"Evie!" Elijah's call of her name cut off with a choked gasp.

Time slowed to a crawl.

Anthony was turning, his hands closing the front of his trousers, but he could still see Miss Stuart's horrified expression as he moved, and his head came up. Elijah stood in the doorway, one hand on the open door, his expression going from concern to confusion to rage in the mere blink of an eye.

"Get out!" Miss Stuart shrieked, but it was too late. The damage had been done. No one looking at him and Miss Stuart, in their current state of undress, would believe nothing had happened between them.

Elijah's gaze dropped to where Anthony was still holding the front of his pants together. His lips tightened. Jaw clenched.

He took two steps forward, and even though Anthony knew what the other man meant to do, he did not balk. Time was still moving so slowly, he saw every tiny motion. He could have blocked it. Could have dodged. But he did not.

One blow.

Elijah would get one blow for free to vent his frustration.

It hurt like hell when Elijah's fist slammed into Anthony's chin, knocking his head back so hard, he heard his neck crack.

"Elijah!"

Time suddenly resumed its normal pace as Miss Stuart flew between them. Anthony did not need to see her expression to know she was glaring at her cousin. He took the opportunity to reach up and rub his jaw, working his head back and forth to release the tension in his neck.

"How could you?" Elijah's demand ignored Miss Stuart, his eyes locked on Anthony, burning with the fury of a thousand suns. In the open doorway, others were appearing, though Anthony could not focus on them right now.

"How could *you?*" Miss Stuart shrieked, grabbing the front of her cousin's jacket. "You barge into *my* room without so much as knocking, then assault my lover?!"

Anthony considered intervening, but he did not think Miss Stuart would appreciate it.

"Your..." Elijah's voice cut off, his face turning that odd purple shade Anthony had never seen before.

"Lover?" The slightly horrified question came from the Marquess, and Anthony felt his face heat with embarrassment. The man had been his employer and sometimes a father-like figure in Anthony's life over much of the past decade. Seeing his reaction to finding them reminded Anthony, much though he might wish it, of what was between him and Miss Stuart was not *only* between them.

"Yes, my lover." Miss Stuart put her hands on her hips. "Now, everyone, get out so we can get dressed."

"It is not that simple, Evie." Elijah looked up as if asking the heavens for patience. "He cannot just be your lover. He has to marry you now."

"I am not going to marry someone just because *you* want me to." Miss Stuart sniffed derisively.

The tension in Anthony's chest relaxed. She had not said she did not want to marry him, just that she would not bow to family or societal pressure, which was so very her. His vixen's claws were out, and they would not be sheathed until she got what she wanted.

"It is not about what I want."

"Of course, it is. Did you marry every woman you took as a lover? No, no, you did not, or you would have gotten married years ago. Come to that, if I was going to marry the first man I ever took as a lover, I would have been married years ago."

"I do not want to hear this," the Marquess muttered from his place in the doorway.

"Then get out of my room and out of my decisions. Captain Browne and I have an understanding, and it does not include any of you."

Coming up behind her, Anthony put his hand on her shoulder. If looks could kill, Elijah would have slain him on the spot, but he did not care what Elijah wanted. He only cared about what Miss Stuart wanted.

"Miss Stuart is correct. What happens between us *is* between us. This is not the same situation as you, Elijah, unless you and your family plan to tell the rest of the *ton* about what you discovered tonight. There is no scandal unless *you* create one."

The appreciation in Miss Stuart's eyes as she looked up at him in surprise was worth the daggers Elijah and the Marquess were shooting at him with their eyes. Deciding that a change of topic was in order, Anthony pretended everything about this situation was completely normal. It was the only possible way out of this exceedingly awkward moment.

"Miss Stuart found proof of Mitchell's dealings with the Russians. If you can meet us in the drawing room in ten minutes, we will show you."

* * *

<u>Evie</u>

If she had not been in love with Captain Browne before, she certainly was now.

His unerring logic as he turned aside her cousin's insistence that they marry was enough to make a lady swoon, but it left her with a problem. She had just fervently denied marrying him, and he had agreed with her... but perhaps they could continue onward as they had been. This time without having to sneak around her family so much.

Though as they approached the drawing room and heard arguing inside, she had a feeling her family was not going to suddenly see the light.

"You *chose* to marry me. You will not attempt to take that choice away from your cousin!"

"I did not really have a choice when you think about it."

"Of course, you did. You could have let Joseph marry me, and thank goodness you did not, because that would have been awful. Sorry, Priss. But the point remains that you still chose to marry me."

"Wait, why did you just apologize to Priscilla instead of to me? I'm the one you insulted!" Joseph sounded outraged.

"And she's the one who has to live with you." Josie was not having any of it.

Evie pressed her lips together with amusement. Captain Browne sending them to the drawing room had given her friend the time to set forth her own arguments. If anyone could wear Elijah down, she could.

If Joseph said a single word, Evie would eviscerate him. He not only was able to choose his bride—because Elijah had saved him from the scandal Mitchell had tried to concoct as a distraction—but after finding him with Lady Cross... well. Evie would not tolerate any lectures on morality or marriage from him.

Uncle Oliver was the one she dreaded dealing with. It was one thing to disappoint him by taking on missions he did not want her involved in and proving her worth. It was another to disappoint him by tarnishing his honor. As her guardian, he was supposed to be looking after her— that was how he felt—and while she thought it was nonsensical that *his* honor could be judged by her actions, she knew that was how he would feel.

She glanced up at Captain Browne, whose impassive expression gave nothing away, then braced herself before pushing the doors open.

Everyone in the room turned to look at them, all still dressed in their ballroom finery. Evie had donned a soft gown rather than a ballgown or her maid's outfit. While she did not care what she wore, she knew her appearance would have an effect on how she was heard, whether or not they meant it to.

It did not escape her attention that Adam and Lucas were not in attendance, but everyone else was there, ranged around the room.

"Letters between the ambassador and Mitchell," she said, lifting her hand with the small packet of paper before anyone could say anything. She let go of Captain Browne's arm and stepped farther into the room, heading to her uncle, seated in his usual spot on the couch. "There is nothing incriminating in the ones I can read, but it proves there was correspondence. Some are written in cipher."

Uncle Oliver's eyes lit up, which made her smile. No matter how he felt about her and Captain Browne, he was glad to have the information. The proof that they needed.

"We can make copies and send them to my best codebreakers to figure out the cipher," he said, taking the packet from her. Some of the lines on his face relaxed as his relief showed. "Knowing Mitchell and the Russians are connected might be enough to have the delegation sent home. Thank you, Evie."

Well, that was a surprise. She had expected to be soundly scolded for leaving the ball and sneaking into the embassy with Captain Browne, not thanked. From the look on Elijah's face, he still wanted to scold her.

"I think it has been a very long night." Uncle Oliver got to his feet, holding the packet in one hand and his cane in the other. Diana stood with him, one hand hovering just behind his elbow in case he needed her support. "I am going to bed and recommend the rest of you do as well."

Everyone murmured what sounded like acquiescence, but no one moved. They all stood as he left, Diana by his side. Her cousins avoided her gaze. Her friends were staring at her with rapt attention. Even Priscilla looked wildly curious.

"Game of billiards?" Joseph finally asked, his gaze skipping around the men who were assembled.

Evie rolled her eyes. How predictable.

All the gentlemen nodded, and everyone received a kiss from their spouse before leaving the room... everyone except Captain Browne.

He and Evie were not married, and after everything she had said tonight, they probably never would be.

Unhappiness tightened her gut, but there was nothing to be done. She would take none of her words back. She would not be forced into marriage with a man just because her family had discovered they were lovers.

"Well, I suppose we all may as well sit down and talk." Josie flounced over to the couch where Uncle Oliver and Diana had been sitting and plopped down. Evie winced at the thought, causing Lily to raise her eyebrows since she was looking at Evie, watching her reactions.

"I do not think Evie wants to sit," Lily observed, a slight smile curving her lips. "I take that in addition to indulging yourselves, Captain Browne also made his displeasure known over the change in plans?"

"You are correct," Evie said ruefully, reaching back to tenderly rub her bottom. Still sore inside and out, she did not particularly want to sit down. At least the rags for her monthlies were also catching the seed leaking from her rear entrance. Otherwise, she would not have dared sit down at all for fear of staining the furniture.

"You are lucky you got off with merely a spanking after pulling a trick like that," Josie said, shaking her head.

"Captain Browne spanked you?!" The shocked, soft question made them jerk their heads around to look at Priscilla, who was sitting with her mouth hanging open. The only one who was not looking at her was Mary, who was shaking her head.

Mary, who was used to being overlooked, her presence forgotten as people loosened their tongues in front of her. They had just done the same thing to Priscilla.

Though, in Evie's defense, they had taken Priscilla so much into their confidence at this point, she had rather forgotten there were things the woman did not know.

Oops.

CHAPTER 28

Explanations

E*vie*

Explaining their husbands' proclivities to Priscilla was both enjoyable and daunting. Evie had never seen so many facial expressions from the other woman. They'd finally shattered Priscilla's perfect reserve. All it had taken was talking about erotic punishment.

Who knew?

They also told her about the Society of Sin, which skirted very close to telling her about Joseph's involvement, but they did not go there. Yet. At least now, it should not be such a shock when he admitted his desires to her.

"I would have never thought..." Priscilla shook her head, her eyes unfocused. "Do you think Joseph will want to do that to me?"

The question was asked anxiously, but Evie could not tell if it was because Priscilla found the idea unappealing or because she was intrigued. Hopefully, the latter if it was a choice between the two. She and Joseph could work out an understanding. There was a couple in the Society who visited together so they could *both* be spanked. Or perhaps Joseph would find as much satisfaction in the doing as he did in the receiving.

"Well, he has attended in the past," Mary said slowly, which was true. Even his last time at the Society was now 'the past,' even though it was not as distantly in the past as it should have been. "Do you think you would be interested?"

Priscilla bit her lip.

"I do not know," she confessed after a long moment. Her gaze flitted between the other ladies. Evie, the only one standing, is where Priscilla's gaze landed last. "How can I know? I have never even heard of it." There was a plea in her gaze, asking her husband's cousin for understanding.

"That makes sense," Evie said soothingly and smiled. "I did not know, either. If you had asked me before the first time Captain Browne spanked me, I would have told you I had no interest in such a thing."

Nibbling on her lower lip, Priscilla's anxiety seemed to mount even higher.

"Perhaps Rex could hold an event soon," Mary said, leaning over to take Priscilla's hand. "You could come watch. You do not have to *do.* In truth, watching on my first visit made me realize I had an interest."

"It did not hurt that Rex supplied you with an immediate demonstration when you were caught." Lily's eyes sparkled with mirth.

"Actually, that hurt quite a bit," Mary replied primly. It only took a moment for them to understand her joke, then everyone burst into laughter, breaking the tension that had been slowly growing in the room. If Priscilla's giggles bordered on hysteria, no one was going to mention it.

"I think a Society gathering sounds like a wonderful idea, thank you," Priscilla finally said when they got their mirth under control.

Evie rather liked the idea. Perhaps she and Captain Browne would finally be able to have an unhurried encounter without worrying about her family or anyone else catching them.

As if she had read Evie's mind, Josie turned to look at her and asked the question Evie least wanted to answer.

"What about you and Captain Browne? You two are the only ones unwed among us, and you clearly have a connection."

"A connection does not necessarily mean marriage." Evie held up her hand to forestall her friends' protests, and they sat back, except Priscilla. Evie had known they would argue with her. "After tonight, even if he had the slightest interest in proposing, that has been nipped in the bud." Her voice did not quiver in the slightest, no matter the chill that wrapped around her heart. Evie was not made for marriage, that much she knew. She never had been.

So, this was for the best.

"That does not answer the real question," Mary said, leaning forward. "Do you want him to propose?"

Evie did not have an answer—not one she was willing to admit to, anyway.

* * *

Anthony

Billiards was nothing more than an excuse for Elijah to demand an explanation from him and Anthony knew it, but he was no coward. With Miss Stuart adamant she would not be pressured into marriage by her family, the next best tactic for Elijah would be to recruit Anthony to his side.

Anthony had no intention of marrying Miss Stuart because she had been pressured or bullied to the altar and would not hesitate to inform Elijah of that decision. What he had said in Miss Stuart's bedroom had not merely been for show. It was how he truly felt. If he somehow convinced her to marry him sometime in the future, that would be between the two of them.

But first things first. They each chose a stick, got the balls set up on the table, and broke them apart before anyone spoke. Granted, perhaps arming Miss Stuart's cousins was not the brightest move, but he thought Rex and Nathan would back him if things turned violent.

"So..." Elijah straightened up from where he had been bent over the table. "How long have you been... consorting with my cousin?"

"I do not believe that is any of your business." Especially since their first encounter had been years ago when he'd mistaken her for a whore in a French brothel. Regardless, Miss Stuart's choices were her own, and he knew she would not appreciate him sharing her secrets with her cousin.

She deserved her privacy.

Joseph glared at him from across the table, and Anthony ignored him even more easily than Elijah. He was one of the people keeping Joseph's secret... for now. The man should understand the importance of discretion.

"I suppose you are right," Elijah said gruffly to Anthony and everyone else's surprise, though his next words were not a shock. "It does not matter how long it has been going on. What matters is that you do the right thing and marry her."

"I think what matters is that I do the right thing and respect her wishes, which are clearly not to be pushed into a marriage she does not want."

"He has a point," Rex said, speaking up. "Why would you want your cousin married to a man who does not love her?"

Anthony appreciated him braving Elijah and Joseph's ire, but something gripped the inside of Anthony's chest, and his tongue tangled in his mouth. Shockingly, Elijah said the words for him.

"He does love her, which is why it is ridiculous he is not making an offer for her hand."

All eyes shifted to stare at Anthony.

He stared back at them.

"Oh my God, he does love her." Nathan ran his hand over his face, scrubbing his eyes, then looking at Anthony again to be sure he was not seeing things. "Then what is the problem, man?"

"The problem is she is not going to marry me just because everyone else thinks she should," he snapped. "I do not know if she wants to marry at all." He glared at Elijah. "Which is something you confirmed, by the by."

"Well..." Looking uncomfortable, Elijah leaned on his billiards stick. "She could have changed her mind over the years. I have seen the way you two look at each other, although I did not know things had progressed to the point they have."

"There are a lot of things you do not know about your cousin," Anthony muttered.

Elijah flinched, as did Joseph, though the words had not been specifically directed at him.

"True enough. I do not know where she has been most of this past

Season since she would not tell us, even after she returned. I did not know she was on a first-name basis with the Tramp. And I did not know you two were…" He raised his hand. "However, I know her temperament and know she would not appreciate you anticipating her answer. She would want to be given her say."

That meant asking her, putting his heart on his sleeve, without knowing if she would reciprocate.

Perhaps Anthony was not as brave as he thought. The very thought made him flinch.

"I think she must love him. Otherwise, she would not have been so infuriated at Elijah's insistence that she marry him," Joseph said.

Anthony rocked back on his heels in surprise. The other man's glare had lessened considerably, but that was still an unexpected observation.

"How do you figure?" Nathan asked, his brow wrinkling in confusion. The billiards game had been abandoned, none of them making a move towards the table as they discussed Anthony's marital prospects.

"If she did not love him, she would have laughed, dared Elijah to make her. Instead, she was furious at the idea she might have to marry because we'd… walked in on you." He glanced at Anthony, then looked away. "If she did not want to marry you at all, she would have said so. Instead, she was insistent she would not marry for the reason Elijah stated."

Oh.

Oh.

Anthony blinked, poleaxed. Perhaps she *did* want to marry him. What Joseph said made perfect sense. There was still a bit of doubt, but not as much as there had been before.

"Then how do I convince her to marry me?"

Elijah looked at Nathan, who looked at Rex, then all of them turned to Joseph. Despite the shortcomings of his marriage, he was the only one who had managed to successfully court and propose to a lady. The other husbands in the room had attained their wives through scandal and had never had to properly woo a woman to the altar.

Scandal would not sway Miss Stuart. Pregnancy would have, but he doubted she would risk such a thing again—besides, deep down, he wanted the same thing she did.

To know she had *chosen* him.

For a wild creature like his vixen, that was the only true victory.

"Do not look at me." Joseph held up his hands. "Priscilla required nothing more than the usual poetry, flowers, and dances. I do not think any of those things would convince Evie."

No, probably not. Though flowers would not go amiss. She deserved them, if nothing else.

"I could try some of that," he said, rubbing his chin. Not the poetry. He was abysmal at poetry. "Gifts. A dance."

"All of which she might appreciate, but... Evie is very straightforward. Perhaps you should just ask her."

Elijah was pushing, but Anthony did not mind, as long as Elijah was willing to let him do things his way and let Miss Stuart answer for herself. Therefore, the best time to ask her would be when they had some privacy, which was hard to come by. He would need help.

"I need to do this alone, without any of your family around." He gave Elijah a pointed look. "She needs to feel as though there is no pressure on her whatsoever, or she may balk."

"So, not here," Joseph murmured, then grimaced. "There is always someone around, even if it's just the servants, and I highly doubt Father would be convinced to leave the house now that he knows."

"True." Elijah made a face as well. "Personally, while under this roof, I would prefer you not... propose or do anything else until you are married. Perhaps it's semantics, but..."

"Understood." Anthony did not blame them in the slightest. They were likely correct about the Marquess.

"I could do a Society gathering," Rex offered. "That would give you the space to... discuss whatever you needed to discuss without being under her family's roof."

Elijah and Joseph groaned, and Joseph covered his eyes, but they did not argue the point. Unsurprisingly, it appealed greatly to Anthony. Likely, it would be easy to coax Miss Stuart into attending.

Then he could get her alone and persuade her to his way of thinking before finally proposing.

CHAPTER 29

An Unexpected Apology

E *vie*

Copies of the correspondence had been made and sent off to Uncle Oliver's code breakers and cipher specialists. Lily had also requested a copy. Uncle Oliver had handed one over to her and Nathan without protest. Evie had asked for one too, just to look at, even though she had never been very good at codes or ciphers. While she could follow one well enough, when she knew the rules, trying to figure out the rules of one she did not know had never been her forte, but she wanted to try.

It gave her mind something to do other than worry over Captain Browne and her feelings for him, especially as he seemed to have lost interest in coming around.

That or her cousins had chased him off. It was difficult to know since she had not seen him since that night. Joseph and Elijah were keeping mum, and she refused to ask them about it. If Captain Browne had been thwarted by her cousins in the wake of that night, he was not the man she had thought he was, and she was better off without him.

At least things were moving forwards with regard to Priscilla. Mary had kept her word and convinced Rex they should host a gathering for the Society of Sin. Joseph had told Elijah, who told Josie, he planned to visit his club that evening. As he did not know Priscilla had been invited to this event, that was for the best. She doubted her cousin would appreciate them introducing his wife to the Society, the bloody hypocrite.

Likely he would be sulking at his club over not being able to meet with Lady Cross. Evie had very little sympathy for him since his problems could be solved by way of a simple conversation with his wife. If they were not a love match, it would be one thing, but Elijah had married Josie *because* Joseph was so in love with Priscilla that marrying another woman would break his heart.

So, the fact he had not told the woman he loved of his desires and had snuck around to get them met without her knowledge... No, Evie had very little sympathy for him. She loved him, and he was her cousin, but she was firmly on Priscilla's side since he had still not talked to her about his desires. It would be another thing if he had spoken to Priscilla and she had rejected him.

He was lucky that all Evie and the others were doing was showing Priscilla what was possible instead of ratting him out.

On the third day of puzzling over the cipher, Uncle Oliver announced it had been broken. Some of his men, as well as Lily and Nathan, had cracked it. The decoded letters had proven the Russian involvement in Mitchell's plot, as well as their promises to him upon a successful outcome. They had indeed wanted to use marriage to the princess to leverage influence against England. Instead, the Russian delegation was being sent home immediately, along with the ambassador. The Tzar would likely claim he knew nothing of the plot and send a new one, but it would be up to the Crown whether they accepted the excuse.

Evie knew her uncle would never believe it. Neither did she.

"I suppose that is it." Captain Browne caught up to her and walked beside her down the hall after exiting her uncle's office.

Ahead of her, Elijah glanced over his shoulder and narrowed his eyes at them. She resisted the impulse to stick out her tongue at him and was grateful when Josie tugged on his arm, bringing his attention back to her.

"Yes," Evie sighed. "We probably will not know the full scope of the fallout for months." It would take time for the Russian delegation to return home and for new negotiations and a new ambassador... if there would be one. A messenger had already been rushed off to summon England's ambassador home from Russia.

While she did not think the two countries would come to blows since the attempts had failed, there would be an effect on trade. There would be many talks. Likely the princess would find herself married off as quickly as possible to keep anyone else from trying to advance their interests in such a manner.

Funny how important marriage could be when it came to the power plays of countries. She would have never guessed it was the motivation behind everything, but it made sense if one was playing the long game.

"Are you going to Hartford House tomorrow?" Captain Browne asked.

The Society of Sin event Mary and Rex were hosting. Evie gave him a sidelong glance. Her body tingled every time she looked at him, especially her bottom, despite the fact she was fully recovered from her punishment.

"Yes."

"Good." Aggravatingly, he said nothing else, and they had reached the foyer.

After everyone said their farewells, Evie would have retreated to her room or perhaps the gardens to think about what 'good' meant when she felt like he had been avoiding her the past few days, but Elijah caught her eye.

The door closed behind their guests, and Evie tilted her head at him.

"Evie, may I speak with you for a moment?" he asked, sounding stilted and formal.

"Of course." She suppressed her smile as Josie nudged him from behind. Her friend knew what he meant to talk to her about and approved, which allowed Evie to relax a bit. She was not in the mood for a row with him.

Josie headed up the stairs while Evie and Elijah stepped into the drawing room. Wandering around the edges of the room, she glanced out the front window, but Captain Browne was already gone. She made a face when she realized she had been hoping for a final glimpse of him.

Pathetic.

She was *not* going to moon over him.

"Evie, I owe you an apology."

Well, that caught her attention. Of all the words she might have guessed would come out of Elijah's mouth, that particular combination would never have occurred to her. Eyes wide, she spun around to face him, searching his expression for some sign he was joking, but he appeared to be perfectly serious.

"You do?" While she thought he did, she didn't think he'd ever agreed with her on the matter. She was not sure what he thought he was apologizing for now.

"I do. So does Father and Joseph, and I would not be surprised if those apologies come sooner rather than later." One side of his mouth twisted up in a half-smile as he placed his hands on the back of the chair in front of him, leaning on it. "Sometimes, I forget you are not the usual sort of debutante."

"I am not really a debutante at all," Evie countered. She had never wanted to be one.

"Exactly." Elijah sighed. "But you should have been. I always wanted you to be able to have everything you were supposed to have to make up for the years we could not find you." The sadness in his eyes, on his face, was utterly sincere, and Evie felt her heart clench.

She had never—never—blamed her uncle and cousins for not being able to find her. At the time, she had not wanted to be found. Had not known what was waiting for her if she had been.

All of her fears had been assuaged when Uncle Oliver found her, took her in, and treated her as his own daughter, and her cousins acted as though she had been their sister all along. It was why she could never stay truly angry at them, even when they made her want to scream with frustration. They were doing their best, and they had not had to.

In fact, many of their peers might have even counseled them against doing so had they known the circumstances when she had been found. A street rat, mudlarking to survive... many would have told her uncle to pretend he did not know her. To leave her to her fate.

Hypocrites, all of them.

They would have also soundly reputed her uncle if they had discovered he had left her there, but deep down, they would have agreed with his decision. Would have done the same. Evie knew what their set was like. At best, those who would have done their duty would have done so by sending her off to a boarding school. They certainly would have washed their hands of her the first time she ran away in defiance.

Not that she had run away... exactly. She had gone on an unauthorized mission without permission from her superior. That was how she had put it when she had returned home to Uncle Oliver, incidentally with the proof he had needed that there was a French spy on the princess' household staff. They'd used that knowledge to drip all sorts of misinformation in the footman's ear for months.

"I have everything I want," Evie said, moving to place her hand atop his. "Well, almost everything," she amended. "I would be even happier if you and Uncle Oliver were not always fighting me on being able to assist you, but I understand why you struggle and do as I please, anyway."

"Yes, you do." His smile was wry and not entirely happy, but she would take it. A good deal of his issues, and her uncle's, stemmed from the years when they could not protect her. "If nothing else, being able to actually *watch* you work has proven that."

Evie squeezed his fingers.

"You could have seen me work a lot sooner if you had not been trying to push me out," she answered mildly.

Elijah made a face.

"Yes, I know. But I am watching now." Sighing, he straightened and pulled her in for a tight hug. "We love you, Evie. I always want what is best for you, even if I go about it in a blundering, bossy way."

Laughing, Evie hugged him back.

"Is that how Josie described it?"

"Possibly."

She squeezed her cousin tight, happy she was finally being seen and accepted for who she was. Hopefully, he was right, and Uncle Oliver and Joseph would soon follow, though Joseph had never been nearly as bad as her uncle or eldest cousin. She had noticed Elijah had not mentioned Adam. Apparently, he knew his youngest brother did not try to stymie her the same way the rest of them did.

"Apology accepted. I am sorry for all the times I gave you fits by disappearing."

"Are you?" Doubt colored his voice.

"Of course. I never enjoyed putting you and Uncle Oliver through any stress. I do not regret the choices I made and would not change them, but I do wish I had been able to keep you from worrying."

"Fair enough."

She squeezed him tighter, her heart full of happiness. If there was one good thing to come out of this whole affair, she was glad this was it.

* * *

Anthony

Staring at Mitchell across the table, Anthony had no sympathy for the clearly broken man. He was singing like a canary now that he had been caught, and the proof of the letters between him and the Russians had been presented to him. Whether it would be enough to keep him from being drawn and quartered rather than hung remained to be seen.

As the choice of death went, Anthony could not blame him for trying to avoid the former. He would as well, though he would never be in Mitchell's position.

"I almost had you once, you know," Mitchell said, his eyes focused on Anthony, a burning hatred filling them. The unshaved stubble on his cheeks and his unkempt hair made him look maniacal, like the person he was within was finally visible on the surface.

"Had me?" Anthony kept his voice mildly interested. As he had continued questioning Mitchell, he had found a combination of disinterest and intense interest, switching off between the two, garnered him the most answers.

Disinterest made Mitchell work harder to catch Anthony's focus, then slowly showing increasing interest encouraged him to keep talking. While Mitchell might want to escape the more gruesome death, he still wanted what he had always wanted—attention, adulation, and recognition. If denied, he searched for it, and once he had Anthony's attention, he did his best to hold it.

At least for a while.

Before his resentment caught up with him again.

Which meant Anthony had to continue the cycle, going back and forth with his own interest to keep the information flowing at a steady pace. Annoying but fruitful.

"In France. You were supposed to wear a specific color cravat and flower in your lapel to meet an agent in a brothel." Mitchell waved his hand, but his eyes burned hotter. "Instead, General Moreau was going to find you there. How did you escape?"

By his question, Anthony could only assume there had been some who had not escaped such traps. He burned with anger, wondering how many good men had died because of Mitchell's machinations.

How had he escaped? Miss Stuart. She had gotten word that the general was going to capture a spy wearing a red cravat and blue flower, and she had gotten to him first. Brought him upstairs and pushed him down on her bed to have her way with him, assuming the soldiers who came to capture an English spy would not suspect a man in the middle of coitus.

However, he would not tell Mitchell any of that.

"Luck."

It was true.

"You should be dead," Mitchell sneered. "You should be dead, and I should be free."

Hardly the first time he had said those words during this meeting, but Anthony now understood why he said the first part with such conviction. He had set Anthony up to die, yet here he was—alive, free, and hopefully soon-to-be engaged.

He really needed to get moving.

"I think that's enough for today," he said mildly.

Panic flashed in Mitchell's eyes.

"Wait! I know more!"

Anthony was not the only one who regularly came to question him. Someone else would be by tomorrow, perhaps Elijah or the Marquess, to appeal to Mitchell's sense of inflated self-importance, but it did not seem to matter who was there. Mitchell did not want to go back to his cell.

"Then you can tell it to whoever comes tomorrow," Anthony said, turning his back on the man. The rattle of chains did not threaten him, and he kept walking, nodding to the two guards who came in through the door. Mitchell's pleas not to be returned to his cell echoed in his ears. Anthony did not hesitate as he left. Mitchell was facing the consequences of his own actions, which were long overdue.

In the meantime, the world did not revolve around him, and Anthony had his own life to live, which included convincing Miss Stuart to marry him.

Tonight.

CHAPTER 30

The Chase

nthony

Hartford House gleamed like a jewel in the dark. Anthony had decided not to accompany Miss Stuart. He was unsure if the Marquess had been fully apprised of the plans for the evening, and… well… He had not faced the man, though he would.

After he secured Miss Stuart's hand.

He knew it was supposed to be done the other way around, but he figured he had a better chance of a 'yes' if he did not circumvent her. Besides, once she said yes—if she said yes—her uncle would hardly turn around and say 'no.'

God, he hoped she said yes.

He pressed his hand against the small box in his pocket, which held the ring he had purchased from Bond Street earlier that day. While he could have contacted his parents and asked for access to the family collection—and fully anticipated his mother scolding him for not doing so once he spoke with her—there was no time.

When he had stepped into the jeweler's shop, he had not been sure he was going to buy. He thought she might enjoy choosing her own piece, either from his family's collection or from the shop.

Then he had seen this one—a square-cut emerald, the exact shade of her eyes, sparkling between two diamonds on either side of it, with a simple gold band. It was beautiful but straightforward, stunning yet simple, and multi-faceted like her. Anthony had thought of her the moment he had seen it.

If she wanted something else, he would accommodate her, but he was fairly certain she would like it. He hoped she would. Hoped she would say yes. Liking the ring was not a guarantee of that, but it would be a positive sign of things to come.

Knocking on the door, he smiled when Rex's butler Cormack opened it.

"Captain." Cormack stepped back, allowing him inside. "Rex said to tell you to come to the library when you arrived."

Miss Stuart and the others must have already arrived. Anthony quickened his pace, heading for the library, passing where others were gathered, with some of the doors opened. The goings-on did not distract him in the slightest, though he glanced in each room out of habit. Quite a few of the doorways were closed, indicating those inside who wished for privacy.

The library's door was open. Soft moans and the crack of something hard against flesh gave way to a scream as he approached. Anthony's eyebrows rose. There must be quite a demonstration happening in the library.

The scene that met his eyes when he reached the doorway was even more unexpected.

Miss Stuart, along with Josie and Priscilla, was across from the door, watching as Lady Cross circled around a gentleman with a large leather paddle in her hand. Stepping inside, he could see Elijah was standing beside his wife, and Mary and Rex were on one side of Priscilla, with Miss Stuart on the other. Josie was next to Miss Stuart and peeking around her to see Priscilla's reaction.

Priscilla's eyes were wide, but she did not look terrified or appalled. Shocked, certainly, and very curious. She did not seem to be able to look away from Lady Cross' demonstration.

He wondered if she knew Lady Cross had engaged in similar activities with Joseph.

Likely not. He was fairly certain they were giving Joseph a chance to tell her on his own. Probably. That was not his business or his problem, though. No, he was here for the black-haired beauty with the green eyes, who haunted his dreams and plagued his days.

As if she sensed him, Miss Stuart met his stare directly. Holding her gaze, Anthony prowled around the couple in the center, ignoring the spanking as he strode through the observers, heading straight for Miss Stuart. As usual, she faced him head-on, watching him stalk her with all the haughty pride of a lioness being approached by a potential mate.

His vixen had run from him in the past, but no longer.

When she stepped back from her friends to meet him, Josie slipped into place beside Priscilla, closing the gap.

In the shadow, she waited for him. The green dress she wore was just short of scandalous, her breasts threatening to spill from its low neckline with every breath she took. The gauzy green overlay was fairly sheer, allowing him to see the nude underdress which made her appear nearly naked beneath it. Anthony's cock hardened as he approached, his desire thickening his shaft with every step.

Miss Stuart tilted her head back to look up at him.

"Captain Browne."

"Miss Stuart."

Out of the corner of his eye, he saw Elijah glance at them, then turn away. It appeared he was ready to let his cousin make her own decisions.

Good.

"Did you want to finish watching the demonstration?" he murmured, not wanting to disturb the others around him.

Arching a delicate eyebrow, Miss Stuart shifted closer so her skirts brushed against his legs, their bodies almost touching. Anthony's cock pulsed against the front of his trousers, but he did not reach out to touch her. Not yet. This felt like a challenge, and he did not intend to lose.

"I do not have to finish watching... though I must admit, it has given me a few ideas." The tip of her tongue flicked out to wet her lips, and it was Anthony's turn to raise his eyebrow.

"You want to trade places?" The disbelief in his voice made something flash in her eyes, and he groaned inwardly. That had been the wrong tack to take—she would not back down from a challenge from him any more than he would from her.

Perhaps this was not so much a challenge as her desire for him to wrest control from her. She seemed to enjoy the battle for supremacy that happened so often between them.

"Why not?" Her chin tilted up. "I could easily be in Lady Cross' position."

Yes, she could, but Anthony did not think she would enjoy it nearly as much as being under his hand, and he had no inclination to trade parts. He had tried it once, years ago, and being on the receiving side did nothing for him.

However, she had given him an idea.

"Very well... let's play a game. I will give you a ten-second head start. If you can stay free of me until the clock chimes the top of the hour, you can do whatever you want with me." He lifted his hand, fingers curling under her chin, thumb pressing against the center of her lower lip. His voice lowered, deepened. "But if I catch you, I get to do whatever I want with you."

Sensual need flared in her eyes. He had no doubt her two desires—to win and to let him dominate her—were at war. Though he had no intention of allowing her the former, he rather thought her internal struggle would add spice to the proceedings.

Lowering his head so his lips hovered over hers, he dropped his voice to a whisper.

"Go."

* * *

Evie

Pulling herself away from Captain Browne, Evie quickly stepped through the crowd towards the door, feeling his gaze on her the whole time. She glanced at the clock on the mantle on her way.

Ten minutes until the top of the hour.

All she had to do was stay out of his hands for ten minutes, and she would get to do whatever she wanted to him. Though the idea of spanking him, the way Lady Cross was doing to Mr. Dillingworth, held no appeal, there were a good many other things she would enjoy. Like tying him to a bed and playing with him to her heart's content.

On the other hand, the excitement that fizzed through her when he said he would catch her and have his way with her was also undeniable. What would he do to her that he had not already done?

He must have something in mind. She had seen it in his eyes.

The chase was on.

She glanced over her shoulder as she went through the door, and he was moving. It would take him some time to get through the people watching, just as it had her, which meant she had to move quickly.

Evie dashed down the hall.

She was familiar with Hartford House, which had a similar layout to many of the other houses around it, making things easier. The real question was where Captain Browne would think to look for her and if he had seen which direction she had gone.

She had to assume he had.

At the end of the hall, she did not look back despite the overwhelming desire to see if he could still see her. She ran to the right, giving her access to more rooms than going left would have. Her mind was racing, along with her feet, trying to think of the best place to go, an area of the house that Captain Browne might not know about or would not immediately guess as her direction.

Was it better to hide immediately and hope he passed her? Or to get as far away from him as possible so that he was forced to search through each of the rooms on the way?

Would he stop to search through the rooms? Or had he seen her turn down this hall?

She made another turn, slowing when she was confronted with other members of the Society in the hallway, talking to each other. Blast. If she ran, they would probably notice where she was going. Wait, was that Lord and Lady Spencer? Never mind, she could not stop to look, though she grinned, knowing the lady had finally had her wish fulfilled. She'd told Mary to send Lady Spencer an invitation.

She would have to look for them later.

Evie went through the first opening she saw, a staircase on the left, and headed down rather than up. More than one person had turned to look at her before she had moved, which meant they knew where she went. Her heart was pounding faster in her chest.

She was getting away from the Captain... she was fairly certain...

But not entirely.

Going down the wooden stairs as quickly as she could, she realized she was descending into the kitchen. The twisting curve made it impossible to see too far behind her, but that was good since she could not be seen from the top of it either.

The wood, without carpet to muffle the sound, made it impossible for her to be silent—her or anyone else. Evie's head jerked up when she heard heavy boots descending behind her.

Blast!

Was it Captain Browne or one of the other Society members following her down the staircase after seeing her rush away?

Either way, she would not hang about waiting for them.

Evie rushed the last few steps, landing in the kitchen, which was empty. Thankfully. The door to the outside was closest, but she would consider it cheating if she left the house. Pausing to take stock, she rushed to the next closest door, hoping it would lead to the dining room or another area of the house.

Damn!

The larder. A dead end.

The bootsteps had reached the bottom of the stairs, and Evie whirled around to see Captain Browne's grinning face. Heat, need, and frustration rose up inside her. She glared at him from across the counters.

"Found you," he said.

"You have not caught me," she retorted and dashed towards the door.

Out of the corner of her eye, she saw the man move quickly, hopping up to slide across the counter rather than going around it the way she had expected. She shrieked as she felt his arms come around her, lifting her off the ground and pulling her away from the door. Her fingers pulled away from the knob, opening it wide enough, she could see the hall and the freedom she had almost gained.

Evie did not know whether to feel excited or disappointed.

"Caught you." Pressing her against the counter, he pushed her shoulders down, bending her over, her hands on the cool surface, his hard cock throbbing against her buttocks.

Feeling his erection through their clothing, her muscles spasmed in response. Evie wriggled against him, knowing she was trapped. Captain Browne's hands moved, sliding up until he could close them over her breasts. She gasped as she felt her dress' neckline give way to his fingers, her nipples spilling from the fabric to rub against the counter.

Teeth bit down on her shoulder as he squeezed the soft flesh, grinding his groin against her bottom, emphasizing how little escape she had. The pinch of her nipples between his fingers made the little buds harden further, and she whimpered as the tips brushed the counter. His hands kneading and squeezing her breasts sent flashes of heat through her body straight to her core.

When his mouth released her skin, he licked his tongue over where he had marked her, and Evie moaned.

"Now," he said, thrusting his hips against her, hands still working her breasts. "What should I do with you?"

"I think you are already doing it," she retorted, bumping her hips against him and arching her back.

"Oh no, vixen." His voice was low. Dark. Dangerous. "I am just getting started."

CHAPTER 31

Say Yes

nthony

Trapping Miss Stuart between him and the counter, Anthony was contemplating whether to remain in the kitchen or find a different room to ravish her in. While there was some appeal to the idea of putting her over his shoulder and carrying her off, there were also quite a few things available in the kitchen that he couldn't access elsewhere.

The peeled ginger, sitting in a tub of water on the counter just behind him, was too tempting to ignore and swayed his decision to remaining in the kitchen.

There were several thick fingers of the stuff and, as though someone had known participants of the Society might end up in the kitchen, they'd been carved perfectly for a specific use.

One hand going to his neck while his other plumped her breast, Anthony tugged at his cravat, undoing the knot with ease of practice. Pulling it free, he straightened slightly, moving his other hand to take control of her wrists. Miss Stuart wriggled as he pulled her arms behind her back and looped the fabric around her wrists, tying them together.

He knew she could escape given the opportunity—that was how she had gotten away from him the second time they'd met, when she had been disguised as a maid, and he had tied her, then left her alone—

but he had no intention of walking away. He rather liked having her tied and at his mercy, even if it was a bit of an illusion.

"Perfect," he said, rubbing his groin against her backside as he moved his hands back around to her front, filling his palms with the soft plush of her breasts. Miss Stuart moaned, shuddering as he used his unfettered access to roll her hard nipples between his fingers, then pinch them hard enough, she cried out. "Such pretty breasts. One day, I'm going to slide my cock between them and enjoy watching myself fuck them."

"Why would I let you do that?" Despite the tartness of her tone, she could not suppress another moan as he manipulated her nipples, pinching and pulling to his heart's content, while his fingers massaged the plump flesh around the tiny buds. "That does not sound like there would be anything in that for me."

"You could watch, too," he offered, a hint of wicked amusement in his voice, but he knew what she said was true, and it gave him the most delightful idea. "Or, better, have you seen one of Nathan's machines?"

Her full body shudder told him she had.

Anthony's voice dropped to a whisper as he moved against her, simulating fucking her without the actual penetration, teasing both of them as he fondled her breasts and tormented her nipples. The fabric of his trousers slid over his cock as he rubbed himself against her backside, stimulating him, though not nearly enough.

Fuck, he needed more.

As much as he enjoyed taunting her—filling their minds with the depraved image of him fucking the valley of her breasts while she lay beneath him, arms and legs tied wide open, so she could be fucked by Nathan's machine—he needed more. Giving her nipples one last hard pinch, grinding against her as he did, he let his hands fall away as he knelt behind her.

Taking hold of her skirts, he pushed the fabric above her waist, then pulled her drawers down, baring her pretty bottom. The green fabric of her dress draped over her hips and hung on each side like a frame. Between her thighs, the pouting lips of her cunt were glistening her arousal, swollen with need.

Placing a hand on each cheek, his thumbs at the creases between her bottom and thighs, Anthony dove in with his mouth. Miss Stuart's cry of surprised pleasure echoed through the empty room as he licked the hot crevice, his tongue exploring the folds of her pussy, all the way from the little button of her clit up to the dry, crinkled hole between her bottom cheeks.

That last got the most reaction, her body jerking forward as his tongue lapped the entrance, the tiny hole he had deflowered so recently. Anthony pressed deeper, licking and teasing the little opening. This was the only lubrication she would receive before he fetched the ginger.

* * *

Evie

Oh... oh, goodness... he put his _mouth_ there _again_. The sense of wrongness, of engaging in a forbidden act, had not dissipated at all.

It felt utterly sinful.

With her hands tied behind her back, jerking as the hot pleasure moved through her, Evie could do very little... and she loved it. Loved the freedom of being tied in place, loved being at his mercy, loved how her breasts and nipples still throbbed from his attentions, even though he had moved below her waist. She wriggled for him, her pussy clenching emptily as his tongue explored her, igniting her wanton pleasure when it probed her anus.

She was more than a little disappointed when he pulled away, leaving her panting and needy. Thick clouds of desire coiled inside her, hazing her brain, focusing her needs to a single point—her need for his cock inside her.

A hand pressed against her lower back, pinning her in place.

"Relax, vixen."

His low command was not reassuring, but Evie relaxed, then felt something probing the tiny orifice he had just been pleasuring with his tongue. It was not his finger... it felt softer, though still hard. Thick enough to make her wriggle as it slid into her bottom, stretching her slightly but not nearly as thick as his cock.

"What is it?" She lifted her head to crane her neck over her shoulder, but of course, she still could see nothing. Well, she could see Captain

Browne, staring at whatever he was putting into her arse, his eyes hot with passion as he watched it penetrate her. Her lower body clenched in reaction, and the oddest sensation of heat flared in her bottom.

"Ginger."

Ginger? He was putting ginger in her? Evie wondered why, but even as her thoughts whirled, her body already knew. Her fingers flexed as she leaned against the counter, squashing her breasts as the sensitive tissues around the finger of ginger began to burn.

"Ow! Ow! Take it out!"

"No."

Why that calm declaration made her clench all over again, Evie had no idea, but the clenching made everything worse. When she tried to reach for it, stretching her arms backward and arching her back, Captain Browne easily pinned her wrists against the small of her back, holding her in place.

"Naughty girl."

His hand came down hard on her arse, a firm, crisp swat that made her cry out, her muscles rippling... and the burn increased again. Evie shrieked, struggling against him but getting absolutely nowhere as he held her down, his hand descending again and again on her upturned bottom.

Try as she might, she could not keep from clenching, and every time her muscles squeezed the ginger, the burn increased. Add in the growing heat as Captain Browne spanked her, and it felt like she was burning up from the inside out. The blaze of her desire grew from both, conflicting with and adding to the painful chastisement of her bottom.

The overwhelming sensations, the fire licking her inside and out, were more than she had ever imagined. Her legs kicked upward, her heel connecting with his shin, but all that did was motivate him to spank her harder—making her muscles clench harder around the ginger, searing the inside of her already pained bottom.

Several tears slid down her cheeks, and for the first time, Evie's pride allowed her to speak up. Maybe because this was not a punishment. It was supposed to be fun... and even though she was aroused, she was not sure this qualified. If he'd been punishing her, she would have struggled to ask for mercy. But he was not.

"Stop!"

"Say you'll marry me, and I'll stop."

"What?" The word fell from her lips before the question truly registered.

His hand came down again hard, and she shrieked.

"Yes or no. I'll stop either way. Marry me."

This was the worst proposal she had ever heard of, yet...

Another hard slap against her arse had her whining. Clenching. Throbbing.

When her family had wanted to push them into a marriage after catching them together, Anthony had pushed back. He had refused.

So, the only reason he could be asking now...

"Why?" She tried to straighten up, but he easily kept her pinned, so she only managed to turn her head, catching a glimpse of his face. "Why do you want to marry me?"

It was not her imagination—he hesitated. Only for a moment. Which made her feel his next words were sincere.

"Because I love you." The gruff tone of voice did nothing to detract from the admission. His hand came down again, once on each cheek, as if admonishing her for forcing him to the confession. "Now... Will you marry me?"

He had finally gotten round to an actual proposal.

As infuriating as he could be, there was only one answer she wanted to give.

"Yes, I will marry you... if you take that damned ginger out of my arse!"

Laughter exploded out of him.

Evie sighed with relief when he slid the ginger out of her clenching hole. Unfortunately, the interior burning did not go with it, but at least it would not get any worse.

Something tugged at her wrists, and her hands were free, but she could not do much with them. Anthony flipped her onto her back, stepping between her thighs and gripping her hips, pulling her down so her sore bottom was at the edge of the counter and the underside of his hard cock was pressing between the folds of her pussy. Rocking his hips, his cock rubbed the length of her womanhood, through her swollen lips and over her clit, making Evie moan and arch her back.

She wrapped her legs around his waist, which was far more comfortable than letting them hang down, as he had likely known it would be. Hot desire blazed in his eyes as he stared down at her, and she blinked with surprise when he grabbed her left hand.

A moment later, a ring adorned it. She caught a flash of brilliant green and the clear sparkle of diamonds before she cried out—the moment he had secured the ring on her finger, he had shifted and thrust his cock into her eager pussy. Being filled so suddenly was almost painful, but her body was so ready for him, craved him so badly, the intensity of having that need met was even more overwhelming.

Trapping her wrists in his big hands, he pressed them down on either side of her, using his weight to keep her on the counter as he rode her with hard, fast strokes. Evie cried out, clenching and shuddering around him as he moved, each thrust causing her chastised cheeks to bounce against the counter, reigniting the painful sparks from her spanking.

His cock slid back and forth in her slippery channel, her muscles clenching to no avail. Part of her wondered how it would feel to clench around his cock and the ginger, and the thought nearly set off her climax.

"Anthony…" She shuddered, lifting her hips to meet his thrusts, her legs tightening around him, wanting him deeper inside of her. "Oh God… Anthony…"

Her breasts bounced as he thrust harder and harder, pounding between her thighs with the fervor of a man possessed.

Evie screamed his name as her orgasm finally exploded inside her. Fiery passion consumed her, every part of her throbbing and pulsing with an exquisite mix of agony and ecstasy and the knowledge that Anthony loved her.

* * *

Anthony

Feeling Evie come apart around him, watching her face as she was catapulted into abject erotic rapture, was more than Anthony could take. Tormenting her had been pure pleasure for him, and now he was fucking her for all he was worth, his balls tingling from the remnants of ginger juice his sack slapped against every time he slammed home inside her. He thrust forward, leaning his weight into it, and felt her pulse around him, her muscles clenching him, milking him.

Unlike before, it was no accident when he erupted inside her, spurt after spurt of hot seed filling her.

This was a confirmation of his right to do so now that she had said yes, and his ring was on her finger.

This was a claiming.

They moaned, shuddering together as he emptied himself inside her until he was drained and spent, his head resting against her fabulous bosom. He could feel the frantic beating of her heart slow under his ear as their breathing returned to normal, their bodies still entwined but no longer frenzied.

She tugged her hand upwards, and he let it go, turning his head slightly and smiling as he watched her examine the ring. Though her expression changed little, he rather thought she liked it.

"If you want a different one, we can pick it out together, but I thought this one would suit you."

He had been right about it matching her eyes, the color as well as the sparkle.

"I think it does, too." Her lips curved in a sleepy, satisfied smile. "I love you, Captain Anthony Browne."

Cupping his face with her hands, Evie lifted her head to give him a passionate kiss. Wrapping his arms around her, Anthony brought her to a sitting position, their bodies still interlocked, his half-hard cock reluctant to leave the warm haven it would now call home.

He had tamed himself a vixen.

Epilogue

HAPPILY EVER AFTER

E<u>vie</u>

The banns had been read, St. George's had been reserved, and the day of the wedding dawned with enough clouds to obscure the sun and cool the heat of the day. As far as Evie was concerned, it was the perfect day to be married.

"It is rather ironic that Evie is the first of us to be married without sparking a scandal, is it not?" Josie's eyes sparkled with delighted mischief as she helped secure the veil to Evie's curls. Lizzie had outdone herself with Evie's coiffure before going downstairs to help with the final preparations for the wedding breakfast. "You are the most scandalous among us, yet yours is the most conventional engagement and marriage."

"At least her proposal was properly unconventional," Mary said, making them giggle.

Evie smirked. That it had been.

She and Anthony told everyone he had proposed after they took a walk together at Hartford House, but she had told her friends the truth.

Looking in the mirror, she could hardly believe, after a childhood of tragedy, she had grown to have all the things she had never thought she would have as an adult. A future. A loving husband. Friends and family who loved her for who she was.

And work that she loved.

Uncle Oliver was going to be handing over the reins of spymaster to her and Anthony, with Elijah's blessing. He was willing to assist, but he said the pair of them would make better leaders than he would.

The very first thing Evie had done was add her network of informants, mostly women, to her uncle's. She had also spoken to Lily and Lucas about adding their continental contacts to the network. Not that her uncle's had been lacking, exactly, but now it would be even more impressive than before.

She would also be looking for anyone else who had worked with Mitchell. Before he was hanged, the man had claimed there was no one else, but Evie would be looking into it, regardless. Warwick was another she would keep a close eye on, even though her uncle had already sent a man to have a discussion with him.

She had discovered her uncle had found all the women on Warwick's staff who had been terrorized by Mitchell and ensured they were in good positions.

There was a lot of work still to do, but she was grateful and relieved he had stepped up to rectify the mistake he had made with Mitchell.

But that was not her focus for today. No, all she wanted to think about today was the man she had fallen in love with and that she was about to be married to him. She glanced down at the ring glimmering on her finger and smiled. He had done well picking it out.

Her only complaint was, after their engagement, they had not had a moment alone. The needy ache between her thighs would finally be assuaged today, and she could not wait.

"Is this the part where we tell you what to expect on your wedding night?" Lily joked. Their giggles filled the room, and Evie's face hurt from smiling so much.

A knock on the door sobered them. Mary opened it, her shoulders relaxing, and saw Uncle Oliver standing in the doorway. He looked particularly handsome in his dove grey morning suit, which suited his salt and pepper hair admirably. The silver waistcoat and crisp white cravat set off his handsome good looks as well.

His expression when he took in the sight of her in her wedding dress of white lace and the veil adorning her dark curls, she had never seen before. Everything about him softened, and tears sprang to his eyes.

"You look like your mother," he said, his voice gruff.

That was all it took to turn the room from giggles to slightly weepy teary-eyed young women. Even though none of the others had ever met Evie's mother, it was impossible for those who loved Evie to be unaffected, especially when they looked at her and saw the emotion roiling in her eyes.

"Sorry." Uncle Oliver cleared his throat. "I did not mean to bring down the mood. She would have been so proud of you, and so would your father." He tugged on his jacket, even though it did not need straightening.

Smiling, Evie came forward, hands outstretched to take his.

"Thank you, Uncle Oliver. I would not be here today without you."

"Oh, you would have done just fine." His smile was more than a little watery. "You are a survivor, Evie. You always have been. Somehow, you would have made your way in the world... I truly believe that, but I am so glad I have been a part of it."

It felt as though her heart swelled inside her chest, banging painfully against her ribs. They squeezed each other's hands, then he turned to offer her his arm. Behind her, her friends were already gathering around like little banty hens, plucking up the train of her dress to carry between the three of them.

Uncle Oliver put his hand over hers where it rested on his arms.

"I love you, Evie. If you change your mind, just say the word."

And just like that, everyone was laughing again.

* * *

Anthony

Was there any worse feeling than standing at the head of a church, everyone's eyes on you, waiting and wondering if your bride would actually appear?

Not that he had been given any indication she would change her mind, but there was that little niggle of doubtful fear, anyway.

"Stop looking so panicked. People will think you do not want to be here," Nathan whispered from beside him.

Anthony tried to relax his face.

Looking up instead of at the doors he was waiting to open, he was surprised when he saw two dark figures standing on the balcony, which had not been opened for guests today. With so much of London emptied out due to the end of the Season and Evie a Marquess' niece, rather than daughter and him being the third son of a viscount, rather than first, they were able to keep their guest list smaller.

One of the figures shifted partially into the sunlight, and Anthony realized he was looking at the Tramp and his lady.

How fitting they had chosen a spot on the balcony.

A grin curved his lips. Evie would be happy to know they had made it. She had sent an invitation but had not had high hopes of an actual appearance.

"That's more like it," Nathan muttered. "Keep smiling like that."

Anthony might have retorted, but the music began, and his heart felt like it stopped in his chest, seizing his lungs.

It was time.

Later, he could not remember anything until the double doors opened to admit Evie on her uncle's arm. That moment he could describe in exquisite detail.

The sun burst through the clouds, creating a silhouette and showing off her figure. She looked like an angel walking down the aisle. Her emerald gaze was fixed on him, never wavering, the smile on her face wide and open.

Evie as he had never seen her.

When she was finally standing in front of him, committing to being his wife and he caught her smirk when she promised to obey. They both knew she would loosely interpret that particular vow, but he had no objections.

"I now pronounce you husband and wife."

His.

She was finally his.

His vixen spy wife.

Overcome by the moment, tired of the wait to hold her in his arms,

Anthony pulled her to him, wrapped his arms around her, and claimed her lips in a possessive kiss.

Father Christopher sputtered, but several cheers and much laughter echoed through the church.

Anthony did not care how anyone else felt, and he did not think Evie did, either.

This was the happy ending they were always meant to have.

* * *

Thank you so much for reading my Deception & Discipline series! In my head, this was always where it was going to end, but as usual the characters had other plans. If you want more, check out the Deception & Discipline Series which starts with A Season for Bliss where Joseph reveals his secrets and Priscilla discovers some surprises about herself.

The End

Acknowledgments

This series would absolutely not be what it is without my beta readers. They are not only my biggest cheerleaders, they also spend a lot of time helping me with my writing and making my stories better.

Candida, Annie, Maria, Marta, Karen, and Katherine – you all are amazing. I am so grateful for you and all the help you've given me.

For this particular book, I also have to give a special shoutout to Marilize Roos and Jennifer Bene, two wonderful authors in their own right who also took the time to help me with this final installment of the series.

Another thank you to my editor Sandy of Personal Touch Editing – I so appreciate the personal touch you always give my books.

Of course I have to thank my husband, who tolerates long working hours and a wife who is constantly wanting to talk about the men inside her head.

A huge shout out to Rebecca Mckernan, who does such a lovely job of bringing this series to life for audiobook.

And, last but not least, thank you dear listener. I hope you have enjoyed all the shenanigans of my four lovely ladies. I'm sure we'll see them again, though their own stories are technically over with the happy-ever-after.

About the Author

Golden Angel is a *USA Today* best-selling author and self-described bibliophile with a "kinky" bent who loves to write stories for the characters in her head. If she didn't get them out, she's pretty sure she'd go just a little crazy.

She is happily married, old enough to know better but still too young to care, and a big fan of happily-ever-afters, strong heroes and heroines, and sizzling chemistry.

When she's not writing, she can often be found on the couch reading, in front of her sewing machine making a new cosplay, hanging out with her friends, or wandering the Maryland Renaissance Fair.

Find her online at www.goldenangelromance.com

Other Titles by Golden Angel

HISTORICAL SPANKING ROMANCE

Domestic Discipline Quartet

Birching His Bride

Dealing With Discipline

Punishing His Ward

Claiming His Wife

The Domestic Discipline Quartet Box Set

Bridal Discipline Series

Philip's Rules

Gabrielle's Discipline

Lydia's Penance

Benedict's Commands

Arabella's Taming

Pride and Punishment Box Set

Commands and Consequences Box Set

Deception and Discipline

A Season for Treason

A Season for Scandal

A Season for Smugglers

A Season for Spies

Desire and Discipline

A Season for Bliss

Bridgewater Brides

Their Harlot Bride

Standalone

Marriage Training

The Duke's Pursuit

Rogue Booty

CONTEMPORARY BDSM ROMANCE

Venus Rising Series (MFM Romance)

The Venus School

Venus Aspiring

Venus Desiring

Venus Transcendent

Venus Wedding

Venus Rising Box Set

Stronghold Doms Series

The Sassy Submissive

Taming the Tease

Mastering Lexie

Pieces of Stronghold

Breaking the Chain

Bound to the Past

Stripping the Sub

Tempting the Domme

Hardcore Vanilla

Steamy Stocking Stuffers

A Sassy Christmas

Entering Stronghold Box Set

Nights at Stronghold Box Set

Stronghold: Closing Time Box Set

Masters of Marquis Series

Bondage Buddies

Master Chef

Law & Disorder

Switch Play

Legally Bound

Shallow Submission

Hidden Away

Giant Tamer

Third Wheel

Dungeons & Doms Series

Dungeon Master

Dungeon Daddy

Dungeon Showdown

Daddies Everywhere

Chef Daddy

Foosball Daddies

Taco Daddy

Little Villain

SCI-FI ROMANCE

Tsenturion Masters Series with Lee Savino

Alien Captive

Alien Tribute

Alien Abduction

Standalone

Mated on Hades

SHIFTER ROMANCE

Big Bad Bunnies Series

Chasing His Bunny

Chasing His Squirrel

Chasing His Puma

Chasing His Polar Bear

Chasing His Honey Badger

Chasing Her Lion

Night of the Wild Stags

Chasing Tail Box Set

Chasing Tail... Again Box Set